A Strong and Tender Thread

JACKIE WEGER

Harlequin Books

TORONTO • NEW YORK • LOS ANGELES • LONDON
AMSTERDAM • PARIS • SYDNEY • HAMBURG
STOCKHOLM • ATHENS • TOKYO • MILAN

When dreams and goals ebb on the tide of life
let love bind you together
—a strong and tender thread

J.W.

———————————————◆ • ◆———————————————

Published May 1983

First printing March 1983

ISBN 0-373-16005-4

Chapter One

"What's wrong with us, Gabby?" Tim's plaintive voice droned in Gabrielle's ear as he plopped unceremoniously in the vacant seat next to her. No Smoking/Fasten Seat Belts signs flashed on and he buckled up. Gabrielle ignored him. Damn! They had been over this before—too many times, and now he was making a pest of himself again, staring at her until she answered him. His scrutiny made her uncomfortable but she resisted the urge to shift away from him in her seat.

Out of the corner of her eye she watched keen appreciation flicker across his features as he drank in the sculpted angles of her face: the wide forehead, naturally arched brows, her small nose centered exactly right between high curved cheekbones—a perfect foil for the long curling sweep of black lashes veiling sensitive brown eyes. Her skin was the color of dark wild honey. Tim's eyes lingered on the fullness of her mouth. Gabrielle frowned when he began to draw a finger up the skin of her arm; she moved her elbow off the thin armrest between them.

"Answer me, Gabby," he said, pleading.

Gabrielle sighed. "There's nothing wrong with us, Tim. There just isn't any 'us,' as you so inaptly put it."

"You can't mean that. I love you," he whispered. His boyish features had a look of petulance, wide mouth drooped into a pout, a characteristic Gabrielle had noticed on their very first date and one she didn't like. Tim used it often, during rehearsals when the choreographer criticized his dancing, or when he didn't get his own way. One reason, she thought, why Tim would never progress beyond the chorus.

She forced herself to look Tim in the eye. "I'm not in love with you, I'm not in love with anyone. I like you as a friend—nothing more. I don't understand how you got

such a different idea into your head.'' There was an independence about Gabrielle that challenged Tim, but after
the fiasco with Luke Bryant, she hadn't wanted a man.
They wanted to dominate her, possess her, order her
about. She wouldn't have it.

"You gave me the idea,'' he accused. "The way you
look at me, the way you dress, the way you walk, even—''

"Stop it!'' she hissed. "I don't look at you in any special
way. I can't help the way I walk. I'm a dancer. We both
are. We're trained to be graceful. You walk as fluidly as I
do. Why can't you just be a good friend? Instead of trying
to— Oh, never mind!'' she said, disgusted, and turned to
stare out the small square window.

A full white moon hung in the sky, as if reluctant to
withdraw its magic. Grayness blanketed the land as the
plane swerved for its approach to the runway, punching a
hole in the muted silver of false dawn. The monolithic
Goodyear sign glared neon-blue on the vast barnlike structure that housed the blimp—an aerial signpost and a
familiar landmark to Houstonians.

Gabrielle felt a tingle of excitement sift through the jet
lag and acrid aftertaste of a dozen cups of instant coffee.
After the Civic Ballet's exhausting tour in London, it was
good to be getting home again. She smiled ruefully. What
had really tired her were the past four days of sight-seeing
and shopping. The troupe had elected to take their off-
days in Europe instead of Houston. And who wouldn't?
Tomorrow was a workday—rehearsals at three. It would
only be a short session to review the tour, what had worked
and what hadn't, for the benefit of those who had not been
among those chosen to make the trip.

One thing had worked beautifully: She, Gabrielle Hensley, a black premiere danseuse in the role of Cinderella,
had enchanted English audiences. Ballet was enormously
popular in London and all performances in Sadler's Wells
Theatre had been sold out.

Gabrielle fell in love with the English people and they
with her. She had been the darling of the theatergoers,
feted with flowers and champagne after every performance, with dozens of invitations to supper parties and

private clubs. She had enjoyed it all immensely. There was even a rumor that the Royal Ballet would invite her to dance *Giselle* next spring. Gabrielle thought the formal invitation might even now be in the director's briefcase—he had been treating her like a prima ballerina for the past week, a behavior, for him, that was quite out of the ordinary.

Gabrielle yawned and covered her mouth with a dainty hand, wondering how long it would take them to get through customs. Receipts for all her purchases were in her tote. Recalling exactly how much the designer outfits had cost made her shudder, and there was still the luxury tax to be paid to make them even more dear.

The thought reminded Gabrielle of the only flaw in her career—despite the glamour, the parties, and the heady applause, the salary was dreadful. To make ends meet she often had to take outside jobs and she realized with a sinking heart she had acted much too hastily when she told Mr. Garrett she wouldn't return to her job as translator after the London tour. She made a mental note to call him first thing tomorrow and ask for her job back. With her finances in shambles she would have to find time, somehow, to work at least part-time.

If Mr. Garrett had already replaced her at his real estate office, perhaps he would recommend her to one of his colleagues. He had praised her often for her work, not only in translating Castilian Spanish formalized in contracts but for her ability to converse with his Chicano clients. Gabrielle had Val to thank for that. Having a Chicano roommate these past three years had helped her with all the nuances and dialect of the spoken language, nuances she could never have learned in the classroom.

The huge jet touched down and rolled along the concrete runway, guided by the pilot to the disembarkation tunnel. Engines screamed, ground down to a piercing whine, then stopped altogether. Silence hung in the air for several seconds before passengers began to stir, stretch, and push into the aisles.

Tim reached over to unbuckle her seat belt. Gabrielle pushed his hands away. "I can do it myself," she told him, asserting her independent nature.

"You broke up with Luke," Tim said without preamble, "because he said you couldn't dance after you were married. Marry me, Gabby. You can dance as long as you want."

She stared at Tim in astonishment. He was obsessed with the idea that she was still in love with Luke Bryant and thought sincerely that was why she refused to be aroused by him.

Gabrielle shook her head wearily. "Tim, I'm tired. You've been awake as long as I have, so I know you must be too. Please, just drop it, will you?"

His eyes were apologetic. "Don't look so upset, Gabby. You're right, we are tired, we can talk about it later."

Gabrielle stood up and stretched her limber frame, searching among the jackets and soft luggage overhead for her tote.

"Do you need a ride home from the airport?" Tim asked as they pushed their way into the crowded aisle.

"No, my mother's meeting me."

Nearly asleep on her feet before she got through customs, Gabrielle threw an angry glance at Davila, who had been ahead of her in the long line. The scatterbrained girl had not kept a single receipt for her purchases, and the ensuing confusion as the customs agents unpacked Davila's bags held up the line for more than twenty minutes.

Relief washed over Gabrielle when she spotted her mother's features above the heads of her colleagues, then she smiled with ironic bemusement. Emily Hensley was elegantly dressed and coiffured even at this ungodly predawn hour. She called to her mother.

"Here I am, Mother!" Emily swiveled her head to locate her daughter, then pushed through the milling crowd to hug Gabrielle briefly.

"Welcome home," she added, smiling her greeting and at the same time signaling for a redcap to carry the mound of luggage at Gabrielle's feet.

"Gabby, wait!" Tim rushed to her side. "May I give you a lift to rehearsals tomorrow?"

Gabrielle watched her mother hurrying the redcap toward the exit. "Oh, all right, Tim, but only if you promise not to discuss anything heavier than the weather."

"I promise," he said with alacrity. "Two thirty?"

"That's fine," she called over her shoulder as she ran to catch up with Emily.

"I'm sorry to rush you, Gab, but if we don't get going now, we'll get caught in rush-hour traffic and be hours getting home."

"That's okay, Mother. I'm dead on my feet." Gabrielle folded herself into the front seat of the small sedan and another wide yawn overtook her. She would forget everything, she told herself, forget Luke Bryant, Tim's persistence, rehearsals tomorrow, the state of her finances, and just sleep. Her lashes drooped against the curve of her cheek and only the far recess of her mind registered the sound of the engine and the movement of the car as Emily drew it skillfully into the outgoing traffic.

"Gabby, are you awake?"

"Just barely, Mother."

"Listen to me for a minute. When I said welcome home, I meant it."

"I know you did," Gabrielle murmured. She was too tired to puzzle about her mother's tone and tried vaguely to recall if they had had another argument before she had left for London.

"You're missing the point. I mean *our* home, your father's and mine."

Gabrielle sat up straight, alert. "What are you talking about? Has something happened to my apartment?"

"Not exactly." Emily hesitated. "You've been pushed out of it, I'm afraid."

"Mother! Will you quit beating around the bush! Didn't Val pay the rent? *How* have we been pushed out?"

"Not both of you," Emily explained patiently, "just you. Val has a new roommate—her husband. She got married this week."

"What!" Gabrielle exclaimed, astounded. She and Val had been roommates for more than three years. Val had missed the London tour because she had sprained an ankle badly only two days before they were due to leave. The director had been furious at the diminutive Chicano, not to mention the wardrobe mistress who had to sew steadily for the entire two days to refit costumes for a larger girl. Val hadn't mentioned anyone special to Gabrielle at all. At least, Gabrielle didn't think she had. Val had been falling in and out of love so often the past three years, Gabrielle seldom listened carefully anymore to her friend's waxing eloquent about her newest beau. Damn! And damn again!

"I think Val said his name is Pietro, and he's not a dancer," Emily continued. "He works offshore. I assume he's on one of the rigs out in the gulf. But you'll have to call her yourself," Emily drawled, "you know how she is when she gets excited. She reverts to Spanish and I can't understand a word she says. I *did* learn Pietro has already moved in with his things."

Gabrielle groaned. "Mother, are you sure? Maybe they're just spending their honeymoon there or Val just wants to stay in our apartment until they can find their own place."

"Gabby, you will just have to call her yourself for the details," Emily reiterated. She glanced sideways at her daughter. "I know how much that apartment means to you, Gab, but your father and I are glad to have you home with us, even if it's just for a few days. We seldom see you anymore."

"Mother, that's not true and you know it."

"Once or twice a month for dinner is hardly what I'd call visiting, especially when you usually eat and run." The freeway was becoming clogged with early-morning commuters anxious to get into Houston before the inevitable flat tire or fender-bender backed up cars for several miles. Emily shot off to an access road, taking a shortcut to the university campus where she lived. "Personally, I think you should think about doing what Val did," she said, after negotiating around the line of cars at the exit ramp.

Gabrielle tensed, hating the familiar and unwanted subject that always came up between them. Tim's pursuit of the same subject had already served to ruffle her usually calm nerves.

"What's that, Mother? Sprain my ankle and miss a tour with the ballet or get married?"

Emily ignored the sarcasm. "Get married, Gabby," she said stubbornly, staring straight ahead and pretending intense concentration on her driving. "You'll soon be twenty-five. It's time you were married. You could have been already," she voiced mild rebuke, "to Luke."

Gabrielle clinched her hands in her lap, feeling an angry knot of tension forming in her stomach. "That's over and done with and has been for some months. Luke is married now. I don't know why you insist on bringing up his name every time we see one another. I wish you wouldn't."

"Well, all my friends' daughters are married. And two have babies already." Emily stated her most practical reasons for discussing the subject at all.

"Mother, do you mind if I fall in love first? Or should I just advertise for a husband, so you can tell your bridge circle that your daughter is married too? What should I say? 'Tall, handsome black man desired for marriage to equally attractive black woman. Virility a must! In-laws anxious to become grandparents.' "

"There's no need to get nasty, Gab. I'm just trying to point out— Well, to tell you the truth, advertising is what you'll have to do if you continue to let dancing be the consuming interest in your life. There *are* other things, you know."

"Of course I know, and I do expect to marry someday, Mother. Someday. Right now all I want to do is dance. I've finally just won a permanent slot in the Civic Ballet and I don't want to give it up. Besides," she declared, "I like dancing, I'm good. I've had lead roles in both *Giselle* and *Cinderella* this year alone." Gabrielle's voice trembled with emotion. "If you didn't want me to dance, you should have never let me have lessons and then sent me to the Fine Arts Academy."

"You dance beautifully, Gabby. I enjoy watching you perform, but you're obsessed with dancing and we—I didn't expect you to make it a career."

Gabrielle closed her eyes in exasperation. Those were the very same words Luke had used. Her mind raced unwillingly to the evening she had broken their engagement. She had been excited about winning the role of Snow Queen in the *Nutcracker*. Luke had been arrogantly amused, telling her to enjoy it while she could, because after they married in the spring, he expected her to stay home and raise their own little ballerinas. Gabrielle had been stunned by his attitude. He refused to listen to her when she said she wouldn't give up dancing. She'd snatched his ring from her finger and left it lying on the coffee table as she walked—no, ran—from his apartment.

A few months later when she learned Luke had married, she discovered she had never really loved him. She had been in love with being in love—romantic fantasy, she realized now. She would never make that mistake a second time!

Luke had been tender, kind, and fun to be with, but there was never the electric, breathless feeling she had always imagined. Even his lovemaking had been tame, never once releasing the butterflies in her stomach from their silken cocoons.

"You are our only child, Gabby. I just want to enjoy my grandchildren—*if* I ever get any—before I'm too old," Emily said and slid a glance at her daughter to see if her words were having any impact.

Gabrielle grimaced, having heard this argument a dozen or more times. "I promise you, Mother, I will get married...one of these days, and I will produce a couple of little darlings for you to oooh and aaah over. Now, can we just let it drop for a while?"

"Humph!" Emily snorted inelegantly. "You won't want two, if the *first* is anything like mine."

Gabrielle laughed, despite her anger. "You aren't very subtle, Mother."

"Subtlety is not one of my finer points," Emily agreed.

"I could try artificial insemination," Gabrielle said blandly, "then we wouldn't have to worry about a husband."

Emily's regal head lifted on her slender neck. "I can wait for...er...for you to...I mean...."

"I'm so glad we finally agree, Mother." Gabrielle laughed.

Emily tossed her daughter a caustic look. "I'd forgotten how troublesome and impertinent you are."

"It's not something I learned, Mother," she answered with feigned insouciance. "I'm sure it must be hereditary—from whom, I wonder?"

"Now who lacks subtlety?" Emily issued the statement as she braked to a stop in the short paved drive of her home.

The cream-colored stucco two-level house perched companionably on the very edge of the prestigious Monroe University campus and, except for its pale beige color, was exactly like the four others on the block.

"I'll get Hattie to help me with your cases, Gabby," Emily offered, seeing how truly weary her daughter was. "You go on upstairs."

Gabrielle agreed. "I'll just take this one, though," she said, lifting the large ivory suitcase from the top of the heap.

Her mother hadn't changed the decor of her room, Gabrielle noted with wry amusement. It was still the same— fitted for the teen-aged ballerina in soft pinks and off-whites. Flowered prints raced up one wall and met with glee the same print in a ruffled canopy over the twin bed. Now Gabrielle preferred muted shades of ice-green and antique browns. Touches of variegated yellows accented her apartment. *Her* apartment. Not anymore though, if all that her mother said was true. She would call Val first thing in the morning, Gabrielle thought. Today she just wanted to sleep.

But first there were her new clothes to unpack. Lifting the suitcase onto the quilted pink satin spread, Gabrielle smiled and stroked the jeweled, waist-length jacket before holding it up to the new sun filtering through the blinds. Stones colored emerald and garnet were delicately embroidered against heavy black satin; they caught the light and shimmered. A double layer of the same fabric lined the entire jacket, including the slightly belled three-quarter sleeves. "You cost me a month's rent," she said aloud as she draped it on a padded hanger.

With a quick flick of her wrist Gabrielle shook wrinkles

from the Chinese silk shirtdress. She had especially liked
the Mikado print against a green background. It set off to
perfection the golden, raw-honey tone of her skin. Her
wide brown eyes sparkled with approval again as she unpacked an off-the-shoulder tunic of black chiffon shot
with tiny strands of copper. This alone, she decided, was
worth the loss of her privacy; but only for a short time, she
amended. The matching ankle-length pleated culottes were
intriguing. Their inner seams were cleverly concealed in a
gossamer swirl of slender silk-lined pleats. Gabrielle's
fourth purchase was a daring black chiffon blouse that
could be worn with the culottes in case she tired of the
tunic. She had hesitated to buy the blouse when she noticed
the amount of cleavage it exposed, but the thin copper
circlet that locked it around her neck convinced her. She
could cover her bare shoulders with the jeweled jacket.

This small task completed, and too exhausted to bathe,
Gabrielle swept the empty case to the floor and crawled
wearily between cool sheets on the narrow bed.

A FLOCK of wild, chattering parakeets invaded the jasmine,
taunting Micah Davidson as he peered out wooden-shutter
louvers. He watched raw steam percolate from the verdant
jungle, forming a torpid mist on the peak of the equatorial
mountain. His eyes flicked expectantly from the small
clearing floored with peeled logs to the slender spur hacked
through thick, tangled foliage. The dark green mass hovered tunnellike over the one-lane road. Here and there a
shard of sunlight found an opening, piercing the shadowy
dimness.

The early-morning sun shifted, slipping between the
wooden shutters to trace a narrow, striped pattern across
the polished wood floor. As the sun rose, the pattern waf-
fled, leaping over natural burlap coverings on enormous
ottomans between matching twin sofas, either of which
could contain Micah's more than six-foot length with a
comfortable margin.

The bands of sunlight kept reaching toward the black
man as he leaned into the cool interior of his house. They
streaked across close-cropped hair framing his carved

mahogany face, spotlighting a wide brow that narrowed to ash-black sideburns, cut precision straight across the top of his strong, square jaw. A straight nose separated stark brown eyes shuttered with a thick sweep of dark lashes. Parallel ridges under his nose were partially responsible for the sensual curve of his full lips; an ironic smile brought to the surface by an indestructible inner awareness heightened the sensuality.

Micah sat relaxed, displaying the arrogance of an immobile stalker, a stalker with knowledge about the habits of his prey and determined against useless motion. A single splinter of sun snagged on an ancient gold medallion that lay against his solid muscular chest.

A white German shepherd lay on a priceless savonnerie, his ears perked forward at the sound of a motor straining in low gear. The dog stretched and yawned, padded over to Micah, and stood under his hand, accepting as his due the stroking of lean brown fingers behind his ears.

A Jeep struggled over the sharp rise on the mountain and the driver carefully negotiated the small bridge spanning a deep chasm. Micah moved with lithe animal grace closer to the shuttered windows, startling the parakeets into flight. His eyes followed them as they soared with loud squawking and beating of wings, sorting themselves into a neat formation to disappear over the red-tiled roof.

The Jeep came to an abrupt halt in front of the jasmine. Micah watched the thin, faded man as he climbed from the Jeep, and a trace of sadness flickered across his face, softening the harshness. He and Benton were the same age—thirty-eight—yet Benton looked far older; worn and bent from the ravages of injuries received while they were on a midnight patrol in the jungles of Vietnam. Life played strange games with humanity, Micah mused, and the thought brought a tight smile to his hewn lips.

For months after Micah had joined the elite special services group in Asia, he and Benton, the only two blacks in the platoon, had fought one another viciously, very nearly killing each other on more than one occasion. But when Benton had been ambushed by the Vietcong, Micah couldn't stand by and watch his adversary die; it was as though he resented the enemy stealing the pleasure he had relished for himself.

Their relationship had changed after that, as Benton slowly shriveled into a shell and began to cling to Micah. With a subtlety unknown to both of them, Micah became his brother's keeper. Benton, though, refused to be pitied, much preferring Micah's anger, enjoying it and, very often, deliberately provoking it—as though driven by some remnant of his former self. Micah wiped the sadness from his face, remembering only that he and Benton had been together for more than twelve years, with Benton acting as his secretary, and a damned good one at that.

Benton's footsteps, slow and measured, sounded on the wide veranda. Micah's movement was certain and fluid; supple muscles and tendons flexed in the silent forward thrust of his body. His long powerful fingers grasped the knob, jerking the door open.

"What took you so long?" he demanded, raking Benton's sweat-drenched body with a careful appraising glance. Controlled anger waxed the low resonance of his voice.

Benton shoved his glasses high on his brow, sighed wearily, and pushed past Micah into the cool, shadowed interior.

"I thought you were at the river camp. I went there first. Then there was a problem with oil pressure in the helicopter. Max had to stay in Coco Solito," Benton wheezed, sucking in air to expand the cavity of his single lung. "I had to borrow Jinks's Jeep to drive up here." Carl Benton smiled slightly at the angry glint in Micah's eyes. "I also had a devil of a time doing these translations myself."

"Is there some problem with the radio? You could've called me." He took the sheaf of contracts from his secretary's outstretched hand, quickly scanned the handwritten figures, then tossed the papers onto his desk.

"Yes, it's working. I thought about calling you, but what the hell...I wouldn't have been here any sooner." Micah glanced up and noted the battle-ready gleam in Benton's eyes. He smiled, refusing to be baited.

"We need someone who can translate these contracts into English without so damn many mistakes. Leave off one zero"—his voice was low—"and it would take a year

to make up the loss.'' Micah snapped at Benton, ''How
many contracts are there altogether?''

Benton wheezed and pulled an already damp handkerchief from his pocket to wipe away the beads of perspiration on his narrow upper lip before he answered. ''About
eighteen major ones, then there are subcontracts for loggers, engineers, and heavy equipment operators. The land
lease and conservation agreement with the government of
Panama are the two most critical. Registration for the
cargo ship should be translated too. Captain Dressler
called, by the way; the *Upsure* is safely berthed and dry-
docked in Houston. Refurbishing and refitting should be
completed no later than the first of the year.''

Micah lowered himself onto the thick cushion of the
burlap-covered sofa. No skirting marred the pristine lines
of the furniture, nor any piece in the house—a foil against
any pests with the audacity to seek hiding in the cool,
squared structure.

''What about the lumber mill on Chico Bayou in Pensacola?''

Benton wheezed and sucked in air. ''They've agreed on
forty- to sixty-foot logs. And to take all the cedar, provided we give them an exclusive deal on mahogany. I said yes.
We off-load in Pensacola Bay and tugs push the logs up
the bayou. We're responsible for forming up rafts and any
debris left in the bay. They pay for the tugs.''

''Deadlines and schedules?'' Micah scissored the words.

''None but our own. I explained that we'd have to float
the logs down the Mamoni River during the rainy season.''
Benton hesitated for a fraction of a second before continuing. ''Micah, what we really need on these contracts is
someone from the outside.

''If you use a translator from Panama, word will get
around that we've got this logging project off the ground.
That will bring in a crush of speculators more than anxious to cater to the needs of the loggers, not to mention
an element or two that we definitely don't want. Or do
you?''

Micah exploded. ''Hell, no! We'll have enough problem
housing the married men without adding to the problem.

The less women in the logging camps, the better for all of us.''

"Oh, well, I was just checking," Benton said. "We're not set up to handle it anyway. We couldn't hire a security force big enough to keep people off the Cuna Indian reservation. That might create a problem for us. The government wants the Indians eased into civilization—such as it is—slowly. Any great influx right now and I think you'd get your land lease voided. There is one other thing: with General Torrijos dead, the National Guard is wary of a lot of strangers in the jungles. You get two men together and right away they think you've got a rebel force trying to overthrow the government."

"All right," Micah said, "I'm paying you for solutions. What is it?"

Benton's glasses slid down to the tip of his nose; he used the moment to glance at Micah's face. Seeing only a calm facade, he sighed. "Bring someone here until the contracts are translated, typed, and signed. Then if there are any problems, your attorneys won't have any difficulty sifting through the legalese. The job requirements are really very simple—Spanish, English, and the ability to type. A temporary position, three months at the outside, even if any renegotiations are necessary. The important thing is to bring him here to Chepo on a tourist visa; we'd never get approval to bring in an American translator when the embassies here are full of them."

Micah's sweep of lashes concealed his eyes. "You could be right. Take care of it."

Benton grunted, taking care to hide his disappointment that the suggestion did not provoke an argument. "You want me to go through a personnel agency or see if we've got somebody in our Atlanta office?"

A slender smile tipped a corner of Micah's mouth. "No, call Professor Nate Hensley at Monroe University in Houston. Tell him what we're looking for. And mention my name. If he has any candidates for the job, you go to Houston and interview them." Micah paused at his desk, stuffing the contracts into a thin leather briefcase. "Are you driving me to Coco Solito?"

Benton looked startled. "God, I hope not. I can hardly breathe in this heat as it is. Max said he'd have the oil leak fixed and be here no later than eleven. I'm going to ask Maria to fix me a light breakfast, then I'm resting until Amand gets here. He's giving me a lift back to Panama City."

"Amand?" Micah's eyes lighted with interest. "Where did you see him?"

"He was in the Mamoni River camp. Helen and Jinks invited him to lunch."

"What was that slick-talking priest doing in my logging camp?" Micah asked, suspicious of the Jesuit's intentions.

"Just the usual." Benton smiled, counting the items on his fingers for graphic display. "Raving about the effects of modern civilization on the Indians, swearing that the logging operation is going to destroy any clues that might lead to documenting the influence of Chinese culture on the Chibchan, and trying to coax Jinks into vaccinating some children on the Cuna reservation." Benton folded his fingers down. "Let's see—the last two things he was doing was begging the use of Jinks's razor and waiting to dine on the wild pig Helen was cooking." Benton shrugged, a sad, resigned gesture of one who loves to eat but can't. "Sure smelled good too."

Micah picked out the only item in Benton's recital that interested him. "Just who's supposed to pay for my medical team to vaccinate these Indians?"

"Oh, you—who else?" Benton said with a smile.

Micah grunted, noting the smile, and snapped the briefcase shut. "I have a bit of baggage for you to drop off at Tocumen Airport on your way in."

"Okay. Amand is driving his Jeep. There'll be plenty of room. What is it?"

"Vanessa," Micah said dryly.

"Vanessa! I thought that was over lo—"

"It was. She invited herself," Micah said over his shoulder as he strode out the door to the inner courtyard. He kept to the shade of the roofed veranda, skirting the mosaic-tiled footpaths. Still he had to lower his lashes against the searing glare of the brilliant tropical sun; it beat down in waves on the spacious inner yard, planted with native trees and shrubs.

Maria came out of her kitchen and threw a handful of crumbs to the parakeets complaining among themselves in a roof-tall mango tree; its spreading limbs were laden with green fruit.

"Don't do that, Maria!" he called to her. "We have enough pests around here without you encouraging more." Maria nodded and smiled, standing at the banister until Micah entered his bedroom, then brushed the remaining crumbs from her plump brown hand. The parakeets fluttered down, salvaging every tidbit.

The bedroom was dim, still shuttered against the light. A ceiling fan rotated lazily, stirring the cooled air. The throbbing of its motor droned and lulled, unheard by the sleeping woman in Micah's immense square bed. Her voluptuous form was vague through the white mist of mosquito netting draped from its foot-round pivot in the heavy cedar beam more than nine feet overhead.

Micah pulled the netting aside and gazed at the lovely bronze woman. The expensive, flowery scent she wore wafted over him, reminding him of the lusty response she had evoked in him last night. He felt the stirring in his loins, and for a long moment he thought of undressing, then he swore softly, a muffled oath under his breath. A hard glint shrouded his eyes as his lean brown fingers shook her shoulder.

"Micah?" The question voice was low and husky with sleep. She turned on her back, exposing a full tawny breast, provocative against the white muslin sheet.

"Who did you expect?" he asked wryly. "Or have you already forgotten whose bed you spent the night in?" There was no humor in the slant of his smile.

Vanessa smiled coyly. "Oh, I know, all right—you're still the best, Micah."

"I'm sure you say that to all your discards." He let his eyes slide coldly to her exposed breasts, then lifted to meet her gaze. "Get up and get dressed—don't bother to unpack. Benton and Father Chardin are giving you a lift to the airport."

"Airport? What do you mean? I just got here!" Vanessa flared indignantly.

"And you are just leaving," he said with amused sarcasm.

Vanessa sat up, wrapping the sheet around her nakedness. "What will I tell my father?"

"About what?"

"Why, about us."

"Vanessa, there's nothing about us and you know it."

"There used to be, Micah. We can work it out. I made a mistake, I admit it," she pleaded.

Micah's jaw went rigid. "There's nothing to work out and there's no use trying to dredge up the past. You were the one who left, remember?" he said softly. "You were the one who called the wedding off. I won't be played for a fool twice."

"You owe me, Micah!" she hissed angrily, the beauty of her features disintegrated in a snarl.

"I don't owe you a thing. Get up and get dressed," he ordered, allowing the flap of netting to fall into place.

"You wouldn't be filthy rich today if I hadn't talked Daddy into giving you a loan," she spat at him through the white mist.

Micah's head tilted back as his low, rich laughter sounded against the whitewashed ceiling. "Your daddy," he mimed, "is as greedy as every banker in Atlanta. He never made a loan to me; that was a myth to cover our business arrangement and you know it." Micah eased his supple frame into a carved teak chair, its soft cushions well used to his lean imprint. He lifted the lid of an elegant enameled box on the table at his elbow and chose a cigarette.

"I'll take one of those," Vanessa demanded, her voice trembling with seething anger.

He lighted two. "Come out from under that net if you want to smoke," he ordered. Vanessa wrapped the sheet around her and tucked the thin gauze around the heavy, dark post on the bed. Micah smiled as she snatched the cigarette from his fingers. He rested his head on the high back of the chair and let his long curled lashes veil his eyes. They smoked in silence.

STRANGE that his mind should be so crowded with memories today, first with Benton and Vanessa, and now his homecoming from Vietnam.

Micah remembered vividly walking up the red clay road in Georgia that led to his parents' farm. The road was empty and smelled of dust. Benton had followed, yards behind, puffing and out of breath and resting often.

Pink flowering dogwood hedged the road while resinous sap from tall pines oozed its sharp odor into the air, mingling with the dust. He could glimpse the Flint River through the trees hugging its clay banks as its waters moved sluggishly, tinted brown-red with soil it snatched from the rich farmland.

Windows on the neat clapboard house had been boarded up. A No Trespassing sign was nailed to the door, and a card stapled to the cardboard sign had the name of Vanessa's father and the bank he owned.

Micah had looked under the porch step for the coffee can half buried there and found the key. He had ripped the boards off the windows and he and Benton had stayed in the house for more than a month. Memories of his parents had been strong then. Both of them had died while he was fighting in Asia, first his father and a few months later his mother.

As soon as neighboring farmers had realized he was home, they visited and told Micah of the foreclosure. Soon after that a real estate agent brought a young couple to look at the farm. Micah had greeted them coldly and refused to allow them in. Two days later he was in Atlanta, calling on the banker, Benjamin Thomas.

The banker had been wary of the black centurion towering over him, noting the harshly constructed features, the controlled wrath, and the determined set of his jaw. Thomas murmured soothing comments to no avail, finally proposing a business partnership that included returning the farm to Micah, free and clear. Micah listened to the proposal and finally agreed, for twenty-five percent of the profits. Thomas had stared at him aghast, but in the end he relented.

Thomas was certain Congress would soon repeal the law that kept American citizens from owning and trading in gold. He proposed that Micah go to Europe and Africa to buy the precious metal and literally sit on it until Congress repealed the act and the price of gold rose. The banker placed a half-million dollars into a reserve account in Liechtenstein—no questions asked—and the drafts for the gold were paid from there.

Micah hadn't asked where the half million came from but he suspected Thomas had juggled his books at the bank to make the money available. Luckily the gamble had paid off.

At the end of two years Micah had acquired the gold, purchasing it in small amounts until the entire half million was used up. In another year Americans were owning their own gold, and when trading shot the price from thirty-five dollars an ounce to eight hundred an ounce, Thomas sold. The gold brought in $10,923,571.4. Micah got his share and almost got the banker's daughter. When that fizzled, he returned to the farm, picked up Benton, and came to Panama. Of course, he was far wealthier now. Prudent investments had seen to that.

THE whirring vibration of a helicopter's rotors split the air. Micah ground out his cigarette and moved swiftly to the window, flipping open the gray-brown shutter. Max was setting the machine down on the tarp of peeled logs. He turned back to the woman sitting on the edge of his bed.

"I have work to do, Vanessa. Father Chardin will be here in a few hours. Be ready."

"You can't just brush me off like this, Micah."

He raked her with a cold glance. A wicked grin played about his lips. "You're a lot like your father, Vanessa—greedy. You want all the dessert life has to offer without lifting a finger. I want you out of my house. This is the second time a Thomas has ventured on my property without invitation. There won't be a third time," he warned.

A stream of vile oaths issued from Vanessa's mouth.

Micah smiled to himself as he closed the door. Amand and Benton would have their hands full with Vanessa on the sixty-mile drive through the steaming heat in Amand's open, unair-conditioned Jeep. He chuckled aloud. Perhaps he'd allow his medical team to vaccinate the Indians for the priest—as compensation.

Chapter Two

Late that same afternoon, after ten hours of sleep had improved her disposition and taken the edge off the jet lag she had been experiencing, Gabrielle luxuriated in a tubful of steaming water scented with pure tangerine essence. She sighed heavily as she scooped up a handful of the bubbles—another luxury she would have to use sparingly until her finances improved.

She had called Mr. Garrett today instead of tomorrow, being too impatient to wait, only to learn he had already hired a replacement. He was well satisfied with the woman he had hired and knew of no one needing a bilingual clerk just now. She didn't relish having to pound the pavement looking for another job. Not too many employers were as understanding as Mr. Garrett had been about all the extra time off she needed to meet the demanding schedule of class and rehearsals. Gabrielle felt that Murphy's Law had latched onto her with a vengeance.

Suddenly the bathroom door burst open and Val rushed in, and before the startled Gabrielle could venture a word, Val was hugging her soapy wet neck and chattering a mile a minute.

"Gabby! Congratulations! I just heard about the invitation from the Royal Ballet." Val bubbled over with laughter. "Congratulations are in order to me too," she said and held out her left hand to display a gleaming gold wedding band.

Gabrielle eyed her best friend speculatively. "In the first place, this thing with the Royal Ballet is just rumor... until and if, or when, Von Bateman makes an official announcement, and in the second, I'd like to do more than congratulate you, Val. I'd like to wring your neck!"

The diminutive Chicano, dark eyes flashing, grinned and sat down on the only accommodation available in the small bath. She crossed her legs and leaned engagingly toward Gabrielle. "I'm in love—"

"You're always in love. Why did you have to go and get married this time?"

"Gab, this is the real thing! The kind where butterflies fill your stomach and there's no room for food, the kind where you want to be with him every minute and know he's beside you when you're sleeping and worry when he isn't. Oh, I can't explain it...."

"You're managing very nicely," Gabrielle said wryly. "And I do wish you the very best, Pietro too, but Val, honestly! I don't have a place to live—"

"Oh, but you do. When Pietro goes back offshore—he works for Mobil Oil—you can move back in."

Gabrielle sighed with relief. "I knew Mother had got it wrong. She said Pietro had moved in."

"Why, he has, but he's offshore ten days and home seven, so when he's working, you can stay with me."

"And when he's not?" Gabrielle asked, beginning to understand what Val was driving at and not liking it one bit. Her spirits, soaring only an instant ago, began to sag.

"Well, can't you stay here at your mother's? It's only until after Christmas, then Pietro's getting a shore job and we can get our own place."

"Val, you are crazy! Crazier than a bedbug looking for a cot. Christmas is four months away and I can't live in two places at once. Besides, it's not fair. I'd be paying half the rent—"

"Only a third."

Gabrielle groaned and stood up, dripping water. "Move, so I can get out of this tub, the water's getting cold." She shrugged into a terry robe and pushed Val ahead of her into the bedroom.

"You cut your hair."

"Yes, don't try to change the subject. We've got to work something out. I'll be a nervous wreck living under my mother's thumb again."

"Well, you can live at the apartment too," Val said reluctantly. "Pietro won't mind."

"I mind, Val. It's *our* apartment. It's one thing for you to bring a stray home now and then, but—" Gabrielle sat on the edge of her bed, deflated and contemplating the near future. "Oh, shoot! I'll just stay here until you two get your own place." She looked glum.

"For heaven's sake. What's wrong with staying here? It's where you grew up. It's only for four months."

A lifetime, Gabrielle thought. "You know very well what's wrong with it—my mother. She'll spend half of her life playing bridge and the other half trying to get me married!"

"I'm all for it. You getting married, I mean. That would solve all our problems."

"Valerie Garcia!" Gabrielle said threateningly.

"Guzeldere," Val said, wriggling her ring finger and smiling.

"Guzeldere! No wonder Mother couldn't pronounce it." She gave Val a brooding look. "You are fast going from being my best friend to becoming my worst enemy."

"I thought Davila held that estimable position," Val said, refusing to take Gabrielle seriously.

"Right now you're running such a close second, you could spit and not miss it! I don't have time for marriage. You know that. It's hard enough trying to find time to eat, sleep, dance, and work."

"Did you ever ask yourself why you throw up this wall of excuses every time somebody mentions marriage, Gabby?"

"I don't have to ask myself that question. I know why," she said, slipping her feet into a pair of fluffy mules. She discarded the towel and put on a robe. She didn't have time, that was why.

"The problem with you, Gabby, is that you let things just flow around you like... like a fence post in the wind. You never reach out and grab at a slice of life unless it has to do with ballet. You experience everything in dance and nowhere else. It'll catch up with you one day, believe me."

"What are you using to make this prophecy? A crystal ball or are you reading palms these days?"

"Oh, Gab, don't get mad—"

"Val, I'm broke. You've run me out of an apartment I love, right back into the clutches of my overprotective mother, I don't have my extra job because Mr. Garrett has already replaced me, and you sit there and tell me not to get mad. Just what do you suggest I do, throw up my hands and shout hallelujah?"

Val shrugged. "I can help out with your cash flow. I brought back your half of the rent for this month."

"A hundred and fifty dollars will not get me out of this mess."

Val gave her a weak smile. "Gab, you're still disoriented from jet lag, and everything looks bad now. You'll feel better after you've had more rest. Look on the bright side. You have a roof over your head, you were a smash in London, and now you have some money." She laid the cash on the dresser, swiveled on the white wicker stool, checked her face in the mirror, then stood up to leave. "I've got to go. Pietro is waiting for me to cook supper."

"How domestic."

Val ignored this sarcasm. She paused at the bedroom door. "Look, Gabby, I'm sorry about this, really—I mean, about the apartment and all. But Pietro lived with his cousin before we got married and, well, it just seemed like our place was the answer. I'll see you at rehearsals tomorrow, okay?"

Gabrielle forced a smile. "Okay, Val. I guess I'll ride home with you tomorrow night and pick up a few things I'll be needing here."

"Sure, then you can tell me everything that happened in England."

After Val left, Gabrielle puttered around in her room. She hadn't unpacked yet and still didn't feel up to it. Instead, she rummaged through a suitcase until she found a clean pair of tan slacks and a brown knit top and put them on. She mulled over her options for a while and discovered she didn't have any.

There was that old saying, "No sense crying over spilt milk"—but damnation! Her whole cow had dried up! First, she'd been pushed out of her home and hearth, and second, Mr. Garrett had already hired a satisfactory bilingual clerk. Somehow she would have to muster the cash to rent another apartment, find a second job, and—hardest of all—unearth a reliable roommate to share expenses. She decided her next roommate would have to be ugly, covered with moles, have flat feet, and be man-free, or failing that, the girl would have to positively be as dedicated as she was to her work. Unfortunately, Gabrielle knew of no one right off who fitted either of these requirements.

Hattie knocked on the door and came bustling into the room. She was brown, large-boned, very broad, and a head shorter than Gabrielle and she never pretended to be jolly. She adored Gabrielle when she wasn't exasperated with her, and since Gabrielle had not been in the house for even twelve hours and spent most of those in bed, Hattie was disposed to adoration. She smothered Gabrielle in a bearish hug.

"You were asleep by the time I got your cases up," she said, explaining away this unusual display of affection.

"Thanks, Hattie," she said, sitting down in front of the mirror. "When will supper be ready? I'm starved."

"Humph! If you want to eat in this house tonight, you'll just have to settle for sandwiches—tiny ones," she said with disapproval. "Those bridge women are coming over tonight. We've been settin' up tables in the front room all afternoon."

"What about Daddy?"

"He's eating over at the school. You know he's not coming home till those women are gone."

Nothing has changed at home, Gabrielle thought. Not her mother and her passion for bridge, not her father and his abhorrence of it—or maybe it was the gossipy old women, most of whom were the wives of his colleagues— nor Hattie, who still disapproved of it all.

"I'm just going to brush my hair and put on a little makeup, then I'll be down. I'll eat on the back porch."

Sitting on the back porch in a lawn chair overlooking the small well-kept backyard, Gabrielle was prone to agree with ancient cartographers that the world was flat. It was ironic how she could feel like she was on top of the world one day and the next seem to find herself slipping off its edge. She had never imagined that so much could happen in so short a time that she'd have so little control over. A slice of life indeed! she thought ruefully; her life was more than sliced, it was shredded, but she'd get it all back together and soon. Without another thought, she went into the house, through the kitchen and up the stairs to her room.

She flung herself across her bed, emotionally drained and still under the influence of jet lag, and drifted into a sound slumber for the second time that day.

Chapter Three

Feeling gloriously rested and thoroughly refreshed, Gabrielle bathed quickly and stepped naked and wet into her bedroom and shivered. The room was cool, the drapes drawn against the late afternoon September sun. With deft hands she circled her slender body with an oversize pink bath towel, tucking the corner into curved cleavage between her full brown breasts.

"Gabby?" Emily hooked her head around the door.

"Come in, Mother," she answered as she began sorting cosmetics on the dresser. She met her mother's eyes in the mirror.

"Tim called," Emily said. "He's running about fifteen minutes late, he went over to your apartment to pick you up. Val told him you were here."

"Oh, Lordy, I forgot all about him. Thanks, Mother."

Emily lifted one of the heavy, unpacked cases to the unmade bed. "Want me to sort this out for you?"

"I'd appreciate it, if you could dig through there and find me some clean leotards for rehearsals today. There's a brown set, I think."

"What did Val have to say when she came by yesterday?" Emily asked, curious, her back to Gabrielle and her hands busy with the task in front of her.

Gabrielle laughed ruefully. "She suggested the three of us continue to share the apartment part-time, of all things. I said no." She pushed the thought out of her mind and concentrated on applying her makeup.

Emily watched, fascinated, as Gabrielle dipped plum-tipped fingers into tiny pots of rust hues, stroking swiftly and lightly to darken high cheekbones, then drew a featherlight band to enhance satiny brown skin above arched brows. A single perfect stroke of smoky black liner on each lid transformed sparkling almond-shaped eyes into shimmering orbs of elusive mystery.

"I don't see how you managed that so fast," Emily said, amazed as Gabrielle's features went from gamine to exquisite in less than a minute.

"It takes a lot of practice. We don't have much time between scenes to change our makeup." Her eyes widened and watched carefully through their thick fringe as she outlined her lips and drew pale burgundy over their fullness. "How's that?" She smiled at her mother's image behind hers.

"Entirely too provocative," Emily snorted, yet sounding pleased.

"We old maids need all the help we can get," Gabrielle teased pointedly. "I'm told I look just like you did twenty years ago."

Emily raked a cursory glance over her towel-clad daughter. "Somebody's memory is failing, and badly," she returned, but bristled happily at the compliment. "Here, hand me that curling iron, I'll do the back for you." She ran her fingers through the swag of silky black curls that capped Gabrielle's well-shaped head. "I really like this style. Did you have it cut recently?"

"Yes, in London. It's called a brushed-back wedge cut, à la Diana." Her fingers closed over her mother's wrist. "Just the tips, Mother," she warned. "I don't want to walk out of here looking like a ten-year-old." She yelped in pain as Emily deliberately touched the hot curling iron to her scalp for an instant.

"What's going on in here?" The deep drawl of Nate Hensley's Southern voice carried around the bedroom door. "You decent?" he asked, not waiting for an answer before pushing through the door.

"I'm not," Gabrielle teased and watched her father's image fill the recesses of the mirror not already taken by those of her and her mother. His eyes twinkled in a face drawn in skin the color of deeply browned cured tobacco; laugh lines crinkled around his mouth as he gave her a wide smile that revealed gold-edged teeth. He pushed Emily out of the way and kissed his daughter on the top of her head, then he eyed Gabrielle, securely draped from armpit to ankle in the pink towel.

"I'd say you're a sight more decent now than when you climb into those skimpy leotards." He squeezed Gabrielle's shoulder fondly and turned to his wife. "Emily, will you please tell Hattie there will be four extra for dinner tonight?"

Emily narrowed her brown eyes at the sheepish look of her expensively clad husband. "No, she'll quit." Her frown deepened. "I wish you wouldn't invite all those radicals to dinner every day."

Nate's booming laughter filled the room. "Emily, you think anyone who doesn't drink gallons of coffee and play bridge twice a week is a radical. We merely discuss the economics of unemployment and wars, not create them." He smiled indulgently with amused patience at his wife and swept clean an area on the suitcase-laden bed large enough to settle his girth. "As for Hattie," he said dryly, "she's been quitting every Thursday for the past fifteen years. I think I can live through one more threat."

Emily sneered sweetly. "Brave words from a man who goes all rubbery when he thinks *I* might have to cook." Nate sobered immediately and Emily, happy that her barb had stung, continued. "I'll tell her, but you'd think the parents of your students would teach them some manners before sending them off to college. I just wish they wouldn't chew gum at the table, they sound like a cacophony of bent frogs."

"My Lord! Where did you pick that one up?" Nate winced. Emily had a remarkable penchant for slinging words together in such an awful manner they usually hung in the mind. Too often in class he'd catch himself repeating her; it was embarrassing for a professor of his stature. He threw his wife an exasperated look, then directed a question to Gabrielle. "Do you need any help moving your things home? One of my students has a pickup we can borrow."

"No, I don't. I'm getting some things tonight and Val and Pietro are going to bring the rest over this weekend."

Nate continued to gaze at his daughter. He often wondered that he had been so blessed to have such beauty spring from his loins. Her face with its prominent cheek-bones and wide brow was evocative, hinting strongly that the independent tilt of her chin was more than mere facade. Unlike Emily, he felt no desire to rush Gabrielle into marriage, yet he was concerned about her driving ambition, her seemingly single-minded fervor about ballet. Dedication he could accept as ordinary, even admirable, but Gabrielle went beyond even the extraordinary, carrying it to the point of obsession. She drove herself relentlessly and it worried him. Sometimes he was riddled by a strange, unaccustomed apprehension for no fathomable reason. It had begun several years ago when Gabrielle had sprained her ankle during rehearsals and had been unable to dance or go to class for two weeks. Her eyes had been filled with panic. He had been immeasurably relieved when Dr. Baker had declared her fit for dance once again.

Gabrielle had put herself into bondage with dance and if it was taken from her he wouldn't—couldn't—contemplate what her reaction might be. He had breathed easier, felt the strange apprehension lessen when, upon moving out of their home, Gabrielle had had to work outside ballet to make ends meet. It kept her among ordinary people with day-to-day living experiences and therefore blunted the astonishing world of stage that pulled her so irresistibly, so inexorably, into fantasy.

But Gabrielle was happy with her life and Nate held that uppermost in his mind. He realized she was smiling at him with an inquiring look on her face. "Did you need some money?" he asked then, moving his hand to his pocket.

Gabrielle straightened her back, the smile went off her face, and her chin thrust out. Watching this transformation, Nate added obstinate to his mental image of his daughter and knew she was going to refuse his offer before she spoke.

"No, thank you, Daddy. Val returned my share of the rent I paid before I went on tour, so I have some cash until I get paid again." It would help some, she thought. It wasn't nearly enough, but she wouldn't accept any more help from her parents than was absolutely necessary. For a single instant she regretted the purchase of the magnificent clothes that hung in her closet.

Only slightly daunted, Nate asked, "What about your furniture?"

Gabrielle shrugged. "It stays in the apartment until Val moves out or I can find another place. I can't afford storage on it anyway."

Nate nodded, content that Gabrielle had everything under control, and claimed his wife's attention once again. "Emily, do you recall what I mentioned to you yesterday? About that secretary of Micah Davidson's calling to see if I knew anyone interested in a job?" Emily nodded. "He called back today to say he wouldn't need anyone for a while yet, because Micah has been injured in a helicopter crash."

"Nate! That's terrible." Emily voiced sincere concern and sympathy.

"Who are you talking about?" Gabrielle asked. She lowered the hairbrush to her lap and pivoted on the white wicker stool to face her father. "Do I know him?"

"No, honey, you wouldn't remember Micah. He was a student of mine fourteen or so years ago. He had to quit in his junior year. His father got sick and he went home to help his mother run their farm." Nate's brow rumpled in thoughtful recall. "In Georgia, I think. He was one of my most promising students too. He called me when he got his draft notice, and again when he got back from Vietnam. I hadn't heard from him in seven or eight years, until yesterday—at least not directly. He's practically a legend in the financial circles in Atlanta. Micah lives in Panama now." Nate smiled at Gabrielle. "He wanted someone to translate some contracts having to do with logging timber from virgin jungle. That's a job right up your alley, Gabby. If he calls back, do you want me to put your name to him?"

"Would it be soon? I need to find part-time work right away."

"I think it would be a few months, from what Mr. Benton told me. The project is being put on hold until Micah has recovered enough to direct it."

Gabrielle shook her head ruefully. "I guess that leaves me out. Thanks anyway, Daddy. Now, if you two don't mind, I need to finish dressing. Tim will be here in a few minutes and I don't want to be late to rehearsals."

GABRIELLE inspected her leotard-clad body critically in the mirror. Not an ounce of unwanted fat marred her trim, lissome figure. Thank goodness she didn't have to maintain a stringent diet as many of her friends did to keep in shape for the strenuous dance routines. One could occasionally get an extra pound or two past the director's keen eye, but never past the wardrobe mistress, who knew to the fraction of an inch how much flesh should pad a bone.

She could dance another ten years easily, she thought, and after that, her own studio, teaching and perhaps a few guest appearances in ballets she liked best. After all the hard work, long hours of practice, strained muscles, agonizing over interpretations, she had made it to the top. London had proved it.

"Gabby! Tim is here," her mother called up the stairs.

Gabrielle stuffed her pointe shoes, towel, and baby powder into her tote, then shrugged into a lightweight beige coat and belted it securely around her waist. Tim was leaning lazily against the front door when she reached the wide entrance hall. He pushed himself away from the door and circled her waist possessively.

"I've missed you," he murmured against her ear. He bent his head to plant a kiss on her lips, but Gabrielle turned her face so that his lips raked innocently on her cheek.

"Betty's having a party tomorrow night. How about going with me?" Tim asked, guiding his ancient blue Volkswagen into the afternoon traffic.

"No, Tim, I told you, I'm not going to see you socially anymore, and even if I did, I certainly would *not* attend one of Betty's parties."

"You don't really mean that," Tim whined.

Gabrielle groaned inwardly. "I do mean it. We'll see each other often enough at rehearsals and at group events; that's enough for a while."

"Well, then," he pushed stubbornly, "Betty's party is a group event. Meet me there."

"Group event is right," Gabrielle said, disgust plain in her voice. "Musical beds is not my idea of a fun evening, so forget it." Tim began to jerk the gears angrily, changing lanes in the fast-moving traffic with hardly a glance in his rearview mirror or any consideration for other drivers. Gabrielle regretted that she had accepted his offer of a lift to rehearsals. He began to tailgate the car in front, hitting the brakes with short stabbing motions when he was nearly on top of the other car.

"Tim! Don't take your anger out on me or all the other drivers. It's childish," Gabrielle exclaimed, becoming alarmed at the dangerous turn of his anger.

"You're the one being childish, Gabby—not me. This is the age of sexual freedom, or hadn't you noticed?" he snarled.

"Sexual freedom has nothing to do with it. I want to feel something for a man before I go jumping in bed with him." She tried to speak calmly, but her words only seemed to make Tim more irate.

"You don't feel that way about me—is that it?"

"I'm sorry," Gabrielle said quietly, "but that's exactly it. Now, for God's sake, slow down. That diesel is moving into this lane."

"I can make it," Tim drawled, jerking the gears and flooring the gas pedal.

In the millisecond of a slow-motion drama, Gabrielle knew he wouldn't. As if detached, she saw the scene unfold: The front of the Volkswagen crashed into the wheels of the mammoth truck. Colors and sounds became vivid, vibrant: the sky-blue hood of the Volkswagen, the red rain-washed letters painted on the back of the diesel, the white mud flap behind the monstrous wheel, and then the sickening crunch as metal tore metal, and finally silence. She was aware of the rain splattering on her through the broken windshield, but she felt no pain and couldn't understand why the cloud of darkness clutched her.

She woke the next morning in the hospital, knowing she was in the hospital—the smell of medicine and antiseptic assaulted her nostrils. Every muscle in her body ached, and sluggishly, instinctively, she tried out each of her limbs. All responded to the messages her brain sent but one. Black waves of shock, despair, and panic began to well up in her. *What was wrong with her leg?* She forced her eyes open and found herself gazing into her mother's face, bent over hers.

"Hello, sleepyhead." Emily's voice was quiet; soothing; her face was dark and drawn, but relief was clearly etched in her ebony features.

"What time is it, Mother?" What a silly thing to ask, she thought, when there was something more important she needed to ask about, something she had to know, something fearful. Her mouth felt dry, her words sounded faraway in her own ears, and for a moment she didn't think she had spoken aloud. But she must have; Emily was answering her.

"Eight o'clock tomorrow morning for you. How do you feel?"

"Thirsty, sore. My leg hurts—I think."

"Oh, it does, I'm sure," Emily said, watching Gabrielle out of the corner of her eye as she poured iced water into a plastic cup. "It's broken."

Gabrielle raised up and looked at the white cast on her leg. Plum-pink polish on her big toe looked incongruous against the heavy white plaster that entrapped her leg from heel to upper thigh. Her insides wrenched violently, like an unhinged door swinging abandoned in the wind. Her heart twisted inside her.

"Is it a bad break, Mother?" she asked, her voice broken, shuddering with despair, praying the answer would be no, but sensing in the very depths of her soul that the answer would be otherwise.

Emily, seeing the rising panic on her daughter's face, looked away and, knowing she couldn't lie, nodded her head.

Gabrielle's throat constricted so tightly she could hardly breathe. The tears began to come, rolling down her cheeks and melting into the starched white pillow. She felt numb, as stiff and unbending as the white cast on her left leg. All the years of hard work, the pain, exhaustion—for nothing, a stupid accident. She hated Tim, hated him violently, for doing this to her. She felt a jolt of shame. He could be dead. She asked.

"That scoundrel got off with ten stitches in his head and a citation for reckless driving," her mother told her. Gabrielle let the hate come back. Tim would be dancing, hearing the applause, going to his disgusting parties, while she— Oh, God! What was she going to do?

"Don't cry, Gab," Emily begged. "It's not life threatening. Dr. Baker will explain everything. I—I didn't listen to much that was said after I learned you were alive."

"What's there to explain, Mother?" Gabrielle cried out between sobs. "I have a broken leg. I can't dance, not for weeks, maybe even months." A new wave of panic overtook her and she began to rock back and forth on the bed, moaning.

"Gabrielle," Emily began anxiously, then stopped and watched her daughter cry until exhausted. "Everything will work out, you'll see," she said, but there was little conviction in the soothing words.

Gabrielle was in the hospital for three weeks. She had visitors; everyone from the Civic Ballet came, bringing flowers, candy—even Von Bateman, the director. He didn't mention the invitation for the Royal Ballet and neither did Gabrielle; they both knew she wouldn't be able to dance by spring, not a role as demanding as *Giselle*.

Luke Bryant came, bringing his new wife, Pat. Gabrielle had felt awkward and asked them to leave, pleading a headache. Later she wondered if she had imagined the smirk on Luke's face. Tim came too, but Gabrielle became hysterical and Dr. Baker ordered him to stay away. She felt relief that she didn't have to see Tim again, but not seeing him did nothing to curb the bitterness she felt. He was entirely to blame for this disastrous interruption of her career.

Gabrielle went home from the hospital and for two uncomfortable months hobbled around on crutches. In late November the itchy, autographed cast was removed, and by that time the ballet was in rehearsals for the *Nutcracker*.

Few of her friends had time to visit. She spent most of her time alone.

Gabrielle knew the work that lay ahead of her to begin again and for the first time in her life she was overwhelmed with a sense of desperation. She had no job, no apartment, no money, and she couldn't dance. And fearfully, there was the uncertainty in Dr. Baker's words: "I can't guarantee that your leg will heal strong enough for you to resume so strenuous a career, Gabrielle. Only time will tell. For now, you must be very careful, give the bones all the time they need to knit." Time. . . time. . . time. . . .

She didn't have the time! The ballet wouldn't wait. Another girl would be chosen to dance the leads, *her* leads, *her* roles. Gabrielle didn't care whether she lived or died.

Chapter Four

A lowering sun cast a few last burnished rays through the bare branches of the dogwood tinting gold the dusty red clay lane in front of the farm. Micah sat in the low rocking chair, his long legs crossed and propped on the porch railing. He felt the chill as the sun withdrew its warmth from the mild December evening. A gentle breeze ruffled vines woven in the trellis at the end of the porch, spilling the fragrant scent of late-blooming roses into the air.

He hadn't changed a thing on his parents' farm—his farm now. It relaxed him to come here and to know there was a sameness about it. He never felt lonely on the farm. There was a welcome about the rambling house with its large neat rooms, the starched and pressed antimacassars crocheted by his mother that still protected the arms and back of furniture in the living room, and the fragrance of lavender sachets in the closets. It was home, and one day he would raise his own sons here. He wanted his children always to have that sense of belonging. It was an emotion he had lost once and its absence had filled him with an overpowering void.

When he had left the farm to go to Vietnam, he had been a boy, scared and untried. He came home bitter, cynical, and mad to a hostile reception by the American people for an unpopular war. But in Vietnam life was intense, compressed, and he often thought he would never get another day to live, another day of life. When he came home, life was a series of recoveries, a searching out, and he had learned stamina and independence and tolerance of human weaknesses. These things too he would pass on to his children. The tolerance, though, caused him to be possessed of a secret streak of vulnerability that he endeavored to hide, not only from others, but from himself as well.

The wind picked up, gusting across the Flint River as the

sun dropped behind the soaring pine windbreak, bringing him back to the present. Micah unsnapped the circular leather brace from his wrist and slipped it off his hand, massaging his lean fingers. His burn-scarred palm was beginning to heal, and feeling was returning to his fingers, causing an excruciating tingling sensation. The therapist had devised the soft, fingerless glove, lined with steel in the palm to keep his hand from drawing into a claw. He looked at the exposed tissue and grimaced. He had grabbed the burning frame of the helicopter to pull himself out of the wreckage; it had been an instinctive move, one of survival and one that he regretted today. Not that he had survived, but that he hadn't had enough presence of mind to keep his hands off that searing metal doorframe.

His mind flashed back to that fateful day in September. Max had had problems with the oil pressure in the helicopter the morning he flew to Chepo to get Micah for an aerial survey of his land leases. They had lifted off the pad with no problems and were within two miles of the logging camp when the oil line broke and spewed its contents across the motor housing. The oil caught fire. Max managed to bring the machine down to the tops of the trees before the rotors stopped. And in a single breathless instant Micah felt the helicopter drop to the ground and tumble over on its side. Burning oil swamped the metal frame of the aircraft and dripped flaming into the cockpit, scorching Micah's neck and back. When Max had said calmly "Let's get the hell out of here," Micah did just that.

The welts of unhealed skin on his neck and back were still tender and pink-tinged. He had refused another skin transplant at the burn center in Houston. He already felt like the patchwork quilt that covered the bed in his room. It wasn't the painful process that he objected to so much as the time-consuming grafting and healing that required the sterile environment of hospitalization. He was anxious to return to Chepo.

The logging project was far behind schedule, because he had been unwilling to turn it over to anyone else. Micah had finally agreed to let J.T., the logger boss, take his crews into the jungle, lay out the sectors, and mark the trees to be cut. Still, the logger boss was chomping at the bit and as anxious as Micah to begin the challenge of harvesting the majestic forest from the inhospitable jungle terrain. The next rainy season began in April and Micah wanted to have the mahogany cut and on the banks of the rivers, ready for the high water to carry it into the Gulf of Panama.

Captain Dressler had taken command of the *Upsure* yesterday and had the ship in the Gulf of Mexico for sea and safety trials. If all went well, they would sail for Panama on the twenty-fifth—as good a Christmas present as he could ask for, considering the events of the past year.

Micah cursed softly. Benton *would* have one of his miserable asthma attacks now. That meant a delay in interviewing and hiring a translator. Micah had talked with Professor Hensley by phone before he left the hospital. Nate had promised to have some applicants for Benton to interview but warned the pickings might be slim during the holidays. Well, no matter. It was Benton's idea in the first place, so he would just have to return from Phoenix a few days earlier to handle it.

Chapter Five

Gabrielle sat on the pink-carpeted floor in her room doing limbering-up exercises. Outside, a cold, wet drizzle kept an overcast sky company and made the interior of her room a gloomy gray. She was engrossed in the exercises and didn't want to stop to turn on a light. Only two days ago, after consultations with the orthopedic surgeons who had operated on her leg, Dr. Baker had finally conceded and agreed to these mild floor workouts. Even though she wasn't allowed to do anything remotely construed as a dance routine, she was pleased that she could at least exercise enough to keep her body trim and her muscles toned. She could even walk again in her slim-heeled shoes, a delight after so many weeks of slippers and sneakers, and those on only one foot. Just being able to tug on a pair of hose lifted her spirits and chipped away at the depression she had been battling since she had come home from the hospital.

She paused a moment to catch her breath just as her father hooked his head around her door. "Gabby! What are you doing sitting in the dark? I thought we agreed—"

"I was just exercising," she said, leaning back on her hands and looking up at Nate. He switched on the light, bathing the room in a soft glow, and looked anxiously at Gabrielle.

"You're taking it easy on that, I hope," he said, indicating her left leg stretched out in front of her. "Following Dr. Baker's instructions to the letter?"

"Don't you go mother henning me, Daddy. I get enough of that from Mother and Hattie. Honestly, I don't understand why Dr. Baker won't let me do a few simple routines. If I can walk, I can dance."

"No!" Nate spoke sharply, more sharply than he had intended, and realized it when he saw the surprise on Gabrielle's face. "I'm sorry, Gabby, but I just don't think you need to court trouble. The past few months have been difficult for you and for your mother and myself. We just want you to—to get well and the best way is for you to do exactly as Dr. Baker says.'' Nate walked across the room, needing a moment to compose himself. He stopped pacing and lowered himself cautiously onto the small wicker stool in front of the dresser. Satisfied that it would hold his weight, he looked at Gabrielle.

''Did you talk to Mr. Garrett today?'' he asked.

Gabrielle shrugged indifferently. ''Yes, but he doesn't have any work for me. The woman he's hired is so efficient she doesn't need any help at all. He did offer to inquire about any openings in our area for clerk-linguists—but not until after Christmas.''

Nate continued to gaze at Gabrielle. She had lost weight and her cap of black curls framing her face gave her a vulnerable quality that moved him. He wished he could undo the accident for her, but being practical, he knew God seldom offered this opportunity to parents, no matter how much they loved their children. But he might give her back her independence and said carefully, ''I have something that I think you might find interesting. Do you recall the afternoon of your accident?'' He could have kicked himself. Gabrielle grimaced. How could she forget that day? It was burned into her mind as though branded with a hot poker. When she nodded, Nate continued.

''Your mother and I were talking about a former student of mine that had been injured in a helicopter crash. Do you remember?''

''Vaguely.''

''Well, his name is Micah Davidson and he's recovered enough to get on with the project he had begun, and his secretary, Carl Benton, called again today, asking for the names of anyone I know who would be qualified and interested in doing some translating. Mr. Benton will be here day after tomorrow. I'm allowing him the use of my study for interviews since the university will be closed for the holidays. I wish you would talk to him. Micah told me a couple of weeks ago that they're anxious to fill the position. Frankly, I was only able to provide Mr. Benton with two applicants and I had to get those from the language professor. I don't think either of them is willing to leave the States during Christmas, and getting a passport on such short notice—"

Gabrielle's head shot up and she interrupted. "Leaving the States? Where is this job?"

"In Panama, near the canal. Does that pique your interest?" Nate smiled.

Gabrielle felt a sense of elation. She drew her knees up, locked her arms around them, and smiled impishly at her father. "You know it does. Tell me more. What kind of a salary are they offering?"

"I don't know, but I'm sure it's more than adequate and traveling expenses are included. Why don't you just be around day after tomorrow and I'll introduce you to Mr. Benton."

"I'm going Christmas shopping with Val, but we'll be home right after lunch."

"That will be perfect. Your mother will be playing bridge all afternoon, so I've told Mr. Benton he could set up his interviews for anytime after one o'clock."

ON the day of the interviews Gabrielle was tempted to call Val and cancel out their shopping trip, then changed her mind. With Christmas only a week away she needed to buy her parents' gift. Theirs and a smaller one for Hattie was all she could afford.

For the past two days visions of an exotic, lush paradise had floated in vivid color in Gabrielle's mind. She found herself daydreaming about working in tropical Panama and began to feel a slight tremble of excited apprehension. With her luck, she thought, Mr. Benton would probably hire the very first applicant and she would return from shopping to find the position closed.

Think positive! she told herself and stepped into the tubful of tangerine-scented bubbles. Gabrielle gently massaged her healing leg. Only a thin scar on the inside of her calf marred her skin, smooth as unruffled velvet. When the cast had first come off, Gabrielle had noticed her leg was a sickly gray; she hated it, looked at it accusingly as though it were some alien appendage that she wanted to discard. Now though, it had returned to normal, the rich brown of a new autumn leaf.

Gabrielle took particular care with her dress and makeup. She blow-dried her hair, stretching it out as far as it would go, and swirled the swag of recalcitrant curls away from her face, allowing them full rein only when she managed to lock them at the crown of her head. The curls bounced and lifted until they reached her nape, where they clung entrancingly to her slender neck. Wispy tendrils escaped old-fashioned combs and lay against her small ears, willfully hiding tiny gold circles that pierced their lobes.

Using a sable brush she traced a dark rose high on her cheeks, drawing color lightly to her temples. A tiny sponge smudged gray shadow on the curve of her lids, complementing vividly the sweep of long dark lashes that needed no mascara to enhance her smoky brown eyes. Gabrielle's favorite burgundy over a layer of rose shaded the provocative fullness of her lips.

Gabrielle smiled at her image in the mirror, recognizing the sensation that raced up her spine; it was the same as when she waited impatiently to be cued on stage from dimly lit wings. *This is it,* she told herself, *not a dress rehearsal.* She flipped the collar of the black silk blouse over the beige suit jacket; it drew attention to soft hollows in the curve of her neck.

Gabrielle paced the foyer impatiently, waiting for Val, and by the time the small red sports car pulled to the curb in front of the house, she had imagined herself hired by Mr. Benton a dozen times over.

She made her purchases early into the shopping expedition and tried to rush Val through hers, anxious to return home.

"For heaven's sake, Gabby," Val complained, "this is my first Christmas with Pietro. I want to get him something really nice."

"I know you do, but we've been in every store in the Galleria and you still can't make up your mind. My leg is beginning to feel numb. I haven't been on my feet this much since I had the cast off."

"Well, go sit down and have a cup of coffee by the ice rink and watch the skaters or something," Val suggested pointedly. "I can get more done without you pestering me to leave every five minutes. Thirty minutes—that's all I need. Think you can stay in your skin that much longer?"

Gabrielle smiled sheepishly. "Yes, you go ahead. I think I will have that cup of coffee. But only for thirty minutes, Val," she reminded, "or I'm just going to have to take a cab home."

People turned to stare as Gabrielle walked to the small terrace coffee shop, but she was so wrapped in thought about her upcoming meeting with Mr. Benton, she was oblivious of the appreciative glances she drew.

Later Gabrielle would only remember that this day flew by. Right now the minutes she waited for Val seemed like hours. When Val finally pulled her car to a halt in front of the Hensleys', Gabrielle was a jumble of nerves. A long black limousine was parked in the drive, a chauffeur sat in the driver's seat.

"God, look at that," Val said. "You'd better have yourself a drink to calm your nerves, or you'll be stuttering worse than I do and your Mr. Benton won't know what language you speak, much less translate."

"He's probably already hired someone," Gabrielle said, hoping desperately it wasn't so. She lifted her gaily wrapped packages from the narrow boot behind the seat.

"Good luck, anyway. Don't forget to call me and let me know what happens," Val reminded as she put the car in gear.

Gabrielle carried her packages up to her room and dumped them unceremoniously on her bed. When she was halfway down the staircase, her eye caught a movement in the far recess of the front room. Who was that? She halted, breathless, on the step. It wouldn't do to appear anything but calm if that happened to be Mr. Benton. She sat down on the carpeted tread to gather her wits.

Almost immediately the front doorbell chimed. Before Gabrielle could move, Hattie swished down the wide entrance hall and answered the door. Gabrielle sat still as

Hattie ushered the young man to the study. She heard the murmur of voices, the door closing.

Obviously the tall stranger in the front room wasn't Mr. Benton. Another applicant? No. If he had been, he would have been ushered into the study first. Or maybe he had already had his interview. And where was her father? The stranger's back was to her, he seemed mesmerized by the twinkling blue Christmas tree lights scattering a kaleido-scopic image on the taupe walls. Gabrielle wished he would turn around.

A student? No, she thought, he was too well dressed. He wore a gray tailored pin-striped suit with much more élan than any student could muster. *Turn around,* Gabrielle demanded silently.

As if acquiescing to her silent command, the stranger pivoted and raked the room with a sweeping glance. A wild animal checking its lair for unwanted visitors? Gabrielle felt as if she were the intruder. The man shrugged his wide shoulders in dismissal of some sudden thought. A cup and saucer was balanced in his hand.

He definitely was not a student. He was drinking out of her mother's best china and her mother *never* allowed the fragile porcelain to be used by her father's students.

Gabrielle's eyes traveled upward; on his neck she saw an ugly mottled pink scar. It slid out the open collar of his shirt, straggled up the cords on his neck to nip at his earlobe.

He lifted the cup to his mouth and Gabrielle saw his left hand. A leather fingerless glove wrapped around the knuckles and palm. The dark leather was only a shade lighter than the vibrant mahogany of his fingers.

The man replaced the cup carefully in its saucer and his eyes roamed the room once again. The gesture made Gabrielle sure he sensed he was being watched. She held her breath as he walked toward the entrance hall, praying he wouldn't lift his eyes to the staircase and discover her behind the narrow slats.

She liked his face. It had the look of an unfinished sculpture, as though an artist had roughed it out with his chisel, expecting to return later to soften strong angles and planes of the square-cut chin and jaw. The man's eyes were carved deep and made shadowy by a sweep of thick, black lashes. But even should the artist return, Gabrielle knew he would never be able to improve on the stranger's mouth.

His full lower lip curved sensually into a slight smile and Gabrielle wished fervently that he would turn back into the front room so she could make her way down the remaining steps. Instead, he stood immobile just inside the double French doors, imprisoning her behind the narrow rails.

After several long seconds he turned back into the living room. Gabrielle sighed with relief. She had just placed her hand on the banister when the telephone shrilled, drawing the stranger's eyes back to the wide foyer. Gabrielle froze. Damn!

Hattie rushed in and lifted the receiver. "Professor Hensley's residence," she said into the mouthpiece in her haughty telephone voice. "Gabby's not here. She's gone shopping." A look of puzzlement on her features changed almost immediately to one of understanding. "Oh, well, I didn't hear her come in. Just a minute." Hattie put her hand over the telephone and hollered up the stairs for Gabrielle.

"Shhh, not so loud, Hattie. I'm right here."

"Good Lord, girl! What are you doing hiding on the steps like a two-year-old spy?"

"Hattie," Gabrielle hissed, "please keep your voice down." But the warning came too late. The stranger was looking at them and held Gabrielle's gaze as she stood up and walked the rest of the way down the steps. An eyebrow arched quizzically as an amused, knowing smile hooked the corner of his mouth. Gabrielle offered him a brilliant smile of her own to cover her embarrassment. She raised her voice slightly to Hattie.

"My leg gave out. I had to sit down a minute. I guess I overdid it shopping this morning." Hattie handed her the telephone with a peculiar look on her face.

"I'm not deaf, you don't have to shout," she said grumpily.

Gabrielle skewered her with a "be quiet" look. The stranger was grinning widely now, while his eyes scoured Gabrielle from head to toe in slow, deliberate inspection.

Gabrielle tilted her head up, chin thrust out, and returned his inspection in the same deliberate manner, pretending cool hauteur at his image. She turned her back on him to answer the phone.

"Hello."

"Gab? This is Val. Any news yet?"

"No," Gabrielle said between clenched teeth. "I haven't even met Mr. Benton yet. There's someone in the study with him now." A surreptitious glance out of the corner of her eye confirmed the stranger continued to stand and stare at her from the doorway. Damn. "What was that, Val?" Her friend had reverted to Spanish, rattling off something about a baby. Gabrielle answered Val automatically in the girl's native tongue.

"I said," Val reiterated, "I just heard from my doctor. The tests were positive. I'm pregnant!"

"Val!" Gabrielle exclaimed, her attention riveted to her best friend's words. "That's marvelous. Congratulations."

The study door opened and the young man who had entered earlier nodded to Gabrielle as he made his way out.

"Val," Gabrielle said quickly, "I've got to go. There's this gorgeous stranger staring at me and I think Mr. Benton is free now. Bye!" Gabrielle caught sight of the stranger's back as he too went out the front door. She cradled the phone and turned to the study.

A faded brown, withered-looking man stood just inside the hall. He peered at Gabrielle over the rims of his bifocals. His thin face was hollow, with skin drawn taut into his receding hairline.

"Are you Gabrielle Hensley by any chance?" he wheezed, breathing deeply to draw air into his lungs.

"Yes," Gabrielle said, flashing a nervous smile.

Mr. Benton pushed his glasses high on his brow. "Your father described you to me, but he could have just used one word—exquisite," he said gallantly.

"Thank you," she replied demurely, but she felt not at all demure. The confrontation with the stranger, for all its silence, had excited her. Gabrielle drew rein on her emotions and offered her hand to Mr. Benton.

"I'm Carl Benton," he said, accepting her hand and shaking it firmly. "Your father said he would introduce us but your mother ran out of gas somewhere and he's gone to take her some."

That explained the stranger's presence in the living room, she thought. He had probably been waiting for her father and having waited as long as he could, left. She would ask him about the stranger later. There had been an aura of sensuality about the man, a promise, and Gabrielle felt drawn to him like a bee to honey. But there were other more important things, *now things,* to claim her attention. She listened to Carl Benton.

"Have you decided to interview for the job?" he asked.

"You haven't hired anyone yet?" Gabrielle quizzed, displaying much more calm than she felt.

"No, I haven't. Your father was right. The pickings are slim during the holidays. The man that just left is qualified, but he can't commit the time needed to do the job before school starts again. He's a student. Are you interested?"

"I think I might be." What an understatement, she thought. Aloud, she said, "I'd like to hear about it, my father was a bit sketchy on the details."

"I feel a little awkward asking you to have a chair in your own home, Miss Hensley," Mr. Benton said, as she followed him into the study. Gabrielle laughed.

"Just pretend I'm an anxious applicant, Mr. Benton, and go from there."

"Good enough," he said and smiled, displaying overlapping front teeth. He sat in her father's chair behind the cluttered desk. "Do you have a valid passport?"

"Yes. I was in England earlier this year."

"Good, that's out of the way. I'd like to see it before I leave." He lifted a newspaper from some clutter at his elbow. "Would you pick any column, read it aloud, then translate it into English?" He handed her a Spanish language paper.

Gabrielle scanned it quickly, read the Spanish aloud, and with an impish grin translated a news item about a Panamanian woman giving birth on a *chivas*. The word translated to nanny goat, but was actually the local idiom for bus.

Mr. Benton almost managed to hide a smile behind his hand, but inadvertently displayed it when his glasses slipped to the very tip of his nose, drawing his hand swiftly from his mouth.

Gabrielle laughed. "I'm sorry. I was just showing off."

"I gathered as much." He chuckled. "Are you as familiar with numbers?"

"Yes, very much so. I worked as a bilingual clerk for a realtor. We dealt with figures all the time."

"Can you type?"

Gabrielle hesitated. "It's not one of my better skills," she admitted. "I can, but only on an electric machine and I'm still slow."

"Speed isn't essential, but accuracy is," he declared.

Gabrielle couldn't help smiling. "Being accurate is what slows me down."

Mr. Benton shoved his bifocals on his brow for the third time in as many minutes. "The only other thing required," he intoned seriously, "is that you be willing to travel to Panama and to remain there until all of the contracts and agreements have been translated and typed. This should take about three months. Because we are so far behind schedule, we want our team together and ready to leave the States on the twenty-fifth. Can you live with that?"

"Of December?"

"Yes. Christmas Day. The *Upsure* is sailing late that evening. We'll be on it." He held up his hand to stall the questions he saw forming on Gabrielle's lips. "The *Upsure* is a cargo vessel that Micah Davidson has purchased and had refitted to haul raw timber. She's having sea trials now. Except for Captain Dressler and the first mate, most of the crew members are hired out of Houston. We're not sailing until late to let them have Christmas Eve and most of Christmas Day with their families."

The extension in the study shrilled. Mr. Benton leaned back in his chair. "I guess you'd better be the one to answer that," he said, smiling.

It was probably Val again, Gabrielle thought. The girl

was just too curious to wait. She lifted the receiver. "Hello."

"Carl Benton, please." Gabrielle stared at the phone for one uncomprehending second, then passed the receiver to Mr. Benton. The seductive quality of the voice that came over the wire somehow reminded her of the stranger. How could that be? The man had never spoken a single word. She moved to the far side of the study to allow Mr. Benton privacy, but he waved her back into her chair.

"Benton here." He breathed heavily into the phone, listened attentively. "I'm trying to do that very thing," Gabrielle heard him say. Benton paused. "Tonight? I'll suggest it." He cradled the phone. To Gabrielle he said, "Now, where were we?"

"You've covered most of it, except the salary you're offering," she told him. She hated to bring up the subject, but lack of funds was critical to her. She had to know.

"We are offering forty-five hundred dollars for three months, plus traveling and board expenses. There is one slight catch," Benton said.

Gabrielle's heart sank. *Here it comes,* she thought. *He's going to tell me the very reason why I can't accept the job.*

But all Mr. Benton said was, "You will have to enter Panama on a tourist visa, not as an employee of Davidson Enterprises. You'll be housed at Chepo, Micah Davidson's estate in the southern mountains of the province of Panama. You'll be asked not to discuss your work. This project isn't a secret, but we're not announcing it publicly to avoid certain situations that I don't need to go into here. Can you handle that?"

"Yes," Gabrielle said and felt a sense of exhilaration. Forty-five hundred dollars! More than enough cash to get her life back in order until she could rejoin the Civic Ballet.

"Are you offering me the job, Mr. Benton?" Gabrielle asked, her voice slightly unsteady.

"I am," he declared. "What do you say?"

"I say yes!"

He smiled at her enthusiasm. "You may consider yourself hired. Would you have dinner with some of us tonight?" he proposed. "Our medical team, Dr. Harold

Jinkins and his wife, Helen, his nurse, have arrived from Oregon where they've been on holiday. It will give you an opportunity to meet them and Micah Davidson before we sail.''

"I'd love to," Gabrielle agreed. She was hired. She wanted to shout or sing and dance around the room, instead she sat calmly and composed.

"Now that you are an official member of our family, you may as well call me Benton. Everyone else does."

"I'm Gabrielle," she volunteered, "but it gets shortened to Gabby all the time."

"All right, Gabby, let's get down to business. Our steward will pick up your luggage no later than seven thirty on Christmas Eve. On Saturday, the twenty-fifth, I'll send a car for you at five o'clock sharp to bring you to the pier in Galveston. Oh, and we'll send a car for you tonight too, about seven. Is that fine?"

"It's perfect."

Benton looked at his watch. "I've ordered a taxi for three o'clock, it should be here in about two minutes. Could you get your passport for me?"

When Gabrielle returned with the small flat document, Benton was standing at the front door.

"My taxi is here. May I take this with me?" he asked. Gabrielle nodded and smiled. He handed her a folded check. "Here's a portion of your salary. The remainder will be paid to you when we reach Chepo." The cabbie tooted his horn impatiently. Benton smiled.

"See you at seven, and please tell Professor Hensley I said thank you, and merry Christmas."

Gabrielle watched the taxi pull away from the curb and stepped back into the house. She unfolded the check and almost fainted at the sum—two thousand dollars! Merry Christmas indeed. She sank weakly to the bottom step.

"You seem to have a thing for these steps today, Gabby," Hattie said, glaring down at her. An armload of freshly ironed linen balanced precariously against Hattie's ample chest.

Gabrielle smiled, still in a happy daze. "I sure do, don't I?"

"What's wrong with you, girl? Move over or up, so I can get by—these sheets aren't getting any lighter."

"Oh, I'm sorry, Hattie." She stood up. "Will you help me go through the boxes in the storeroom? I need all my summer clothes. I'm going to the tropics this winter—Panama!" she shouted at the startled Hattie.

Chapter Six

At a quarter to seven Gabrielle was dressed and waiting for the car Benton had promised to send for her. For the umpteenth time she checked her image in the mirror hanging in the hall.

Her breasts peaked unrestricted against the black chiffon; the neck to waist slit in its bodice parted, revealing a seductive glimpse of full, golden-brown breasts. Gabrielle loved the feel of the featherlight swirl of pleats at her ankles; they purloined attention from the entrancing curve of her hips. For the first time in months she was aware of her sensuality; she felt like a woman about to explore the unknown. In a way that's what her new job would be—a challenge. She looked forward to it. And it was made to order; in three months' time she would be back in Houston with the go-ahead from Dr. Baker to begin dancing again.

She smiled at her image again, then frowned when she noticed wisps of curls were beginning to escape the soft chignon she had so painstakingly contrived. She brushed them back into place, refusing to tolerate a single strand to hide the shimmering emeralds that pierced her ears—the matching stones had been a gift from her parents on her twenty-first birthday.

A car door slammed and she glanced out the tall front windows. A uniformed chauffeur walked around the front of a limousine and up the sidewalk. She moved hurriedly to the front door, carrying with her a cloud of fragrant 20 Carats. She waited for only one rap before opening the door.

"Miss Gabrielle Hensley?" the chauffeur asked and lifted his hand to a black cap in a respectful salute.

"Yes." Gabrielle smiled entrancingly.

"I'm Michael. I have instructions to drive you to the Galleria Plaza Hotel," he said formally.

"Thank you," Gabrielle replied, just as formal. "I'll be right with you." Heavens! She stepped back inside to shrug into the jeweled jacket. She unplugged the lights on the Christmas tree against mishap since both her parents and Hattie were out for the evening. The brief thought of her parents reminded her that she had forgotten to ask her father about the stranger. The excitement of being hired and going to Panama had swept it from her mind completely. Gabrielle took a deep breath before she stepped out the door.

If Mr. Benton had wanted to impress her, he had certainly succeeded. She felt like a premiere danseuse once again. The feeling brought a smile to her lips as she followed Michael down the short front walk.

He pulled the car door open when she reached the curb. The interior of the limousine was dark. Gabrielle thought for a fleeting second to mention it, but changed her mind and folded herself onto the thick velvet cushion. She realized immediately that she was not the only occupant. The compelling, mossy fragrance of a man's essence engulfed her.

"Good evening, Miss Hensley," came a seductive drawl from the far corner of the wide seat. Gabrielle's senses quickened; a pulsating prickling sensation flared and raced through her veins. It was the voice of the man who had called Benton during the interview.

"Who are you?" she asked in a soft voice. She was curious, but not alarmed. The chauffeur opened the driver's door to enter the car, and the overhead light came on. Gabrielle found herself staring into the hewed face of the stranger. A warm flush of embarrassment crept up her neck and she told herself it couldn't be. The faintly amused smile that rested on his lips was as vexing and as disquieting as it had been earlier that afternoon. She averted her face, refusing to meet again his twinkling, all-knowing eyes. The car purred into motion, its interior dim once more, and the man answered her question.

"Micah Davidson," he said, dipping his head with indolent grace and moving quite obviously nearer the middle of the seat. The scent of his cologne, which Gabrielle recognized as Aramis, became stronger and impossible to ignore.

"Davidson?" she questioned, and her voice went shallow, almost bereft of its soft musical tone. Her throat was arid.

"Yes, but call me Micah," he told her, leaning forward to touch the switch that closed the glass panel between the seats. "We don't stand on formality—Gabrielle." He chuckled softly. "I was going to introduce myself this afternoon, but you weren't off the phone before I had to leave. How's your leg?"

"It's just fine," she replied, staring straight ahead into the darkness. The mortification she had felt when he discovered her staring at him from the steps returned and as the limousine rounded a well-lighted corner she discovered he was peering at her intently. He laughed outright at her display of coolness. The rich baritone sound filled the car.

"I also like the way you described me to your friend... Val, isn't it?"

Gabrielle found her voice. "You eavesdropped on my conversation," she accused, resorting to anger to cover her dismay and discomfiture. For heaven's sake! He must have understood every word she had said to Val in Spanish.

"Your voice carried," he told her. "And it's no worse than you staring at me for a full ten minutes."

Gabrielle wished she could fold herself up and hide in the little black purse she carried. "Hardly ten minutes," she challenged.

He laughed. "Your white suit was like a flag behind those dark rails," he informed her.

"Beige," she corrected. Oh, God! He had seen her from the very first. She chastised herself for being so stupid. She should have gone back to her room or continued down the steps to the kitchen. Talk about spilt milk!

"Beige, then, but still ten minutes."

"If you saw me, you should have said something," she insisted.

"What, for instance?" he countered. "I thought you were some fifteen-year-old kid on those steps. I must admit," he drawled, "I was pleasantly surprised when you stood up." He folded one long leg over the other and adjusted the tautness of his slacks at his knee. "Why didn't *you* speak up? Considering the time of year, 'Merry Christmas' wouldn't have been out of line."

"I thought you were a friend of my father's." She didn't enjoy the feeling that Micah Davidson was castigating her for rude behavior. She had been neither impolite nor civil this afternoon; there hadn't been time for anything other than surprise, curiosity, and that awful embarrassment.

Micah was badgering her purposely. He found himself bewitched by Gabrielle; the fragile face with the determined chin, the feathery clothes clinging to her slender body, only not so slender in some places, he noticed in the half-light that came into the car as they drove through Houston. Her voice was musical, modulated, her gestures graceful, and he realized he knew little about her beyond the fact that she was the daughter of his former economics professor. For a moment he turned his mind back, attempting to recall if he had seen her before when he and other students had been invited to Nate's. But he remembered nothing of a child and it came to him with a start that he had left college more than sixteen years ago. Gabrielle would have been a baby. Two, perhaps three. He wondered how old she was now and wished he had looked at the passport Benton had brought back to the hotel. Back in the present, he knew only that he wanted to keep her talking. Her voice aroused him.

"I am a friend of your father's," he said. "A former student too."

"I know that now, but I thought you were a colleague, an instructor from the university, and you could've been waiting to see Mr. Benton too," she added.

"That's why you were hiding on the steps? You don't speak to Nate's associates? They're a rather stuffy bunch, is that it?"

Gabrielle stiffened, perturbed at his insinuation that she was a snob. "Yes, I like teachers and no, they are not too stuffy for me. What does all this have to do with *you* glaring at *me* and listening in on my phone conversation?"

"Put it down to curiosity. You're the newest employee of my company. I'm just trying to find out what makes you tick."

Gabrielle thought about that for a minute. Knowing about his employees might simply be company policy, but what made her tick was none of his business. She knew she was getting off to a bad start, but she couldn't seem to help herself. In for a penny, in for a pound, she thought. And Micah Davidson seemed to want his pound of flesh. She had no intention of letting him best her.

"You are all charm, Mr. Davidson," she didn't bother to dilute the sarcasm.

"You think so? And of course, you like men with charm." It was a statement, as though he sensed she was attracted to him. He sounded amused.

"Yes," she snapped, "especially ones who wouldn't have the ill manners to embarrass a lady. You're enjoying it too," she added.

"Touché," he clipped as the chauffeur braked to a stop in front of the hotel. The doorman leaped to open the door of the limousine. Micah slid against Gabrielle in the stream of light that showered them from the lobby. He placed a hand under the jeweled jacket and gently pushed her out of the car. His hand was warm through the thin chiffon and Gabrielle moved away from him pointedly.

She waited just inside the lobby doors out of the chill wind. Micah stayed behind to speak to the driver. There was no doubt in Gabrielle's mind that Micah Davidson played the game by his own rules—and he expected to win. He probably had hordes of women falling at his feet, all of them eager to submit to his arrogant, devilish charm. *But not me,* she thought. Somehow her brain refused to get this message; it demanded to know more about this singular attraction that was causing so much confusion in its well-ordered compartments. Foolishly, Gabrielle conceded. She watched Micah. He leaned nonchalantly against the car, arms folded, ignoring the cold. He wore an expertly tailored brown silk suit, brown tie—knotted, but hung loosely about the collar of a crepe de chine shirt. Gabrielle supposed that the unhealed scars on his neck were much too tender for the uncomfortable strictures of a well-knotted tie and buttoned collar.

He was attractive. She knew a lot of attractive men. He

was the color of rich brown earth. So were a lot of men. Gabrielle told her brain that there was nothing special about Micah Davidson. It digested this information and filed it— under fictitious statements.

Micah's eyes swept over Gabrielle through the clear glass of the lobby doors. He grinned. Gabrielle offered him a withering look and turned her back.

"We're going up to Annabelle's for a drink before dinner," he said, joining her a few moments later. His hand slipped around her waist to guide Gabrielle toward the bank of elevators. She was aware of his fingers, the slight pressure against her back, as though each finger were a separate entity. She walked hurriedly ahead. The fingers grabbed a swath of silk pleats.

"Your leg must be tremendously improved from this afternoon for you to challenge me in a foot race, Miss Hensley," Micah said dryly. Gabrielle thrust her chin up defiantly, but slowed her pace. They joined a large crowd of hotel guests waiting for the elevators.

"Has the cat got your tongue all of a sudden?" he whispered against her ear.

"No," she whispered right back, tilting her head up and aware of the stares they were drawing. "I just don't have anything to say to you, Mr. Davidson."

His eyes caressed her delicate features, then dropped with a slow deliberate taunt of intimacy to the almond-hued flesh exposed by the décolletage of chiffon. Gabrielle feigned disinterest in his inspection until he tugged her into the circle of his arm to allow the others to enter the elevator first.

"Stop that!" she hissed at him as they stepped into the elevator themselves. He smiled at her agitation and held her against his body for the lift to the twenty-fourth floor.

"I can't move now, it's too crowded," he murmured into her ear.

"It is, isn't it?" Gabrielle said sweetly and moved her heels to stand directly on his toes. She heard him grunt with pain. The other guests emptied the elevator on the eighteenth floor, leaving the two of them alone for the few-seconds' ride to Annabelle's.

"You owe me for that little trick," Micah said succinctly

when the doors closed. A look of secretive pleasure creased his face. "I'll collect at my leisure," he warned.

"All's fair in—" Gabrielle clamped her mouth shut when she realized what she had been about to say. And she wondered why that particular phrase had leaped to the tip of her tongue.

Benton was standing at the elevator when the doors swished open. A startled look governed his face as he glanced first at Gabrielle, then Micah. He looked back at Gabrielle and noticed the frigid set of her mouth.

"You two have met, I see," he said wryly. "I was just going down to the lobby to see if you had arrived," he said to Gabrielle. "Helen and Jinks are already in the lounge."

Gabrielle put her arm through Benton's. "Mr. Benton," she began evenly, "I—I need to talk to you about the job." Surprised at her gesture, Benton covered his astonishment by making a pretense of adjusting his glasses. He looked out the corner of his eye at the lovely, willowy girl on his arm. "I may not be able to accept the job after all," Gabrielle declared.

The unexpected statement caused Benton to stop dead in his tracks. Micah bumped into him. When the small flurry of confusion was over, Micah clamped his fingers around Gabrielle's arm and drew her unceremoniously into a small alcove near the entrance to the lounge.

"You go on in," he directed to Benton. "Gabrielle and I will be along in a minute. Order a Dubonnet on the rocks for her and the usual for me." Benton made as if to say something, changed his mind with a shrug of his thin shoulders, and entered the bar. Micah released Gabrielle's arm.

"I never suspected you were a quitter," he said silkily.

"I'm not a quitter, Mr. Davidson," Gabrielle bristled. "I just realized I may have been a bit hasty in accepting the job."

"The salary isn't to your liking, then?" he queried, a trace of hardness in his melodious drawl.

"Quite the contrary. It was more than I expected and very satisfactory." She moved back a step, uncomfortable at the steely glint that pierced her from under his sweep of dark lashes.

"You had second thoughts after you met me. Is that it?"

Her composure slipped at his acute perceptiveness. "That's not it at all," she almost stuttered. For heaven's sake! What was wrong with her? She had handled abrasive men before, and with much more élan than this. Recovering her composure, she continued. "I've just had second thoughts about—about leaving the country," she lied.

"You don't expect me to believe that. Your passport shows you've been out of the United States before. It's not a new experience for you." He arched a cynical eyebrow. "Or is it you expect all men to bow and scrape on their knees at your beauty? You rather like that pedestal you've climbed up onto, don't you? I suggest you come to earth and learn to handle a bit of give and take between a man and a woman." He looked at her from head to toe with deliberate appraisal. "Or is it that you're a spoiled little girl masquerading as a woman?"

Gabrielle trembled with anger at his unwarranted attack. "I don't have to prove anything to you. What I am is none of your business. I quit!"

"You've been paid," he said with angry impatience, "and you gave us a firm commitment. It's going to be difficult to find a replacement for you now. If it's me you don't like, you will work with Benton. But I warn you, he won't have any more time than I to cater to your whims and baby-sit your ego."

"*My* ego! You insufferable toad! You are the one strutting around like you're king of the hill, not me." *What's wrong with me?* she thought. How could she let a snippet of repartee get under her skin? It wasn't like her at all. Just the same, this man was rude and had pushed her beyond the limits of social niceties. "As for you," she told him, "I neither like you nor dislike you. I don't even *know* you."

His eyes dropped to her breasts, as though he could count her racing heartbeats. He smiled. "Well, there's only one way for you to get to know me. Let's have dinner and you sleep on it tonight." He chuckled wickedly. "Perhaps by the morning you'll have decided this insufferable toad has turned into a prince."

"That would be utterly impossible, Mr. Davidson," she said, holding her ground.

"I don't know," he said, the sensual mouth curved as he looked down at her. "There might be some stray mistletoe around here. We could check it out." He tucked her arm into the crook of his elbow, disdaining firmly her resistance. "Helen and Jinks are looking forward to meeting you. At least have dinner." He looked at her expectantly.

Gabrielle was reluctant to succumb to the etiquette of polite pretense in the wake of his smooth practicability. She told herself that she just hadn't been prepared for the abrasive force of the tangible sensuality he exuded, and reminded herself that the job was merely an interim until she could return to dancing.

"All right," she agreed slowly.

The group Micah led her toward was sitting on red banquettes, low sofas curved and facing high over the city. Variegated lights on the ground far below built a collage that moved and flowed. The timbre of disco music added a low, throbbing cadence to the dim atmosphere of the lounge. The music was only loud enough to draw couples to the dance floor without impeding conversation. Dancing pairs swayed to the music, jostling one another while tiny strobes of light embedded in the parquet floor twinkled and blinked, flashing against legs and twirling hems.

"Here she is," Micah said to the smiling group that looked up as they approached. Benton's smile was tempered with relief. Helen Jinkins was cynical, warmhearted, and totally kind. She had pleasant blue eyes bracketed with laugh lines, a complexion fraught with freckles that ran together, and protruding, but not unattractive, teeth. She smiled at Gabrielle.

"Sit next to me," she said after Micah introduced them. "You *are* every bit as lovely as Benton said—no reflection on you, it's just one can never tell what he actually does see through those bifocals of his."

Gabrielle sat. Micah continued the introductions. "That bald-headed man sitting on the other side of Helen is Jinks, the worse half of our medical team. We just tolerate him because of Helen." He chuckled.

Jinks lifted his rotund body courteously and reached over Helen to shake Gabrielle's hand. Wild, bushy eyebrows compensated for his bald pate and rode herd over a pair of faded blue eyes sparkling with friendly chicanery.

"Pay no attention to our leader, miss. He's only envious that I'm the better man."

Gabrielle smiled mischievously. "That's an astute observation, Dr. Jinkins. I quite agree."

The bushy eyebrows waved up and down. "Well, well, a woman after my own heart," he chortled. "Are you listening, Helen?"

"Sit down and quit preening, Jinks," Helen admonished.

Micah shuffled the drinks on the low table and handed Gabrielle a thin crystal of aromatic wine. Their eyes met fleetingly and she smiled. He sat next to her, draping an arm along the curved edge of the banquette behind her back. He leaned into her a bit more than good manners demanded.

"Keep that smile on your lips," he said for her ears only. "I'm beginning to think that's where we need to begin to learn to know one another."

Gabrielle poised in midturn as the meaning of his words sank in. Micah chuckled softly, aware that the provocative words caused her a moment of uncertainty. Gabrielle turned entirely away from him to face Helen. The space was too close for an attentive person to miss the exchange and Helen had been attentive.

"Ignore these men." Helen laughed. "They're either fighting, drinking, bragging or—well, other things," she drew up short. "How did Micah convince you to go to work for him in our pestiferous, bug-ridden piece of jungle real estate?"

"What kind of real estate?" Gabrielle asked, dismay waxing her voice. Visions of exotic lush greenery, swaying palms, cloudless blue skies, and magic sunsets diminished and faded.

"Oh," Helen said, "that's how. He didn't mention it." She patted Gabrielle's hand. "You don't need to worry, Micah's created a bit of tropical paradise at his house at Chepo with the most marvelous indoor plumbing." Helen had a wistful look on her face. "We live in a village called

Coco Solito on the Mamoni River, something more primitive than Chepo."

"A hell of a lot more primitive!" Jinks snorted. "Ocelots digging in the garbage before you can get it buried, monkeys using the clotheslines for a trapeze, not to mention the snakes, spiders and—"

"Jinks," Micah warned, "Gabrielle's not yet *sure* she wants to come."

Jinks leaned forward, around Helen to look at Gabrielle. "He doesn't want me to tell you about the gnats, mosquitoes, and horseflies, some of which are so damn big, even Texas would claim 'em." Helen elbowed him in the ribs. He eyed her with a pained expression on his face. "Well, what did I say? A person ought to know—"

"You're going to know more than you want to in about ten more seconds if you don't button your lip," Helen told him, muttering under her breath. "You'll just love Panama City," she added to Gabrielle, effectively cornering the conversation again. "It's a wonderful potpourri of Spanish and French, with modern skyscrapers down one street and old masonry buildings with lacy wrought-iron balconies down the next. There's hundreds of beautiful shops and boutiques and a very active nightlife. If we can get the men to take us, we'll go to some of the nicer hotel casinos and clubs. The men usually drag *me* to the cockfights and the more lurid, infamous cantinas." Helen glanced over at Gabrielle's jeweled jacket. "With you along, though, I don't think they'd have the courage to suggest a boisterous, dirt-floored beer hall, what with all the *truck* that goes on there," she finished disdainfully. Micah groaned audibly.

"Let's dance," he said to Gabrielle, grabbing her hand and giving her no chance to refuse as he pulled her to her feet and hurried her onto the floor among other couples. He held her primly, keeping a little space between them. "Pay no attention to Helen and Jinks," he began.

"Aren't they telling the truth?" she asked.

He hesitated. "Ah, yes, but—"

"It sounds adventurous to me."

"It does?" He sounded pleased, surprised. "Listen, I'm—I'm sorry.... Somehow we've got off to a bad start—

two bad starts, if you count this afternoon. Would you accept my apology?''

Gabrielle melted. She felt a swelling thrill; the visions of swaying palms returned accompanied by a lure of high romance. Micah had an animal magnetism that was spellbinding. It reminded her forcefully of the ballet *The Spectre of the Rose*, a romantic story in dance about a young girl who, returning from a ball, thinks she has met someone— perhaps *the* someone—who will be the romance of her life. The young girl is not sure of anything, she scarcely knows him, but she has a rose that he has given her. Happily tired, she sleeps and in the maze of her dreams they float in trancelike waltzes. With the music of the ballet in her mind Gabrielle did not hear or notice the pause on the dance floor. She continued to dance. Micah pulled her to him abruptly. Startled, she looked first at him then around her and recognized that she had been in a trance of her own. Micah wore a decidedly amused look.

"You were smiling. Does that mean you accept my apology?"

"I might."

"Good, then you'll work for me?"

"I thought we agreed I would sleep on it."

"Oh, that," he said, pulling her against his solid body. "Do you mind taking a quick catnap on my shoulder right here? I'll wake you up when the music stops."

Gabrielle laughed and recklessly gave her whole being over to the excitement ignited by his nearness. Their bodies locked from breasts to thighs, and those undulated with the tempo of the music as though there were no barrier of clothes between them. Gabrielle inhaled the lulling, hypnotic scent that cloaked him and closed her eyes, oblivious of others around them on the crowded floor. This time no other music intruded. A barrage of erotic sensations began to pound her and she tried to sort them out, catalog them, imprint them permanently on her mind, but her body would have none of this and defied her, absorbing the sensations and feeding them into her veins until her blood raced hot like a river of molten lava gushing from an erupting volcano.

Too soon the music stopped; Gabrielle tilted her head up, moist lips parted, inviting his kiss. She smelled warm mint and whiskey mingling on his breath as his mouth neared hers. An almost inaudible groan escaped Micah's lips.

"Not here," he said softly, acknowledging the compelling urge that sparked between them. "I couldn't stop." Instead, he pressed his lips against her hair, and her curls, sensing this impetuous motion, began to escape the unwanted chignon languidly until they tickled his nose. He chuckled. Gabrielle heard him through her dazed and befuddled mind. She wondered what he was laughing at.

"Nap's over," he said, his voice husky. "You can open your eyes now."

"I don't want to," Gabrielle replied, unsuccessfully attempting to quell the excited vibrations that raged in her body.

"That's all right by me," he taunted. "I'll just lead you blindly to my room where I can ravage you to my heart's content—well, perhaps not my heart, but something quite near it."

Gabrielle lifted her lashes unhurriedly. "Once a toad, always a toad."

"You've got that all wrong," he told her and seemed to think seriously about proving his point as the music began again.

THE atmosphere during dinner was electric. Fortunately for Gabrielle Helen carried the conversation and painted word pictures so accurately that Gabrielle felt as though she knew Father Chardin, the Jesuit priest who, in a lifelong quest, searched for proof of Chinese influence on the cultures of North and South America; she met Frenchie, the Portuguese who ruled the loggers with an iron hand under the direction of J.T., the logger crew boss; and the Choco Indians living in the Darien Gap, still primitive and whose wealth could be counted in how many spoons they owned and who were only recently beginning to wear pants. She learned of the *nele,* the tribal medicine man who visited Coco Solito and stole Jinks's patients and who, when sick himself, slunk in the back door of the clinic to beg modern medicines. Helen mentioned J.B. Maxwell, the helicopter pilot, but adroitly skimmed over the crash that had injured Micah. Gabrielle listened and soaked it all in. She wanted to ask how Helen, Jinks, and Benton came to be working for Micah Davidson, but something held her back. She filed the question away for a later time.

Some part of Gabrielle registered that the food was delicious, although she could not have said what she ate or drank. Benton picked at his food, eating even less than Gabrielle, and this was noticed and remarked upon.

"Benton, my good friend," Jinks said, "do you want me to give you an injection for that asthma? You'll enjoy your dinner more."

"Hell, no! You stay on your side of the table, Jinks. You've done enough damage already." Benton wheezed, feigning horror.

Jinks pointed a meat-laden fork at Benton. "What are you complaining about? I left you all the good parts, didn't I?"

"Jinks, will you please watch your vulgar mouth," Helen hissed, cutting an embarrassed glance toward Gabrielle.

Gabrielle's musical laughter floated in the air, mingling with the soft sound of cutlery and low piped-in music. "Let them be, Helen, it's not any more racy than all the gossip I've heard backstage and in dressing rooms and, if the truth were known, onstage too."

There was silence around the table for several long seconds as four pairs of eyes stared at Gabrielle.

"Backstage?" Helen asked, for all of them. "Are you an actress?"

"No, I'm a dancer, classical and modern ballet," she volunteered. Micah had a surprised look on his face. "Didn't my father tell you?" She looked from Benton to Micah. Both men nodded no. Gabrielle talked about her career, but glossed over the car accident, mentioning it only briefly. She was telling an anecdote about the London tour when she happened to look at Micah. He wasn't smiling and seemed to be glaring at her, his eyes cold and withdrawn from the rest of them. Gabrielle cut the anecdote short and gave up the conversation to Helen again. She listened with only half an ear while she tried to figure out what she had said that had triggered Micah's coolness. She couldn't and after that the evening went somewhat flat for her. After dinner Jinks suggested they return to Annabelle's for brandy. Gabrielle declined, insisting she had a busy day ahead of her tomorrow. She wouldn't, though, unless Micah still wanted her to work for him. She put the question to him after he had ordered up the limousine and they waited in the now-deserted lobby.

"Did I say I didn't want you to work for me? I thought that was settled," he snapped.

Gabrielle wondered why she felt as if she had gone to war and somehow, unintentionally, stumbled behind enemy lines and suddenly discovered she was out of ammunition. She decided to brazen it out.

"Then why get angry at me? What have I done?" she said, her temper rising. "I don't think it is settled. I'm not sure I want to work for someone whose moods change like a yo-yo zipping up and down a string." She shouldn't have said that, Gabrielle thought, but darn it, she'd had enough confusion and disappointments over the past few months and she didn't want to work for someone she had to tiptoe around to avoid his wrath. She got her fill of that from choreographers when she had to be literally on her toes.

Micah rammed his fists into his pockets. The one with the leather brace snagged and wouldn't go in; he jerked it back and rested it on his hip. "I don't like surprises," he informed her and made the silent decision that by the time he saw her again he would know all there was to know about this exquisite creature that had the nerve to question his moods. That was the way he was and she'd better learn to live with it.

"You mean about me being a dancer? That's no secret and I certainly made no attempt to hide it. I planned to accept this job because it was temporary. I didn't discuss it with Benton this afternoon because I thought my father may have mentioned that I had broken my leg and have to spend several months recuperating."

"So the business about your leg this afternoon wasn't just to cover a faux pas?" His voice was coolly sardonic.

Gabrielle smiled. So that was it—he thought she was being coy. "It was, actually," she said. A little tact wouldn't hurt at this point, she thought. "I just used the first thing that came into my mind when I saw you had discovered me sitting there."

Her answer seemed to appease him; the harsh line around his mouth relaxed and he smiled. "I take it dancing is your first love and being a linguist is just a sideline."

"Dancing is my whole life," she answered honestly. "I feel sort of lost without it. But the company won't take me back until I get a release from my doctor and he says I have to wait until spring. That's why this job appealed to me, it will give me a change of scenery. I'm. . . I was very good, I hope to be again."

"What about your friends?" he said smoothly. "Are you leaving behind anyone special?"

"What do you mean?" she answered, understanding him implicitly, but not liking him prying into her personal affairs.

"I mean a lover, a boyfriend?"

"No. Why are you asking me all of these questions? They have nothing to do with my ability to do the job." This was something new to Gabrielle. Other than her mother, no one had ever been so interested in her friends, especially her male friends. Before, during, and since Luke Bryant, there had not been another man in her life. She mentally swept Tim under the carpet. Micah didn't answer the question, but walked her to the limousine, which had driven up to the door. He handed her in. Surprised, Gabrielle looked up at him.

"I won't be seeing you home," he informed her. "Michael will get you there safe and sound."

Later all Gabrielle could think about was that Micah had not kissed her good night. And she had never wanted to be kissed so badly before in her life.

Chapter Seven

Benton was propped up in bed, reclining against fluffy pillows in the suite he shared with Micah. He didn't feel well. He hated and loved Micah to such a degree that both emotions were ambivalent, so interwoven and nestled together in his mind that he no longer recognized one or the other for what it was. He envied Micah his health, his strength, his lethal charm with women, even though Benton himself seldom desired a woman, except perhaps when certain memories caught him unaware, and then his passion was only for *her,* so that no other woman appealed to him. It never occurred to Benton that he was celibate, because to his way of thinking only priests were celibate, and they, Father Chardin had told him, even had to confess enticing dreams. Benton shuddered.

Telling someone about what was in the back of his mind or about a dream or memory locked in some shadowy secret corner of the brain was beyond his comprehension and certainly foolish. Benton had shared a secret only once, and because of that he was loyal, bound by events to his small circle of friends, and his loyalty went unquestioned by him or others.

Now, though, as he went over the past week in his mind, his thoughts were of Gabrielle Hensley, and the bad mood he found himself in was directly caused by the dossier he held in front of him. His bifocals slipped to the very tip of his nose as he leafed through the confidential report. Irritated, he shoved them back to the bridge of his nose with a quick gesture. It wasn't what the document said that made him feel so out of it; it was the fact that Micah had ordered it. Not that the procedure was unusual when they hired someone for a sensitive job, but damn! There wasn't any reason that he could see that Micah needed to know so much about Gabrielle.

She had made an immediate impression on him and one of even greater force on Micah. For some unfathomable reason that he couldn't decipher, Gabrielle had got under Micah's skin—gnawed at him like a herd of hungry termites. Served him right, Benton thought gleefully, but he wished he knew what had transpired between them before they stepped off the elevator at Annabelle's. Benton chuckled aloud at the astonished look he recalled on Micah's face when Gabrielle had suddenly suggested she might not be able to work for them after all. And that little scene in the foyer had Micah chewing nails. Later that same evening, when Micah had come off the dance floor grinning like a drunken Cheshire cat, Benton had assumed that Micah had made another of his conquests. But Gabrielle had left right after dinner and Micah had gone to bed alone.

It was a well-known fact that Micah didn't like independent women, and Gabrielle Hensley, if anything, had a streak of stubborn independence, not to mention her undisputed acclaim as a dancer. The report showed that clearly.

Benton suspected with the clarity of objectivity that Micah had fallen under the spell Gabrielle had cast over them all. The thought shocked him and he bolted up. That was it. He just hadn't noticed. It was as though Gabrielle had spun a golden web and locked Micah in it and for all Micah's prudence, culture, and caution about women he seemed unable to keep from tugging the web closer around him, and webs, after all, were built by female spiders to trap their prey. Hence the reason for the confidential report. Micah had stepped headlong into a snare unprepared, and for once the unflappable Micah Davidson was thoroughly and immeasurably flapped.

A smile flickered across Benton's face. He felt better. Matter of fact he felt damned good! He'd watch the both of them and secretly he'd root for Gabrielle.

Instead of taking a commercial flight to Panama, he would sail on the *Upsure* with the rest of them. Although, somehow, he would have to manage to stay out of Jinks's way. That overrated doctor had an annoying habit of being just a bit too ready with his hypodermics, and Benton, who had been a bully for most of his life, who loved to aggravate others, and who had never backed away from a fight, was absolutely terrified of needles.

There was a decided jaunt to Benton's step as he walked into the living room to give Micah the report and also to tell him of his change in plans. He halted abruptly just inside the room, surprised and uneasy to find Vanessa Thomas lounging indolently on the sofa, browsing through a recent issue of *Vogue*.

"What are you doing here?" he accosted her. It was no secret that he and Vanessa detested one another. He knew she had visited Micah while he had been in the hospital, but the last time Benton had seen her was when Micah had tossed her out of Chepo and she had been boiling over with vituperation. Benton had been embarrassed for Father Chardin who had had to shoulder as much of the vilification as had Benton during the trip to the airport.

Now Vanessa looked up from her magazine, a smile on her vulpine face. "I was invited," she said, stressing the word with indolent vigor.

"You must have caught Micah when he was under anesthetic and didn't know what he was doing."

Vanessa got up and stretched leisurely. She wore an expensive pongee suit, a soft, unbleached tan Chinese silk that clung to her voluptuous figure. She smoothed it down over her hips, eyeing Benton with the cunning of a Hydra.

"Don't bother to waste your charms on me, I'm immune," Benton said, watching her. He thought everything about Vanessa was irksome, couldn't see what Micah had seen in her in the first place. On the other hand, Micah had been young, very young, when he had begun his liaison with Vanessa, and youth could be forgiven its lusts, he thought charitably. Vanessa was beautiful, if you didn't mind the hard edges. She had aged rather well, being only four or five years younger than he, but there were beginning to be telltale lines around her eyes and he noticed she was wearing a heavy layer of makeup. "Where's Micah?"

"Taking a shower. Is that something for him?" She held out her hand for the manila folder Benton was grasping.

Benton remembered Gabrielle. No way would he put this report where Vanessa could get her hands on it. One thing you could depend upon with Vanessa: She was a sneak, downright mean sometimes, and she would do anything to get her own way. He held onto the folder. "I'll give it to him later. It's not important." For a short moment he compared Vanessa and Gabrielle in his mind's eye, deciding Vanessa couldn't hold a candle to the lissome ballerina. He chuckled aloud.

"What's so funny?"

"I told myself a joke," he sneered and headed back to his room.

"Let me make you laugh," Vanessa tossed at his back. "Micah and I are getting married."

Benton pivoted on his heel and stared at her. "Oh, are you shopping for husbands again?" he asked with heavy sarcasm. "Don't tell me you've already spent all that money you inveigled out of the last poor devil you were married to." Benton smiled, enjoying a perverse pleasure in egging her on. Vanessa frowned and he noticed the lines around her mouth were even deeper than he suspected. Living in the fast lane, he surmised, aged one in a hurry, especially women like Vanessa.

"Money has nothing to do with it. I've always loved Micah. It's not my fault we aren't married."

"I've always known you were a pathological liar, Vanessa, but I didn't know you lied to yourself."

"Count your blessings, Benton dear," she retorted venomously, "When I marry Micah, you'll be the first to go."

Benton shook his head in the wake of her denunciation. "Vanessa, you never fail to amaze me. You honestly believe that if you bruit something about often enough, it will become fact. Micah will never marry you."

"You think you can stop him?"

"I don't interfere in Micah's personal affairs. Never have. He'll stop himself if you don't do it first." With that he stepped into his room, closed the door softly, and locked it. He buried the report on Gabrielle under his pillow. Vanessa's thinking was distorted and he didn't take what she had said seriously, but his run-in with her, coming so unexpectedly, caused the bad feeling to return. He needed to cheer himself up. The thing to do was to slip up to Annabelle's for a few drinks. There was a lovely brunette working there named Lisa. She had a sympathetic look about her. This early in the afternoon maybe she wouldn't be too busy and would have a few minutes to talk. The thought cheered him and he went quietly out the door of the suite, avoiding the living room, where Vanessa, undoubtedly sat, preening for Micah.

THE following week seemed interminable to Gabrielle, but the excitement about her new job prevailed and swept her through the whirl of shopping and the peevishness of harried clerks as she bought what she needed for the tropics in the last-minute rush of the Christmas season.

She hoped Micah would call, and after each shopping trip she came home expecting to find a message from him. None came. She decided to take matters into her own hands and call him. As she stood by the telephone, memorizing what she would say, her imagination leaped to the impossible.

"Micah? Is Benton there?... No?... Oh, nothing. I just wanted to ask him about clothes—I need to know what's suitable.... Lunch? I'd love to—"

or

"Helen? This is Gabrielle. Would you like to go shopping with me? I have to go to Lord and Taylor's to pick up a few things.... He does? Well, put him on.... Micah?... You miss me?" Laugh. "How can that be? We just met.... Lunch? I think I have time.... Dinner too?"

or

"Mr. Davidson, this is Gabrielle.... Gabrielle Hensley.... You can't place me?..." Oh, God!

Gabrielle never lifted the phone out of its cradle. Micah's image continuously and persistently invaded the shadows of her mind, clamoring so for attention that she couldn't ignore it. On occasion she was literally overcome with a need to sit down and let her thoughts, his image, take over. Once this happened, she would wait with excited trepidation for her heart to begin pounding—it always did, like thunder bouncing against a blue-sky wall, and as if on signal, the butterflies she had so long denied existence would begin to swarm. The feeling always left her at a standstill, breathless and astonished and not a little confused. It would take her hours to relegate these feelings, to return the winged creatures back into the deep, hidden, secret recesses in her body.

On Christmas Day Micah Davidson lounged in his cabin on the *Upsure* and pondered the report on Gabrielle Hensley for the third time. Something was missing. It nagged at him. He felt pressed to discover what it was; there was so little time before she came aboard. Benton, behaving in an unusually pompous manner all week, had produced the report only this morning.

Micah glanced at the report again, his eyes reflective as he studied the photographs of Gabrielle. Some were newspaper clippings, others programs from various productions she had danced in over the past several years. They both delighted and dismayed him. Everything about Gabrielle stung his imagination with an unaccustomed fascination and Micah found himself thinking about her at the oddest moments—when he drank his coffee in the morning, in the middle of conversations with Captain Dressler, and he had lost completely his track of thought while speaking to Jinks about the clinic. He thought of her at night, and that was the worst—or the most pleasant; certain parts of him particularly reminded him of the way she felt in his arms. He was even immune to Benton's goading. That in itself was an achievement, since Benton had hectored him unmercifully until Vanessa had left.

Micah thought of himself as a man in total control, of himself and of others. He didn't doubt his ability to control Gabrielle. She was different from any woman he had ever known and he had to have her for himself. All he need do was set the scene and use subtle strategy, she would be completely derailed.

He fingered the report again and went over it line by line. Finally he sensed what wasn't there. Medical reports.

She had broken her leg in September. The auto accident had happened on the same day the helicopter had crashed thousands of miles away in the Panamanian jungle. Since Micah didn't believe in fate, this was just an interesting coincidence. He was curious as to why Gabrielle wasn't allowed to do even remedial exercises. That tidbit of information had been gleaned tactfully from her friend Val, by an investigator posing as a reporter. Too late now to run that down unless.... He picked up the telephone and listened for the dial tone. Good. The ship was still hooked up to land lines and he spent a few minutes speaking in confidence to his former economics professor.

GABRIELLE glanced briefly at her watch for the dozenth time. Less than fifteen minutes now before the chauffeur arrived.

"For heaven's sake, Gabby," her mother admonished. "Looking at your watch isn't going to make the time go faster. Calm down, you're making *me* nervous."

"I am calm, Mother, and I'm not worried about the time. I was just admiring my Christmas present from you and Daddy," she said smoothly. In truth, Gabrielle had been ready to leave for hours. If she had known exactly how to contact Benton aboard the ship, she would have begged him to send for her earlier. Traditionally the family had arisen early on Christmas Day, eaten a light breakfast, then gone to church in the university's chapel, where services were held for students who stayed on campus during the holidays. And, as was her father's usual practice, he had invited these students home for wassail and some of Hattie's marvelous pastries. Predictably, no one left until after dinner. Consequently Gabrielle, wanting to be alone with her thoughts, had to push them aside and help Hattie and her mother serve and entertain. It had been a madcap day.

"Phooey!" Emily spewed. "You're as nervous as a cat about to have kittens. If you need something to do, go help Hattie with the dishes," she suggested while moving around the room collecting cups and dirty glasses. She stooped to pick up a candy wrapper from the floor. Her lovely tree had been denuded of candy canes by Nate's students. "One of these days," she prophesied under her breath, "I'm going to stop your father from having open house for all those radicals on Christmas."

"What was that?" Nate asked, coming up behind his wife.

"Not a thing, dear," Emily said sweetly, straightening up. "Gabby is pacing a hole in the carpet, eager to be gone. I'm just trying to calm her down."

Nate sat down on the sofa, fixing a thoughtful gaze on his daughter. He marveled again as he had on so many other occasions at Gabrielle's winsome beauty. Silhouetted in the big double windows illuminated by the Christmas lights, she wore an impatient, pensive look on her comely features. She was dressed in black knit and the fabric shaped her figure as revealingly as a leotard. He feared she was too thin.

The entire household had put in a whirlwind week getting Gabrielle ready for her jungle job. Good Lord! he thought, he'd been listening to Hattie and picking up on her outlandish phrases. Heaven forbid that he'd unconsciously commit such an error in the classroom. Happily, though, he noticed that the air of despondency that had hovered so heavily about Gabrielle had seemed to dissolve. She was smiling more these days and the spirit of tension that pervaded the house had to do with her new job. Every conversation was no longer directed at ballet, but more and more to her new friends, the "team," and, surprisingly, Micah Davidson himself.

"Come look at this," he said to Gabrielle. "I've finally found that old yearbook you've been pestering me about. It has a few pictures of Micah."

"Let me see!" she exclaimed, continually astonished at the way her body reacted every time Micah's name was mentioned. She didn't have to look at the pictures to recall what he looked like. His dark, hewed features were never very far from her mind. He invaded her dreams at night until she often woke and discovered herself taut and beleaguered, aching to feel his lips on hers. She spent hours remembering every moment they had spent together. It wasn't enough, and the fluttering butterflies in her stomach begged to be put to rest.

One kiss, she thought. If he just kissed her once, it would be over, because it couldn't possibly be as exhilarating as she imagined. Her hand trembled as she turned the slick pages of the book. Her father had dusted the covers, but the seventeen-year-old album smelled musty. Gabrielle did some mental arithmetic: Micah must be thirty-seven or thirty-eight. In his prime, she thought. How marvelous.

"Gabby, he's here," Emily said.

Gabrielle stood up and all the blood in her body rushed to her feet, leaving her heart pumping a dry hole that caused her mouth to suddenly go dry and the butterflies to gallop.

"Who?"

"The chauffeur, child, the chauffeur," Emily repeated, watching through the windows as Michael parked the car, got out, and walked up the short walk. "The man who's spiriting you away to begin your jungle adventure," she said eloquently, miming a few of Gabrielle's descriptions that she had learned by rote.

Feeling all arms and legs, Gabrielle shrugged into the fur-trimmed leather coat, buttoning it over the knit dress she had so carefully chosen on a trip to Saks. She hugged her parents good-bye.

"Don't forget to write often," Emily insisted. "Remember, you're our baby."

"Mother! Oh, all right," she acquiesced, not wanting to begin an argument in her last few minutes home. Hattie was hugging her too, while the doorbell rang and rang. Gabrielle pulled herself free and answered the door.

Michael tipped his hat in the respectful salute that she remembered. He picked up one of Gabrielle's handbags, she the other, and with a last good-bye to her parents and Hattie, followed the chauffeur down the sidewalk. Her heart pounded against her ribs. She expected Micah to be lounging in the backseat, it wouldn't be a surprise to her this time. She kept her eyes on the chauffeur's back, not daring to let them give her away by inspecting the cavern of the limousine. Michael opened the back door and there was no one there. Gabrielle sighed.

"Did you have a nice Christmas, Miss Hensley?" the chauffeur asked after they were on their way. She answered him absentmindedly, her thoughts clearly not on small pleasantries. Michael hunched his back and drove in silence.

In an hour he pulled to a halt on a concrete pier. Too excited to wait, Gabrielle opened the door herself and stepped out. She stared up at the enormous ship, awe-struck with the size of it; the ship dwarfed her. A wide red stripe circled the black-painted hull at the waterline; *Upsure* painted in white elongated letters on the curved bow assured her this was the correct ship among the dozens docked on the mile-long wharf. Each letter was taller than she.

Michael set her tote and hand luggage at her feet, wished her good luck. Gabrielle acknowledged his comments with a slight smile and came out of her dreamlike state only when she realized she was standing alone at the foot of the wide metal gangplank.

Chapter Eight

The mile-long pier seemed deserted in the late-evening chill. A stiff breeze ruffled her curls. Gabrielle heard the slap of waves as they washed against the ship, whipped by wind that skimmed briskly across the bay. Her eyes swept the ship and found a figure moving along the rails.

"Gabby! Welcome aboard!" Helen called down to her as she neared the top of the gangplank. She met Gabrielle halfway down the steeply angled walk. "Do you need any help with those?" Helen asked, indicating the two pieces of luggage. Gabrielle held out her overnight case.

"No, not a bit," she said. The puzzled look on Helen's face brought Gabrielle back to reality. "Oh, I mean, yes, thank you and merry Christmas."

Helen laughed. "Thank you, that's the first one I've had today."

"You're not serious," Gabrielle said, uncomprehending.

"I sure am. All hell has broken loose since we came aboard yesterday."

"What's happened?" Gabrielle asked, a slight chill threading her veins as she followed Helen far up into the ship's superstructure.

"Oh, nothing that has to do with you," Helen puffed, resting a moment on a metal stair landing. "On my own side of the fence, Jinks took one look at the *Upsure* and began to turn green. How a man can become so violently seasick when all we've done is barely sway in the tide is beyond me." Helen shook her head in dismay. "Benton got excited at some news and that brought on an attack of asthma, but he's better now. He and Micah are holed up in the radio room. Some fool logger spent the night with one of the Cuna Indian women and tribal law absolutely forbids any interaction, especially sexual, with outsiders.

"Unfortunately the chief discovered them. He's tied the logger to a manchineel tree and he's threatening severe punishment for the woman. Father Chardin is in the village now, trying to sort it all out and arrange for the release of the logger. Micah's waiting to learn if he's managed it." Helen looked back over her shoulder and saw the shock of disbelief on Gabrielle's face. "I told you," she reminded, "once you get away from the metropolis of the city into the jungles, it's primitive—almost like time stood still."

"Why can't the priest just untie the logger when no one is looking, or get the police?"

Helen chuckled. "I can see right now I'm going to have to educate you about the natives, but to answer your questions: *We* know the police mean authority, *we* know there are laws we must follow, but to the Indians their chief is the authority. How can you explain civilized rules and laws to a people who remain primitive? Unlike the Cunas who live on the San Blas Islands and come to the mainland every day to work their vegetable plots, the tribes in the jungle don't recognize a policeman's uniform. If one was to go into a village and begin ordering people about, he would likely find himself in the same predicament as the logger.

"Amand has been moving among the Indians for the past two years. I won't say that they trust him exactly, but they're used to him. He might be able to coax the chief to free the logger, but he would never be allowed near the man, even if he knew where he was, which I doubt. The underbrush on the jungle floor is so thick, and so tall, you could walk within a foot of anything you might be looking for and not see it."

"Well," Gabrielle said, trying to absorb all that Helen had told her, "being tied to a tree doesn't sound like too dangerous a punishment for breaking a law."

"If it was any other tree than the manchineel, I'd agree with you," Helen said. "But this particular tree exudes an acrid, highly poisonous juice, extremely painful and very often fatal to humans. Being tied to the tree for hours will cause certain death and not a pleasant one at that. I'm afraid our logger is a bit worse off than a treed possum.

"Well, forget all that," Helen said, as if Gabrielle could. "Here's your cabin."

Gabrielle involuntarily gasped at the unexpected luxury. Her heels sank into a plush burgundy carpet. A white velour sofa basked invitingly in the soft golden glow of a tiffany lamp. The full-size bed Helen deposited her makeup case on was done in soft whites and antique gold and was nestled comfortably in a built-in nook. Two foot-wide portholes over the bed were her windows to the sea. A gold and white door was ajar at the far end of the cabin toward midship. Her luggage, which had been brought aboard yesterday, was stacked neatly on wooden racks riveted to the wall adjacent to the door.

Helen acknowledged her surprise. "This is part of the owner's suite." She nodded toward the slightly opened door. "Micah designed it himself. Considering the lack of space available on cargo ships for passengers, he's outdone himself. There are six suites on this deck, plus the chart room, and radio room. The captain's quarters are next to you." Helen pointed toward the prow of the ship. "Beyond that and up two steps is the bridge. We can only go up there," Helen warned, "when we're invited. Captain Dressler is a stickler for protocol. Every two cabins share a bath and we have the added luxury of two cabin boys—old men actually—and one steward on this deck. That's about it," Helen wound down.

"I love it," Gabrielle said softly while she inspected her quarters more closely.

"I need to let Captain Dresser know you're aboard, Gabby. He wanted to get under way the minute you arrived. I'll be right back." Helen pivoted at the door. "Oh, by the way, it will just be you and me for Christmas dinner, what with all the muddle—"

Gabrielle laughed. "Just you, I'm afraid. My folks had open house for my father's students and friends and we had a late dinner. But I'll sit with you and have a cup of coffee."

"Coffee!" Helen's eyes lit with amusement. "No way. I've iced a bottle of Micah's Chandon cuvée Dom Pérignon. We're christening this voyage in the proper manner. Back in a minute."

The minute Helen closed the door Gabrielle peeked into the adjoining suite. A gray silk tie was folded neatly over a sofa—twin to the one in her cabin. She spied the leather glove that Micah wore on an ottoman pushed against the sofa. His suite. Were all the cabins connected like these two? she wondered. She tried not to attach any special significance to the fact that she was given the cabin adjoining Micah's. But a pleasant sensation of anticipation radiated from an inner core and spread warmth throughout her slender body. She would see him soon. If not tonight, then tomorrow. Drat that stupid logger! She could cheerfully have throttled him herself. When Helen returned, Gabrielle was busy unpacking and the slightly ajar door at the far end of her cabin gave no hint that it had been opened wide and carefully returned to its exact position.

"We have a really nice dining room and galley between decks," Helen said as she guided Gabrielle down the narrow corridor. "It's to your right and down those steps." She pointed ahead, then pushed the heavy steel door open. Helen waved a freckled hand. "Small, elegant, and comfortable." A gay arrangement of red carnations and white doves was centered between two ornate candelabra on a table laid with white linens and set with delicate china. "My contributions to the festivities," Helen mentioned, noticing Gabrielle's appreciative glance. "The room is nice, don't you think? We can sit at the table and look out the portholes."

"It is," Gabrielle agreed, easing herself into a chair opposite Helen. The ship lurched and the other woman grabbed for the wine bucket, steadying it with both hands.

"Well, I guess that wasn't such a good idea."

"What was that?" Gabrielle sounded a bit anxious.

"It must be the tugboats getting into position. The pilots were already aboard so I think Captain Dressler isn't wasting any time getting under way." Helen opened the wine with little difficulty.

"Would you like to make a toast, Gabby?"

A tremulous smile curved Gabrielle's lips. "Yes, I will. To friendship." She spoke with sincerity. Their delicate wineglasses pinged musically. The cold bubbling wine was delicious too. Gabrielle savored the first sip.

"Now I propose a toast," Helen said mischievously. "To gossip. Want some?" she asked with the feminine complicity that only another woman could understand.

"Of course not," Gabrielle laughed.

"Good. What would you like to know first?" Helen said with wicked amusement. "Let's see, I was born—"

"Helen!" Gabrielle laughed. "Couldn't you begin a little later? Like when and how you and Jinks came to work for Micah."

"What? And skip the best thirty years of my life? Oh, I'm sure that would bore the pants off you." But the look on Gabrielle's face told her that was exactly what Gabrielle wanted to hear and boredom was the farthest thing from the young woman's mind.

Thoughtfully Helen refilled their wineglasses before she began. "I first heard of Micah and Benton too," she began, "in letters from Jinks when he was a medic in Vietnam—you know, I can only tell you what I've pieced together. I may get something backward."

"I don't care, just talk," Gabrielle said, exasperated. "Whoever expects gossip to be the last word about anything anyway?" she encouraged.

Helen shrugged. "I guess you're right. Anyway, to start with, Benton was the only black in his platoon in one of the special services groups in Vietnam. He was also the wrestling champion in his company."

"Benton? A wrestling champion?" Disbelief etched Gabrielle's voice.

"I know." Helen nodded. "He barely weighs a hundred and ten pounds now, but I'll get to that if you'll let me."

"Sorry."

"That's better. As I was saying," Helen said pointedly, "Benton was a cocky you-know-what and a terrible bully. Then Micah was assigned to the platoon, and Benton bullied him too, or tried to, and I guess Micah beat the stuffings out of him, which brought Benton down a notch or two. But he and Micah continued to squabble—I think they secretly enjoyed it—until they became almost friendly foes. Jinks said their company commander got so disgusted he finally told them that if they would put that much anger out on the enemy the rest of the army could sit back and relax while Benton and Micah won the war.

"For more than eight months Micah and Benton never said a civil word to one another and every time they were even in the same room together, sparks would fly. Finally, their sergeant got so fed up he sent the two of them out on patrol together. One can only wonder what was in the back of *his* mind. The patrol got ambushed and Benton got hit. Jinks was one of the medical team that reached the patrol during a brief lull in the fighting. When he saw how badly Benton was hurt, he was just going to administer morphine to ease the agony of the dying man, but Micah rose up from nowhere, shoved his bayonet to Jinks's throat, and told him to save him right then and there.

"Jinks told me later that he's never been so scared before or since. He said he simply reached inside Benton and started sewing because he knew if the Vietcong didn't kill him, the angry black warrior standing over him would."

Helen lighted a cigarette and inhaled deeply. Gabrielle sipped on her wine, covering her impatience to hear more, but not daring to interrupt. Every word about Micah was a balm, a soothing coating like a smooth cream drenching her skin. Her brain clamored for more, separating and sorting the information like a hungry, devouring computer.

Helen tilted her head in thoughtful recall. "Let's see, where was I? Oh, yes. Some months later, as fate—certainly not lady luck—would have it," she said wryly, "Benton, Micah, and Jinks were all on the same plane coming home. All three ended up on my doorstep, in Oregon. For a month they laughed, cried, and drank—mostly cried and drank. You wouldn't believe the number of empty bottles of Jack Daniel's I threw out." She chuckled under her breath. "To this day I've often wondered what our neighbors thought. Benton had survived with only one lung and a piece of his stomach. While Micah and Jinks drank hard, he just sipped and gorged himself on peanut butter. By then Benton wasn't very strong, and he began to have trouble breathing in the cold Oregon climate. One day Micah left to go back to his parents' farm in Georgia and Benton traipsed after him.

"After that, we just heard from Benton, mostly at Christmas. Micah went to Atlanta...and worked some sort of financial deal with an Atlanta banker and courted the banker's daughter. The next thing we heard, about two or three years later, Micah was a wealthy man and we received an invitation to his wedding."

Gabrielle recoiled, almost spilling her wine over the table. She recovered the glass with trembling fingers. "Micah's married?" Her stomach flipflopped and tumbled into the abyss of her loins.

Helen looked sharply at Gabrielle. "No, the wedding was called off. Then Micah got into this logging project. He asked Jinks to head up the medical team, so here we are. End of story."

But it couldn't be, Gabrielle thought. What happened to the banker's daughter? Gabrielle's curiosity made her breathless. She asked the question aloud.

"Oh, Vanessa shows up now and then, but Micah usually sends her packing. She did visit him in the hospital and he seemed glad to see her. She flew to Houston this past week too."

"This week? You mean since we had dinner last Saturday?"

"Yes, she came in Sunday afternoon."

"Is Micah— I mean, are they back together?"

"I don't know," Helen said. "The closest I ever came to knowing anyting about Micah's love life was that wedding invitation."

The wine in Gabrielle's stomach began to settle like belligerent contraband. There was a definite change in the ship's motion, more roll in the gentle dips, and Gabrielle prayed fervently that she wasn't becoming seasick. They both peered out the portholes into the damp, black mist.

"We must be in the gulf," Helen said. "I'd better go check on Jinks. He'll be two days getting his sea legs, and even then he'll still be wobbly."

Gabrielle pushed her chair under the table and wished Helen a good-night. She would finish unpacking and maybe get a breath of fresh air on deck. She felt just a bit light-headed from the wine.

The adjoining door to Micah's suite had been closed when she returned to her cabin. While her hands were busy unpacking, she mulled over all that Helen had told her. At least now she knew why Micah hadn't called her—he wasn't interested in her. She had been a fool to let her imagination go so wild. With cold logic she forced herself to remember the reason she had accepted this job. Micah Davidson was not one of the reasons. Absolutely not. Think of all that fresh air on deck, she told herself. She needed a lungful in the worst way.

The cowl neck on the black knit dress unrolled into a hood and Gabrielle tugged it out from under the collar of her coat to cover her curls as she stepped onto the unlighted deck.

The chill, wet wind buffeted her as she stood at the aft rail. After a few great gulps of the damp air the wine began to settle in her stomach; her head cleared. Better to suffer a bit of light-headedness with wine than the evils of seasickness, she thought. But the chill in the wind was no less cold than the hard lump in her chest, and in a few minutes the cold reached as deep as her bones. She turned into the gray shadow to make her way back to the comfortable warmth of her cabin and walked headlong into a lean, warm body.

"Aaagh, Gabrielle." Micah's rich melodious voice lifted above the wind. "If you keep spending so much time on my toes, I'm going to insist you go barefoot." His hands gripped her arms lightly, steadying her.

"Micah!" Wind snatched his name over the rail and out to sea.

"You sound surprised to see me, and you're cold too." He felt her shiver, but it had nothing to do with the weather. He pulled her inside the warmth of his wool pea jacket. "Is that better?" he murmured as his arms closed around her.

"It's marvelous," she breathed, inhaling the heady fragrance of Aramis and Ivory soap that seemed to hover like an aphrodisiac.

"I missed you," he said.

The words shuffled around in Gabrielle's brain and moved from imagination to reality; said aloud, they sounded so right, so true. But there was a logical pretense and she couldn't give it up so easily.

"You just say you missed me. I was as close as the telephone and you know where I live." Her voice was muffled under his great coat.

"I thought you would be too busy to see me. It usually takes quite a while to get everything together for a trip out of the country, and then you had all your good-byes to make to your friends." He lifted the collar on his jacket up around his ears and tugged her closer to him when he dropped his arms again. "I had my hand on the phone to call you a dozen times," he admitted.

"Liar," she said and felt him stiffen. She hadn't meant to say the word, but it slipped out, rolled off her tongue like an epitaph. *She* had been the one to go to the telephone more than a dozen times, not he.

"What do you mean by that?"

"You didn't want to call me," she accused. "I—I know you had other things on your mind. An old friend visited you." The banker's daughter loomed large in her mind. "A very old friend."

"Who told you that?"

"It doesn't matter who told me," she countered. "Do you deny it?"

"No, why should I?" he retorted. "I'm nobody's property and I don't wear a chain around my neck." His arms tightened the coat around her, snuggling her to his chest. "Did you sit by the phone and wait for me to call?" he murmured.

"No, I certainly did not. I don't wear a chain around my neck either."

"You," he said caustically, "hardly wear anything around your neck and about a foot below either."

Gabrielle thought for a fleeting second to back out of the circling warmth of his arms, but changed her mind. It was too cold.

"I saw you Wednesday night at Jones Hall. You had on

that pleated skirt, but with a different top—a tunic of some sort. It practically dipped to your waist."

"It did not, and I thought I saw Helen and Jinks. Why didn't you speak to me?"

"I couldn't get near you for all your adoring admirers. I got tired of counting how many men kissed you on this cheek or that cheek or your lips," he said, a trace of envy in his voice. "Every one of them was ogling you. It was sickening the way they gushed all over you."

"They weren't gushing, they were just wishing me well, glad to see me. I have a lot of fans and many of the patrons remembered me."

"You see," he tossed at her softly, "if I had called, you wouldn't have been home anyway."

"I might have been," she said stubbornly.

"You're here now, and this is much better than the telephone," he drawled huskily. "Tilt your head up here, Gabrielle. I'd like to wish you well myself. Those lips have been haunting my dreams all week." Her breath dipped shallowly. She couldn't refuse; she wanted his kiss too badly. His lips touched hers; they were cold, chilled by the wind, tasting of salty sea spray. He lifted them away from her mouth. "You've been drinking my Dom Pérignon."

"Helen gave it to me," she whispered and wondered why he felt the need to talk when there was this other thing upon them, this need to explore, this experiment, this "just once" situation. She slid her arms around him. It was just like in her dream. His silk shirt was smooth, no impediment to her fingertips as they slid, palm flat, up the muscled, lean back.

Finally his warm, moist tongue began to trace the shape of her lips, thrusting gently, teasing, until every nerve in her body came alive. The spark of erotic current, dormant for a week, arced between them, inciting chaos and turmoil. The current shot through Gabrielle, causing an arousal she had not believed possible. His tongue breached her lips impatiently, thrusting against her teeth hungrily, but it was only an aperitif, a succulent hors d'oeuvre that peaked the hunger.

Gabrielle leaned her body into his with wild abandon,

welding her contours to his until she felt his throbbing maleness hard against her soft thighs. She felt as though she was in a foreign land, walking, and each short step carried her from one galaxy to the next and the stars rained down on this foreigner, swamping her body with sensual, urgent needs.

Micah left her lips and began a series of tiny kisses from her ear to the soft, warm hollow in her throat. He savored the pulse he found there; it told him what he wanted to know and returned unsatiated to her lips. The long drugged kiss that followed drenched the immediate spark of wanton desire but did nothing to quell the impoverished ache impaled in his loins.

His voice was ragged, harsh, almost brutal with the desire he felt. "This isn't enough," he said.

"I know, but I don't know you well enough—I hardly know anything about you—" She had not thought beyond the kiss, hadn't expected there to be anything after it. She was taken by surprise and she needed time—time to sort it all out, file it away; time to pick it apart, put it back together. This erotic, historical moment needed a past, a future; her practical self needed more than the present. She couldn't help it.

"I can't," she told him, backing out of the warmth of his coat. He refused to let her go.

"That kiss says you want to," he countered, his voice low, angry.

"You—you just interpreted it wrong. It's just excitement, the holidays and—and everything is so new, challenging."

"Challenge!" he exploded. "Are you telling me you just wanted to see if you could arouse me? Wrap me around that dainty little finger?" The wind snatched his words, tossing them into the churning waters.

"No, that's not what I meant at all. Stop twisting my words. I'm cold. I'm going to my cabin."

His hand gripped her arm, biting through the leather coat. "You'll pay for this, Gabrielle! A tease—you're a tease," he said bitterly.

"I am not!" She yanked her arm from his grip and

walked into the warm corridor of the ship. He maintained a pace behind her.

"Two can play your little game, Gabrielle," he warned, spitting the words angrily at her back.

"I'm not playing a game. I did want to kiss you. We just got carried away. Drop it, please," she pleaded.

The words reminded him of a phrase in the confidential report he had on her. Drop it. She had dropped Luke Bryant, walked away from the man, and now she was doing the same to him. Deep within him something sounded, a note of unmistakable warning to let her go, but his pride wouldn't let him.

"I'll drop it!" He jerked her around to face him. "Right into your lap." He looked down at her, his eyes glaring with molten fire, his voice harsh. "You don't need to play the vestal virgin with me."

"I didn't say I was a virgin."

"I know you're not," he said cruelly. "No man is going to tolerate your teasing for long—least of all me." He yanked her violently into his arms, circling her reed-slender figure in an embrace that crushed all air from her lungs. His mouth violated hers savagely, his lips bruising, his tongue pillaging like a demon warrior insatiable with lust. His hands roamed her body, searching and sure, until he felt her quiver and lean into him, betrayed by her own body. The harsh, cruel plundering stopped and he shoved her away from him abruptly. Gabrielle grabbed hold of the handrail to keep from stumbling, drawing in great gulps of air to renew the fragile thread of composure that threatened to snap. She looked at Micah, shaken and wide-eyed, stunned by his rage and cruelty.

His mirthless smile made no allowance for the bitterness in his voice. "Work a challenge around that. I dare you." His voice was so low and smooth Gabrielle barely heard him. "You start work in the morning, Miss Hensley," he added, stalking down the corridor.

Gabrielle straightened her coat around her shoulders, drawing dignity from the innate small act, and made her way slowly to her cabin.

Chapter Nine

Sunday morning Gabrielle woke early, and for an instant she was dizzy with a feeling of unreality. The ship seemed motionless, but the low hum of powerful turbine engines told her they must be moving swiftly through the south Atlantic. A leisurely stretch was cut short by an aching tautness in her abdomen. The events of last night slammed into her mind, filling her with a mixture of acute and conflicting emotions. Desire remained locked in her veins, as though fed intravenously without her knowledge, and it was coupled somehow with Micah's anger. Gabrielle accepted that an erotic compulsion lay between them like a tiny torch ready to billow into flames—waiting only for the catalyst. She was positive she could not allow the catalyst to be anger. Instinctively she tried to reassure herself that she could manage any situation. But how could she endure three months of this?

Her cabin was suddenly filled with music, too loud, and the sound purged her reverie. She leaned over the side of the bed and looked at the dials on the nightstand. One read Volume. She twisted the knob, it brought the sound down. She listened to the tune a moment, a perky, gay piano melody that made her smile. A much better way to begin her day, she thought rationally, than worrying over her relationship with Micah.

She clambered to her knees on the bed and looked out the porthole. Buttermilk clouds floated lazily in the blue sky. Gray-green water sparkled in the sun, its surface broken here and there when an eager wave lifted, discovering only too late it had reached its peak and settled disgruntled into a swish of white frothy foam. She opened the porthole and a warm brisk breeze ruffled her swag of curls. Standing on her bed, she poked her head out the round window and inhaled the clean sea air. A jean-clad seaman was coiling a manila rope as thick as her arm on the deck below. He looked up and waved. Gabrielle smiled and watched him continue his task for a minute. Her stomach rumbled, reminding her she had had nothing to eat since late afternoon the day before. She laid out her clothes; gauzy cotton pantaloons that buttoned just below the knee and a matching tunic that belted at the waist—both a marvelous shade of peach that accentuated her dark skin and highlighted the depth of her brown eyes. She added a pair of embroidered espadrilles to the clothes on the bed.

The mossy, tantalizing fragrance of Micah's cologne rushed over her when she entered the small efficiently appointed bath. The compelling scent brought him to mind as effectively as if he had been standing next to her. A thick bar of Ivory soap on the tub held damp lather, so that she knew he had showered not long before. With determined effort she closed her eyes and forced the tremors that raced through her body to come to a halt. When she felt sufficiently recovered, she inspected her features in the mirror and was amazed to see that the mirror reflected only a cool image. She shook her head wonderingly at the resilience of the human body, especially hers.

The tangerine essence that she delighted in bubbled up under the steaming rush of water and Gabrielle let the welcome warmth flow over her body. She rested her head on a folded towel and propped her toes on the spigots. When the frothy bubbles drifted against her lips she blew a gentle stream to coax them away from her mouth. She soaked, eyes closed, trying to restrict her restless mind from wandering to erotic bits and pieces that brought Micah vividly to the surface of her consciousness.

The bathroom door flew open, Micah crowded into the tiny room, filling all its space. He reeled with the embarrassment a situation like this caused and blurted the first thing that came into his mind. "What the hell— My Lord! It smells like a fruit basket in here!"

"Get out!" Gabrielle yelled, sinking as far under the water as she could go without drowning, causing bubbles to coast in waves and slide over the edge of the tub.

Micah didn't budge. He was thinking: *I want her. She has a look about her in the morning, a sleepy sexuality. I wonder if she's aware of it.* His conscience prodded. *I should apologize for last night, but I won't right this minute. I don't want to remind her of it now.* The present circumstances called for a different tact. His lower lip curved with sardonic amusement as his gaze swept over her, stopping at her bubble-coated toes propped on the spigots.

"Make me," he taunted and sat down on the edge of the tub. "Want me to wash your back?" He trailed a hand in the water, stirring away the concealing blanket of bubbles.

"No! Get out of this bathroom—this minute!" she uttered, her voice low with anger and hating him because he was obviously enjoying her predicament. A wave of warmth scorched her neck and shoulders at his nearness, the open desire reflected in his eyes. This was her own fault; she had succumbed to her imagination, letting it take hold, building his charm, his virility, to such heights that he could have been some dark Greek god descending to earth at her command. She had put him on a higher plane than his intentions warranted. He and Tim Stone were cut from the same cloth. "Get out," she repeated.

He ignored her demand. "We share this bath. You're supposed to lock the doors when you're in here to avoid embarrassing situations—just like this one," he said chuckling. He raked a hand along her leg from toe to knee, gathering froth, then dipped his fingers under the water and allowed the bubbles to float free.

Gabrielle jerked her knees up to her chest and clasped her arms around them to keep from floating to the surface. The shift in position lifted her full rounded breasts nearly out of the water. "Keep your hands off me, and next time knock before you go breaking in on somebody's privacy!"

"I don't want to keep my hands off you," he murmured, his eyes riveted hungrily to the exposed fullness behind her knees. He edged closer to her, ignoring the soapy water that dampened his gray slacks as he slid down the rim of the tub. He wasn't wearing the leather brace; his shirt was unbuttoned to the waist with the shirt's collar pulled far back from the scars on his neck. Gabrielle watched him warily, determined not to submit to the intimidation Micah seemed bent on. He drew a finger down the curve of her neck and pressed gently the vulnerable vein in the hollow curve. It was pulsating with every beat of her heart—running amuck.

"We're playing a game, remember? You provoked me deliberately last night—it's my turn now." His hand slid behind her neck. Gabrielle twisted her head, but firm pressure from his lean fingers forced it back. "Shame on you," he said huskily. "Can't you take what you dish out?"

"Stop it," she said, furious at his effrontery and too aware that she might not be able to cope with the ardor clearly visible in his face. She smoldered while he caressed her with his eyes, savoring her nakedness.

"Stop? You don't really want me to stop," he said, quirking an eyebrow in cynical amusement. Gabrielle's words, her tone of voice, her demeanor, unleashed some forgotten fractiousness in Micah. With a sudden flash of clarity he realized he must *win* Gabrielle's affections. Never in the past had he had to put himself out so for a woman. The thought struck at his powerful amour propre, tainting his words and making him say far more than he intended. "You're not even playing hard to get. Did you hope I would fawn over you, cater to your whims, and wait, panting, while you decide when to reward me? Is that how you handled your liaison with Luke Bryant? And your dancer friend, Tim? Isn't it?"

"No!" Gabrielle gasped, shocked. "What. . .how do you know—?"

He smiled triumphantly at her astonishment; he wanted her off balance. He was far from steady himself. "I check out my employees. *Thoroughly.*"

Outrage leaped beyond Gabrielle's anger, beyond her fury, and filled the small space between them. "You had no right! That's an invasion of my privacy." Her eyes bored into his; she no longer felt his hand on her neck.

"Oh, but you're a public figure, a prima ballerina. . .or you were, until the car accident."

At the mention of the accident Gabrielle went cold. "No wonder you didn't call me this past week, you've been too busy snooping," she said, shaken. "What good will it do you?" She realized his hand had slipped to her shoulder; she brushed it away angrily.

"Quite a lot. You'll be twenty-five soon, too old to start all over, which is what you'd have to do. I know your dancing career is over. You jilted Luke Bryant, left him a bitter man, and you wrapped your dancer friend, Tim, around your little finger; you made him beg. I know what you're doing and I won't let you use me like that. I won't beg," he said silkily, "but you will." He grasped her wet shoulders, chuckling throatily when she tried to twist out of his hands. "Careful, Gabrielle," he warned as she thrashed about, "or you'll be entirely out of that water." His fingers bit into her like steel prongs, while with unerring mastery he lowered his mouth to hers, smothering her protests.

He forced her lips apart with his tongue, slowly, alert for her response. When none came, he thrust his tongue harder and deeper, like an itinerant beggar searching amid rubble for lost gems, loitering there, reluctant to stop seeking lest he miss the treasure. He broke off the kiss and straightened up and studied Gabrielle. He seemed unaffected and as totally in control of his emotions as she pretended. "Stubborn little thing, aren't you?" he said, amused, but Gabrielle noted that a ragged edge of desire chased his words.

She felt the knot of anger and outrage as it began to form in her stomach, sending a rush of adrenaline to her brain. Her eyes locked his, holding them as though compelled by an arc of magnetic force. With utter calm that often accompanies deep anger she stood up, ignoring her nakedness. It was unimportant now. Tiny droplets of water sought each other, formed rivulets, and trickled down her lissome body. For a memorable moment she poised, like a lovely goddess risen from the sea. She saw, more than heard, Micah's intake of breath as she reached for a towel. She held it by the corner and let it unfold before draping it around her body, then stepped from the tub. When she spoke, every word was precise and in its place.

"How dare you imply that I tried to seduce you. And beg?" She arched a perfect eyebrow. "For what?" The look she bestowed on him would have made a lesser man cringe. "You have nothing—do you hear me?—nothing I want. You're so full of shabby arrogance, it's disgusting. I made a mistake when I called you a toad. You are really a worm, a low, earth-grubbing, dirty old worm." She turned from him and left the bath, closing the door solidly behind her. She forgot something and opened again. "I'll be ready to begin working in about twenty minutes." This time she closed the door softly and left Micah standing in the bath, a look of stunned incredulity on his face and wondering how on earth his plan had gone so wrong.

Gabrielle's whole body ached; she wanted to scream, throw things, pound on the wall. Instead, she counted to ten, then to twenty. She threw her clothes on, brushed her hair without benefit of a mirror, and locked her curls in place with old-fashioned combs. Her mind ran wild and she fought against the tiny seed of doubt that Micah had sown about her dancing. It was true about her age, but she was willing to work hard. She had not fooled herself about the difficulty that faced her. She wouldn't wait until spring to begin her routines. As soon as she got to Chepo, she would spend every spare minute strengthening her leg.

Within the time she had allotted herself Gabrielle entered the dining room. A sweeping glance told her Micah wasn't there and she let loose a sigh of relief. A white-jacketed steward busied himself at the buffet riveted to the wall. Helen and Benton sat opposite one another at the table. The portholes were open and the fresh, salty air mingled with the tantalizing aroma of fresh perked coffee.

"Good morning, you two," Gabrielle said, manufacturing a weak smile.

"How do you take your coffee, Gabby?" Helen said by way of greeting and got up to pour Gabrielle's and refill her own cup and Benton's.

"Cream only, thank you."

The scene with Micah had taken its toll and Gabrielle

was in no mood for polite conversation, but Helen talked nonstop and Gabrielle's contribution to the conversation was merely a nod or an encouraging smile. Breakfast was nearly over and Gabrielle wondered whether she should broach the subject of work to Benton. Micah may have insisted she begin work today just to emphasize that she was only an employee, but the sooner she completed the translations the sooner she could go back to Houston. She smiled at Benton.

"How do you feel this morning?"

"Much better, considering the events last night and this morning," he said. Gabrielle started. Was he aware of the clash between her and Micah? Benton saw the look on her face but mistook it for apprehension concerning the situation in the jungle.

"Helen shouldn't have said anything to upset you," he said, cutting a sharp glance at the other woman over his bifocals, "but she never knows when to shut up."

"She didn't upset me," Gabrielle said soothingly. "She just mentioned that one of your men had been detained by a native."

Benton grunted. "Detained, is right. He's gone to his reward by now, I imagine."

"You mean he's dead?" Gabrielle said, shocked. Helen sniffed and sent Benton a glance that suggested he had succeeded in doing exactly what he had just accused her of doing—upsetting Gabrielle.

"Exactly that, I'm afraid. We got a radio message from Amand a few minutes ago. The *cacique* or chief, wouldn't back down on our man. He eased up on the woman though. Her children have been taken away from her and divided among her relatives and she's been banished from the village. Although, I suspect, once everything cools down, she'll just disappear with no one the wiser."

"But that's so cruel. Can't the police do something?"

Benton chuckled through a soft wheeze. "The authorities will go up there to document the case eventually, but they'll do nothing to the *cacique*, if that's what you mean. Our man broke a very strong taboo and got caught. He paid the price."

"But with his life!" she exclaimed, still horrified.

"Well, we only hire natives," Benton said with a practical tone, "except for J.T., the crew boss, and they all know the rules."

"I still say it's terrible. Don't you, Helen?"

"I used to think some of the customs were harsh, but after you've lived down there a while, you begin to see things and learn to accept them. The chiefs are just trying to preserve the only way of life they know, and for all its harshness, the Indians do have a well-ordered society."

Gabrielle shuddered, still unconvinced of the righteousness of the tribal laws. "Well, I think I'll read up on their customs and tribal laws, but for sure," she said sincerely, "I'm going to stay as far away from any manchineel tree as possible." Benton and Helen laughed. "What's so funny?" she asked.

Benton answered. "Except for the beds almost all of the furniture at Chepo is built of manchineel."

"What?"

"It's true," Helen acknowledged. "It really is a beautiful wood. It just has to be handled carefully; strip the bark, let it dry, and the tree is as safe as any other."

Gabrielle shook her head, pondering the fickle ways of nature, that it could wrap a bitter layer of poison around a beautiful inner core. Perhaps that was the same with Micah, she thought. Had he cloaked himself with a protective shroud of bitterness that could be stripped away to reveal a tender, understanding man? Gabrielle decided no. He was hateful to his very core. She dismissed him from her mind.

"Micah told me you're anxious to begin work, Gabby. Is that true?" Benton asked.

"Yes," she said. "Just show me what you want me to do and where to work."

"You can work right here or in your cabin. Just don't take these contracts up on deck. They might blow away." He grimaced at such a disaster. "All you can do right now is translate into English on legal pads; you can type them on the forms when you get to Chepo."

Helen pushed her chair under the table. "I guess I'd better get back to Jinks and get out of this housecoat. I wasn't expecting you to show up to breakfast so lovely and spry this morning."

"Thanks." Gabrielle smiled. "How is Jinks this morning?"

"Moaning and groaning—asking me to put him out of his misery." Helen laughed. "But he's improving." Helen pointed to the door at the opposite end of the room. "The galley is just there. Naturally, the cook's name is Cookie. If you want anything and a steward isn't around, just stick your head in the door and ask."

After Helen left, Gabrielle refreshed her coffee and, brushing a stray curl off her forehead, sorted through the contracts in the briefcase Benton had left with her. She read through a few to set their language in her mind. The originals were initialed in several areas by both Micah and Benton and often entire sections were written in firm, bold cursive that she came to recognize as Micah's. After two hours she knew him to be an astute and shrewd businessman who paid attention to the smallest detail and she became somewhat in awe of the sheer quality of power he wielded.

The borders of the contracts were rife with his questions and remarks, pointing out some flaw or adding a detail where he felt necessary. The sums mentioned in the papers were staggering, yet Helen had mentioned that this logging project was almost a casual affair to Micah—"his mud-mired dream," she had said, referring to the wet, humus-padded floor of the jungle. Gabrielle decided Micah was an enigma and understanding him was beyond her.

"You are working very hard." Gabrielle looked up at the sound of the voice. The man standing in front of her wore a white uniform trimmed with black epaulets. He was very dark, very attractive, and sounded very French. "I'm Nigel Mino, First Mate," he said, sitting down.

"Gabrielle Hensley."

"Ah, a lovely name. It fits you." He smiled, showing bright, gleaming white teeth.

"Your accent is French—" Gabrielle began.

"Haitian. And yours is southern United States?"

"Texas."

"Ah! An entire country by itself."

Gabrielle laughed. "You've met Texans before, I take it."

"A few, not too many. We have several aboard in the crew, but everyone knows of their feelings here," he said, thumping his heart to accent the words.

"What does a first mate do?" Gabrielle asked.

"Follow orders at all times," Nigel snapped with humor, laughing, a low, delightful sound that filled the small dining room. "And what is your job?" He fanned his hand over the papers scattered across the table.

"I'm a working girl, a linguist." That served the purpose, she thought. She wasn't in the mood to go into anything about her dancing or the accident that brought about the circumstances she found herself having to manage.

"Free?" Nigel asked.

"Free?" Gabrielle said, puzzled. "What do you mean?"

"Are you married, engaged?" Nigel smiled, but waited expectantly for her answer.

"I'm neither of those and you're much too nosy," she teased.

"Yes, well, I wouldn't want to step on anyone's toes and get mine squashed in the process," he answered. "I thought perhaps you and the owner of the *Upsure* were special acquaintances," he said smoothly.

"We are not," Gabrielle said swiftly.

"Good! For me. I was just going on deck for a few minutes before I report to the bridge for duty. Would you like to walk with me?"

"I'd love to," Gabrielle agreed. "I haven't been topside in the daylight yet. Just give me a minute to get a scarf for my hair and my sunglasses. I'll be right back," she said, gathering up the papers and stuffing them into the briefcase.

In less than five minutes they were strolling around the deck with Nigel explaining the ship to Gabrielle. The sun was bright, the sky blue, and the stiff breeze that whipped Gabrielle's pantaloons around her knees felt fresh, clean, and salty. She sighed and leaned against the rail. If she didn't know better, she could almost close her eyes and imagine that she was on some idyllic cruise with the ship wandering among the tropical vacation islands that dotted the south Atlantic. Unfortunately the *Upsure* was making no ports of call. Captain Dressler expected to reach Balboa no later than Tuesday.

"Did you understand all that?" Nigel said, breaking into her thoughts. He propped his elbows on the rail and watched her face.

"Yes," Gabrielle laughed, "the starboard is the right side of the ship, the port is the left, the front is the prow, underneath is the keel, and at the back is the aft...stern, and fantail."

"You are very good," he said, astonished at her recall. "Ah, you are playing a joke on me. You've sailed before."

"No, I haven't," she assured him. "This is my first time aboard a ship."

"The first time! And no problem with the malaise?"

"Seasickness? No, not a bit." So far, she said to herself and offered up a silent, thankful prayer that she had been so fortunate.

Nigel looked at his watch. "I'm sorry, Gabrielle, but I must go to work now. I'm on duty again at eight tonight. Would you like to come up to the bridge?"

"May I do that? Helen—Mrs. Jinkins said we could only go on the bridge at Captain Dressler's invitation."

"You may go on the bridge at any officer's invitation," he corrected her, smiling widely.

"Thank you. I will, then, that is if I don't have to work."

"I hope you will come," he said. He took his hat from under his arm and set it at a rakish angle, then with a debonair swish of his arm saluted smartly. Gabrielle tilted her head, acknowledging his respect with an entrancing smile. Show-off, she thought and watched him disappear around the forward deck. Another flash of white caught her eye and for a moment she thought Nigel had circled the superstructure and shot back through the corridor from the port side to wave at her again. On closer inspection she saw it wasn't Nigel. It was Micah.

He strolled toward her casually. He had changed out of the gray slacks he had worn earlier and was striking in elegant white trousers, a white pullover with a deep V neckline and rope sandals. *He struts,* Gabrielle thought, refusing to endow him with the forceful magnetism he exuded. She wished she were anywhere but here at this very minute. There was no place to run to, no place to hide, so she turned back to the rail and clutched it tightly with both hands as he approached. She wondered what vitriolic comments he had ready to torture her with this time. He paused a few feet from her, cupping his hands against the breeze to light a cigar clamped between his teeth.

"It's a beautiful day, isn't it?" he said and moved to stand beside her at the rail.

What kind of trick was this? His voice was low and pleasant. He wasn't looking at her but concentrated on the cigar he rolled between his fingers. Was he setting a trap? A word trap? Just trying to get her off balance? Gabrielle answered him cautiously.

"Yes, it's hard to believe that just yesterday we were in Houston, bundled up against the mist and cold."

"Did you have a nice stroll around the deck?" he asked, his voice still pleasant.

Here it comes, she thought. *He's going to make some nasty crack about my walking with Nigel.* "Yes, the first mate was kind enough to show me around." Might as well be in for a pound as a penny, she thought and added, "He's invited me to the bridge tonight, to show me the wheel and the navigation instruments."

"Nigel won't have much time to show you anything tonight," he said firmly, drawing deeply on his cigar. The wind snatched and dissipated the plume of smoke, leaving only a trace of the fragrant tobacco aroma.

"Oh? Why not?" she answered with arctic coolness.

"Because we're running into a storm, a pretty big one, coming up from the Antilles. Captain Dressler is plotting a course to keep us ahead of it, or at worst to skirt the edges. That's why Nigel won't have time for you tonight," he said softly.

"Well, perhaps another time," she replied, making an effort to keep a neutral tone of voice.

"Perhaps," he said, just as calmly. "How are the translations coming? Benton told me he gave you several contracts to work on."

"Just fine." At least this was a safe subject, and she regretted that she had clipped the words out. The musical cadence of the ship's bell rang out, announcing the time. Gabrielle glanced at her watch. "Only eight bells?" she said aloud. "My watch says twelve noon."

"Eight bells is a nautical noon. Captain Dressler is only calling the watch during the daylight hours," Micah informed her. "Are you ready for lunch?"

He slid his hand under her elbow, but Gabrielle pulled ahead, reluctant to let him touch her, even in so casual a manner. Micah lifted an expressive eyebrow but said nothing until they were in the corridor and she a few feet ahead of him.

"I sure do like the way you walk," he murmured to her back. Gabrielle stiffened. "Don't get mad, I'm just trying to be nice."

"Be careful that you don't strain anything!" she snapped over her shoulder and stepped through the door into the dining room. If he made a retort, she didn't hear it, which was just as well. It wouldn't do to get into an argument in front of Helen and Benton, who were already being served at the table.

Lunch was not only delicious—avocados stuffed with a succulent shrimp salad—but also a lively affair lasting more than an hour. Just after Micah and Gabrielle had been served, Jinks ambled through the door wearing the wildest orange robe Gabrielle had ever seen. His bushy eyebrows were in more disarray than she remembered and his tan had lightened somewhat. She could tell that he had been ill, but his spirits were high.

"Jinks!" Helen exclaimed when she saw her husband. "If you had to crawl out of your sickbed, did you have to put on that horrible thing?"

"What's wrong with this?" Jinks asked, pirouetting

clumsily and taking exaggerated care to keep the robe from flapping open. "Your sister made it for me. It's my Christmas present," he announced to the rest of them proudly.

"She doesn't even like you, Jinks, that's why she gave you that obnoxious rag," said Helen, obviously disgusted with her husband's shenanigans.

"I suspected that when I saw how she sewed on this pocket." He lifted the garish fabric, displaying a pocket sewn way off center and at an almost vertical tilt. "My cigars keep sliding out," he said glumly.

"I'll tell you what's wrong with that robe," Benton snickered. "It shows too much leg. You know, Jinks, I never realized just how bony your knees really are."

"What are you talking about? I have nice legs." Jinks attempted to emphasize his point by peering over the mound of his stomach.

"How do you know?" Helen asked dryly. "You haven't seen them in years!"

"I didn't come in here for an anatomy lesson," Jinks told her, stung by her remarks. "I came for some decent food. I'm tired of watered down consommé." He sat down in the seat next to Micah.

"You'll be sorry," Helen warned. She turned to Gabrielle. "The problem with Jinks is he's his own worst patient."

Jinks ignored Helen and zeroed in on Gabrielle to enlist her aid in his point of view. "Disregard anything that old redhead says," he said, making a production of retying the sash on the robe. "What do you think about my smoking jacket?"

"Who, me?" Gabrielle stuttered, positive she wouldn't be able to make even a small tactful comment about the horrid garment.

"Yes, you." He smiled. "And I want the truth," he insisted.

Gabrielle paused, pretending to give the robe critical attention. "It's ghastly, Jinks," she said, laughing.

"Sorry I asked." He feigned dismay. "What do you think, Micah, old buddy."

"I think it might come in handy," Micah said solemnly.

"You do? For what?" Jinks asked, falling into the verbal trap.

"If we have to abandon ship," Micah said, holding back a smile, "it can be used as shark repellent."

"I hope it doesn't work and he's in the damn thing," Helen muttered.

"Just for that," Jinks glared at Micah, "don't come running to me the next time you fall out of a helicopter." The steward put a plate mounded high with shrimp salad in front of Jinks, which had the immediate effect of quieting him down, and he ate with relish while Helen grimaced and shook her head with dismay.

"How are you doing on the translations? Any problems?" Benton asked Gabrielle.

"No, no problems. I finished the one for the Mamoni River surveyors that has to do with the engineers."

Benton's jaw dropped. "You finished! You mean you translated an entire contract this morning?"

"Yes, that's what you hired me to do, isn't it? It's in my cabin if you want to check it."

"Yes, I do," he said and stood up from the table. "You coming?" he asked her.

"Why, no," she said, astonished at his excitement. "We're having glazed strawberry pie with real whipped cream for dessert, and I'm staying put until I've had mine. The briefcase is on the luggage rack if you want to have a look by yourself," she offered. "Why is he so excited?" she asked no one in particular after Benton rushed out.

"He's probably remembering how he agonized over the couple he had to do," Micah suggested. He quirked an eyebrow questioningly. "Did you really complete an entire contract? That one had more than eighteen pages, as I recall."

"Yes."

"Why so fast? You can take your time."

"I understood you were eager to have them done; besides, the sooner I get them finished, the—"

"Sooner you can get back to Houston?" He finished the sentence.

"Exactly," she said firmly, looking directly at him. His

handsome dark features drew into a frown, but he said nothing more.

Helen followed their conversation with interest, slightly puzzled at their tart exchange. "Don't let him talk you into slowing down, Gabby. The more free time you can manage, the more time we'll have to sightsee and shop. Would you believe I haven't even been to see the Golden Altar in the Church of San Jose? Or any of the ruins at Panama Veija. These guys won't go near a church, much less the ruins, simply because there's no *chicha* to be had at either."

"Because there's no what?"

"*Chicha*. It's the national drink, fermented from nance fruit. You can buy it on practically any street corner. It's delicious, but potent, so be careful if you're offered any by one of these scoundrels."

"Helen," Jinks butted in with heavy impatience. "We get entirely enough preaching from Amand Chardin without touring the churches, and at least we can drink the *chicha*, whereas all you can do with holy water—"

"Jinks!"

"Quit Jinks-ing me. I'm just telling you we spend most of our time in the jungle already. When we do get to town, we want some real civilized comfort, which does *not* include tramping around in the sweltering heat and thirsting to death in some four-hundred-year-old ruins and tunnels."

Gabrielle had the distinct impression this was an old argument being aired for the umpteenth time. Micah had leaned back in his chair and relighted his cigar, watching her through the spiral of smoke. Gabrielle pretended not to notice, but if it hadn't been for the lure of the strawberry pie, she would have excused herself right then.

Helen sputtered into her coffee cup. "Your ideas of civilized comforts, Jinks," she was saying with eloquent sarcasm, "are watching fan dancers in brassy nightclubs and playing the slot machines in the casinos with a cocktail glass of Jack Daniel's stuck handily in your shirt pocket."

"That's what I said, civilized comforts," Jinks repeated, undaunted by Helen's anger. He forked the last morsel of shrimp off his plate into his mouth, then reached for the unfinished portion Benton had left on his plate. Helen slapped his hand hard.

"That's enough. Come on, it's back to bed for you," she ordered. The tone of her voice was that of a head nurse who brooked no nonsense. Jinks recognized it and his protests died on his lips. He looked longingly at the strawberry pie in front of Gabrielle.

"No way!" Helen said, following his gaze. "You're going to lie down and let that food digest, if it will," she said hopefully. "We're in for some bad weather tonight. Rough seas and shrimp won't mix in that stomach of yours." Helen reached over and patted his nonexistent waist. Jinks got reluctantly to his feet.

"I'm the doctor," he said peevishly.

"You're the patient," Helen countered, pushing him ahead of her. She waved to Gabrielle and Micah from the door. "See you two later."

There was an awkward little pause as Gabrielle and Micah stared at one another across the table, the constraint between them so keen it was almost visible. Self-consciously Gabrielle took up her fork again and finished her strawberries. Courtesy and gracefulness were bred into her, so as she reached for her sunglasses and scarf, which lay near the edge of the table, she felt some comment was necessary. "I'd better get back to work myself," she said, directing the words to Micah with the briefest of glances. His hand shot out, covering hers, pinning it to the table.

"Stay for a few minutes, I want to talk to you." Gabrielle slid her hand from under his and folded them both in her lap.

"I'll talk to you about work, nothing more," she said emphatically, "unless you mean to apologize for your brutish behavior last night *and* this morning."

His dark brow lifted, mocking her tone. "All right. I apologize," he acquiesced, "but I warn you, you *are* going to have to learn to get along with me." It was as though he were issuing her an ultimatum—his way or no way.

"I can get along with anyone," she flared, glaring at him contemptuously. "*You* are the one with the loutish manners, you're the one pushing. I want you to stop—stop—"

"Stop what?" he asked softly. "Making love to you? Is th—"

"*No!* You don't know the meaning of the word," she said, hedging. "You're always trying to bait me, egg me on, back me into a corner." She resented his attitude that she found him irresistible, that she would submit willingly to his brash charm, that she would stroke his monumental ego.

He was laughing, a low rumble under his breath, watching her expression, her eyes sparkling with animation. "You do that to yourself, you know. I'm just trying to get you to meet me halfway."

"Halfway to where?" she asked, her bearing positively glacial. "The bed?"

Micah's teeth gleamed in a wide smile. "That would do, but I'd rather we settled our differences before we get that far."

"Get that far!" Gabrielle's fury was a leaping bonfire. "I don't want to go one inch in that direction with you," she said, spreading a trembling thumb and forefinger to display the smidgen of space while she glared at him archly.

Micah tilted back in his chair and blew a series of smoke rings. Gabrielle was different; his strategy had backfired twice. *Twice!* But he clung to it with the pertinaciousness of an oyster that clings to a rock. He was as satisfied with himself as a cat that's cornered his prey and, intent on resting a while, toys with his catch until he leaps in for the kill.

Seeing the self-satisfied expression on his face, Gabrielle realized he had succeeded in what he meant to do—raising her ire deliberately, causing her to lose control. Micah watched comprehension dawn on her through a thin slit of lashes.

"Well?" he said, leaning forward.

"Well, what?" Her eyes were blazing and her voice was not as level and calm as she would wish.

"Are we going to be friends or not?"

Gabrielle didn't like the seductive inflection he placed on "friend." They were back to square one. "I'll work for you, that's all!"

"No, that's not all," he prophesied. His dark eyes pierced hers, holding her rooted to the chair while he stood up and ground out his cigar, then his eyes dropped slowly to examine the rapid rise and fall of her breasts through the thin peach tunic.

Alert to his every nuance, Gabrielle held her breath to still her bosom. Micah smiled, a crooked little smile, observing the useless maneuver.

"What are you afraid of, Gabrielle? Me? Or is it something more? I know you better than you think I do. You've skimmed through life on your toes—the ballet is a fantasy world; you withdrew into it every time you meet the realities of life head-on. I'm the only reality in your life right now and there's no velvet stage curtain, no bright lights to hide behind on this ship or at Chepo. And even if there were, I wouldn't let you."

"You wouldn't let me?" she gasped at him, appalled at his words. He had spoken with such passion, such force, rasping out the pronouncement as if it were a warning arriving too late to avoid the inevitable. She sensed instinctively that he was trying to control her, mold her in some fashion she couldn't name to meet his needs—whatever they might be. He forced her to acknowledge his sensuality, the aura of power that surrounded him like a cloak of fire-tempered steel.

"That's right," he said, sauntering nonchalantly to the door. Leaving her with that woebegone look on her face didn't sit quite right with him. Micah wondered why his emotions were so at odds with his common sense. Every time he got near Gabrielle there seemed to be a hollowness where his lungs ought to be, a peculiar tension in his belly—sensations he couldn't put a name to, like those odd flutterings that galloped across his chest. He was a man who liked things simple, cut and dried, down to earth. He wished Gabrielle would quit making everything so complicated. He was all ready to apologize to her this morning for his behavior last night, but the sight of her in his tub had chased all thoughts of apology from his mind. What was the use of making apologies anyway? They didn't hold water, like now. It was a useless waste of breath. He wished Gabrielle would stop playing these coy little love games. She had more to say. He knew it without looking back; he could hear her filling her lungs with air.

"What do you want from me?" she cried and sensed immediately the angry, restless words were a mistake the moment they ricocheted off Micah's back.

He turned in the companionway, his hewn features confident and masculine. "I'm sure it won't take a woman of your intelligence long to figure it out, but just so that we understand one another, let me spell it out for you. *I want you,* plain and simple." *Only you're making it hard, so hard,* he thought. No other woman had ever baffled him so completely.

"You want me?" Gabrielle echoed softly as she watched Micah disappear into the corridor. He was crazy, she thought, and he had a peculiar way of showing that he cared for her. Attacking her all the time. There would never be any love between them; it would take a miracle to get past his anger or hers.

Chapter Ten

In her own cabin Gabrielle threw herself on the velour sofa and felt the tautness in her stomach gradually relax. The briefcase lay on the cushion next to her, where Benton left it. She pulled herself wearily together to continue working.

She had difficulty concentrating on the contracts, and several hours later the words began to blur, run together, and finally disappear entirely as Micah's dark good looks swam before her eyes. She tossed the contracts aside with a long exasperated sigh. Was it her fault that she and Micah clashed head-on each and every time they got within two feet of one another? If only she could stop overreacting to everything the man said or did.

His comment that she hid from life stung; she didn't. It was just that she was more dedicated than most to her dancing, and that didn't leave a lot of time to get emotionally involved with anyone. If she didn't know better, she would think he was jealous. But of what? Luke Bryant, whom she had planned to marry and didn't? Tim? Surely not. Her career? What could her past possibly mean to Micah Davidson? Or her future, for that matter.

Micah's image, his deep, melodious voice, his male scent, the touch of his hand, were all potent reminders of his vibrant masculinity. Gabrielle refused to analyze her feeling toward him and pressed her fingers to her temple in an effort to erase these thoughts from her mind. With sudden insight she understood that her defensive posture was not to protect herself from Micah, but from her own ragged emotions.

Rain slammed against the ship, forming a black curtain beyond the portholes as the ship entered the storm. The *Upsure*'s wide keel rocked violently into the deep troughs in the high, rough seas. The storm worsened and Gabrielle's stomach began to behave alarmingly. She felt tiny, prickly bubbles of nausea begin to burst in her throat. It only took her a few seconds to realize the wretched misery in her stomach was seasickness. Wave after wave of nausea twisted and racked her body until finally she changed into her pajamas and crawled, exhausted, between the cool welcome sheets on her bed.

The sound of the raging storm was muted inside the luxurious cabin, but to Gabrielle, in her acute misery, every raindrop lashing against the portholes seemed to beat out its own pattered tattoo while the wind rushed and ebbed, creating a ragged melody of nature gone awry.

Another surge of nausea gripped her and she wished fervently that she had asked Helen for some Dramamine earlier in the day instead of being so optimistic that she could weather the storm without the seafarer's malaise.

She wondered, vaguely alarmed, that if the ship began to sink, would anyone remember to come for her? Soon, though, she was too miserable to be alarmed by anything and lay in her bed, groaning softly, drifting in and out of a light sleep.

Someone switched on the tiffany lamp and its soft light bathed the cabin in a golden glow, belying the tempest that raged outside.

"Miss Hensley?...Gabrielle?" The musical lilt of Nigel's voice split the nightmare Gabrielle was suffering. "I'm sorry to barge in on you like this, but I knocked, and when you didn't answer, I peeked in and heard you moan. I came to tell you it would be impossible to have you on the bridge in this storm, but I can see you're in no condition to visit anyway." Nigel had given his little speech from the middle of the room, and when Gabrielle didn't answer right away, he walked closer to the bed.

"Please," Gabrielle said, her voice hoarse, "could you ask Helen Jinkins to come in here?"

"Right away," Nigel said, patting her hand comfortingly.

It wasn't Helen who answered her summons for help. Micah shouldered his way into her cabin, a harsh frown of worry creasing his brow.

"Why didn't you let somebody know you were getting

sick before you got so ill you can't move?" he scolded. Gabrielle struggled to raise her head, fighting the wash of dizziness and brilliant shattering lights that blocked her view of Micah.

"I didn't know I was going to get sick until I already was that way," she muttered weakly and let her head fall back onto the pillow.

Micah bent over her, his eyes dark and shadowed in a face that for a moment held a trace of tenderness, then he was all business. He wiped her face with a cool cloth, refreshed it, and laid it across her forehead. He pulled the sheets back, inspecting the bedclothes.

"Have you had any accidents in the bed?" he asked.

"No," Gabrielle said, humiliated and embarrassed at his question.

"I'll be right back," he said, lifting the sheet to her chin. He strode out of the room, but returned quickly with Dramamine and a tall glass filled with ice, soda, and green crème de menthe.

"It may be too late for these," he said, ordering her to open her mouth for the tiny pills, "but you can sip on this, it'll settle your stomach," he promised, setting the glass aside while he lifted her carefully against his chest and propped the pillows behind her head. He eased her back and folded her fingers around the glass of green liqueur. Gabrielle lifted it to her lips with trembling fingers; the sweet mint flavor bubbling with sparkling water soothed her raw throat. For one fearsome moment she felt it begin to rise up out of her stomach, but she swallowed and it stayed down.

"Sip it, not gulp," Micah admonished, scowling, seeing her difficulty.

"I was so thirsty," Gabrielle said, her voice perhaps somewhat stronger than it had been a few minutes ago. Micah sat down on the edge of the bed and grinned at her.

"This serves you right, you know. It ought to let you know you belong down here with us lesser mortals instead of that pedestal you keep climbing up on."

Gabrielle's lashes fluttered to her cheeks before she answered. "I don't put myself on a pedestal, and anybody can get seasick, especially in this storm." As if to em-phasize her words, the ship lurched, dipped into the sea, and rose suspended for a breathless moment before crash-ing into another huge wave. Gabrielle clung to the bed-clothes with one hand while she tried to keep the liquid from sloshing out of the glass she held in the other. Loose objects scattered themselves across the cabin.

"God! Are we going to sink?"

Micah's forehead furrowed in a grimace. "Don't be silly. Captain Dressler has everything under control, but this is the first major storm the *Upsure* has had to weather since she's been refitted, so it's going to take him a while to catch her mettle." Micah fluffed her pillows, which had begun to slide, and went around the bed, tucking the sheets between the mattresses to hold Gabrielle firmly against the rolling and tossing of the ship.

Her eyes followed him as he performed the task. "Why are you being so nice to me?"

He grinned at her, brown eyes twinkling and for once unmasked. "I never kick a man when he's down."

"That's good to know. I think I might be sick for the next three months. I like you better when you're not being such a bully."

Micah laughed and tweaked her toes. "I'm not a bully and what you really like is being waited on hand and foot. And there are some things I'd like to do to you whether you're sick or not, so don't push your luck."

"You're flirting with me, Micah," she said, suddenly overcome with a warm, happy feeling.

He shook his head, smiling. "I'm just trying to take your mind off what's going on around us, and flirting is hardly the word I'd use, but now is not the time to discuss it. Do you think you'll be okay for a few minutes? Helen has her hands full with both Jinks and Benton right now—they're far worse than you, and every available hand is needed elsewhere. I've got to go below and check on my car."

"Your car?" Gabrielle's eyes widened in astonishment, her illness momentarily forgotten.

"Yes, I ordered it two years ago and finally got delivery

before we left Houston. It's in the hold and, I hope, still chained and roped in place. I want to be sure."

Gabrielle was loath to be left alone and a trace of petulance crept into her voice. "I'll be all right...I guess, but aren't I as important as an old car?"

Micah smiled as he made his way across the cabin, picking up the scattered contracts, ashtrays, and makeup pots as he went along. He piled them all onto one end of the sofa before he answered her. He seemed to consider her question seriously. "You might be," he drawled with wicked amusement, "but I've had to wait two years for the car; I don't expect to have to wait quite so long for you." Gabrielle sputtered into the crème de menthe, but he was gone before she could form a retort.

Micah's teasing words, his cheerfulness, sent a twinge of excitement thundering into her very hollow stomach, which took that moment to remind her with sharp insistency of the nature of her illness. She forced herself to lie placidly and drink the rest of the minty liquid. It helped enormously; she felt much better. Her insides seemed prone to stay where God had ordered them instead of lurching all over with the movement of the ship. Resting, with the cloth over her eyes, Gabrielle reflected that she liked the side of Micah he had displayed tonight, a tender caring side she wouldn't have believed existed unless she had seen it for herself. To her, Micah was like a jigsaw puzzle: the compassionate piece went here; the loving piece went there; the angry piece was obviously a corner, it pricked so easily; and his sexuality—Gabrielle had no trouble placing that piece in the labyrinth.

Now that she had solved the riddle of Micah, she felt her anger diminish, she forgot her determination against his bold charm, forgot his harsh words and taunting behavior. An hour ago might as well have been a millenium ago; it sank in obscurity. The winged creatures in her stomach suddenly felt massive, no longer fluttering gently; they began to prance alarmingly.

Micah would be back soon. Abruptly Gabrielle wondered what she looked like. Not too sickly, she hoped. Just to make sure, she threw the covers back, got out of bed, and managed to walk on unsteady legs to the bathroom. *Oh, this is awful,* she thought, seeing her image in the mirror. *Sick people don't have to look sick, do they? No, of course not,* she told herself. She washed her face and hands, brushed her teeth, and sorted out the tangled mass of curls with the hairbrush until they gleamed like a dark, glowing halo. She looked at her wrinkled blue pajamas. Suppose the ship sank? Not likely. But just in case.... Would she want to be rescued wearing dirty old pajamas? She thought not. As it happened, there was this glorious yellow satin nightgown in her luggage. There was lots of gossamer lace, delicate ribbons, and the lovely slits up *both* sides, all the way to her waist, were trimmed in the same yellow ribbon. Gabrielle stripped off the wrinkled pajamas and slid the cool satin over her head. She was almost back to bed when she remembered that sickrooms always had a horrible antiseptic smell. She just might be able to combat that with a dab of Chloé. She retraced her steps to the bathroom. A little of the perfumed emollient behind her knees, in the crook of her elbow, on her neck—nothing obvious. Feeling much better, actually not at all ill, she got back into bed, and waited expectantly for Micah to return. For an hour she fought drowsiness and when she discovered she could no longer hold her eyes open, she cursed the sandman for his treachery and her last, dreamy thought was: *Oh, this isn't fair.*

In her scattered dreams a strong sinewy arm stole around Gabrielle's body and she snuggled close, buffered against the raging storm. She curled content around the dream, inhaling softly a sensual, evocative fragrance. Her mending leg cramped and she stretched it out, encountering another leg; they crossed and held, warm and soothing.

Hours later unconscious panic threaded her dreary visions as she tried to shake off the heavy, still weight that seemed to be pressing down across both her legs. She couldn't move and the thought that something was terribly wrong brought her abruptly awake. She struggled to sit up and discovered herself half trapped beneath Micah's solid, muscled body.

"Quit cavorting around like a Gypsy," he murmured sleepily.

Gabrielle's senses registered the open portholes, the weak sun filtering through, and the gentle, steady rocking of the ship. The storm had passed. She looked at Micah.

"What are you doing here?"

"I just happened to be in the neighborhood and I thought I'd—"

"Very funny," Gabrielle said, moving off the bed.

Micah threw his arm around her, forcing her back under the covers. "I *was* sleeping," he said.

"You have your own bed," Gabrielle muttered, trying to unlock his grip from her rib cage. She felt the muscles along his arm pull taut with a surge of strength as her fingers bit into his arm.

"Cut that out, and go back to sleep," he said lazily, pulling her into the curve of his body. When she refused, he raised his lids a fraction of an inch and explained, "I didn't want to leave you alone, the storm got a lot worse after midnight."

Disbelief etched Gabrielle's features. "If it had been that bad, I wouldn't have slept through it, I'm a light sleeper."

"Like hell you are. You snore too. But you slept through it because there was a sedative in the crème de menthe."

Gabrielle bristled. "You had no right to drug me, and I don't snore."

Micah groaned. "It was strictly for medical reasons. Jinks prescribed it for himself, you, and Benton." Suddenly he leaned over on top of her and reached down to the floor on her side of the bed and lifted an orange life preserver in the air. "See this?" he said, tossing it aside. "It was my job to get you into this thing and to the lifeboat if things had got worse."

She tried to wiggle out from under his weight. "That's just an excuse. You could have slept on the sofa."

Micah chuckled. "That damn thing is three feet too short." He gazed down into her eyes. "Keep squirming like that," he murmured with low menace. "It feels good."

"Get off me," Gabrielle said without conviction, because

the passion that built in her was a hunger that needed to be satisfied, and the same hunger smoldered in Micah's eyes.

"In a little while," he agreed throatily as his fingertips slid under her gown and began to explore her smooth flat stomach and beyond, stopping to cup a full velvety breast and circle gently its dark peak until aroused and hard against his palm. His lips moved against her ear, warm and soft, while his tongue flicked moist little forays along her temple, her cheek, then dropped to her breasts. When he took her hard peaks into his mouth, Gabrielle gasped with pleasure and arched her body into his. She was dimly aware of his hands moving her gown below her waist, under her hips, as the magic of his tongue sent a thousand stabbing explosions of joy in every intimate and moist part of her body.

Just when she thought the ecstasy was unbearable, his mouth covered hers, his lips nibbling and taunting gently, then with more hunger until he was biting and eating her lips with a greed that sent the electric, sensual message into her at every point their bodies touched.

A hot prickling sensation coiled around Gabrielle's spine and her hands began to explore Micah until she became aware of the hard, throbbing need of his flesh. Her hands circled his neck, her fingers tracing softly across the unhealed scars on his neck and back. Micah groaned deep and Gabrielle jerked her hands away.

"Did I hurt you?" she whispered against his mouth.

"God, no!" His voice cracked as he reluctantly drew back from her voluptuous mouth. He pulled himself up to lean against the headboard. "Come up here," he said thickly and drew her up to his shoulder with shaky but determined strength. His eyes devoured her nakedness and the lovely body seemed to drive him wild. He lifted Gabrielle and settled her hips over his. She felt the force of his hard maleness as his hands grasped the curve of her hips and rotated them slowly, with maddening, scorching accuracy until Gabrielle shuddered with pounding waves of intense longing.

Micah's fingers trembled over her face, stopping at the pulsating veins in the hollow of her neck before sliding to her breasts. He kneaded them erotically, stroking and manipulating them, meeting pleasure with pleasure until a soft, inarticulate whimper escaped Gabrielle's lips. Micah closed his eyes and Gabrielle watched his face as the compelling, physical hunger of her flowed from his body, then she slumped against his chest. Their thudding hearts began to slow, beating gently against one another languidly. Gabrielle was shaken by the incredible fiery depth of their desire and as if he sensed it Micah stirred and began again.

LATER Gabrielle rested her head on Micah's shoulder trying to fathom how they had got past their anger. She hadn't believed it possible. Never had she been made love to with such fierce, wanton passion, nor had she ever responded with the same ardent intensity. The memory of their lovemaking drew a wave of tremulous excitement across her thighs.

"Gabrielle"— Micah's voice thickened with renewed desire— "stop that. I'm spent, I'm weak, and I didn't have a full night's sleep."

"I'm not doing anything." Her breath was warm against the thick cords of his throat. He bent his head and smiled into her curls.

"Well, stop whatever it is you're *not* doing and find your gown. I need some coffee." When she didn't move, he pushed her away, creating a little space between their bodies. "Open your eyes and look at me," he chuckled, seeing her head droop limply on its slender column.

"I already tried to open them, they won't. I'm numb."

"No more than I am." He laughed. "Now, move it or I'll order the steward to bring our coffee in here. What do you think he'd say if he walked in and found us like this, glued to one another with love-sweat?"

"I don't know and right now I don't care," she whispered, calling his bluff.

Micah leaned over and switched on the speaker to the kitchen. "Cookie," he said, loud and clear, "send a pot of coffee, service for two, to Miss Hensley's cabin."

Gabrielle gasped and moved off him to the edge of the bed. "You're disgusting," she said over her shoulder.

"And you are beautiful," he said, pressing his lips to the base of her neck. His hand rummaged amidst the rumpled sheets and drew out her gown. "Put this on," he ordered in a no-nonsense tone and threw it over her shoulder. Gabrielle tossed him a scorching glance and involuntarily gasped at her first good look at the ugly scars that began under his arm and wound over his back and shoulder. She had not realized how extensive his injuries had been.

"It's not a pretty sight, is it?" Micah said, slightly unnerved at the look on her face.

"No, it isn't. Does it hurt?" She looked at him with compassion.

"Sometimes," he answered abruptly.

There was a rap on the door. Gabrielle raced for the bathroom. "Micah," she whispered hoarsely, "don't let him see you in my bed."

"Okay," he said, getting up and walking naked to the door. Gabrielle felt a warm flush of heat rise to her cheeks.

"Animal!" she spat at him before she slammed the bathroom door. Micah laughed, but stopped at the sofa to retrieve his trousers and tugged them on. At least, he thought, smiling to himself, he'd been promoted up from a grubby old earthworm.

He was pouring their coffees when Gabrielle came out of the bath. She headed straight for the bed and climbed in.

"What the hell! Get out of that bed," he snapped.

"No, I'm going back to sleep."

"Oh, no, you're not. You've got some packing to do." He jerked the pillow out from under her head.

"Packed? What for?"

"We'll be docking in Colon late tonight. I want everything ready for customs so we can get an early start in the morning."

"Colon? I thought Benton said we were going to Balboa."

"This ship is, but we disembark at Colon. It may be two days before Captain Dressler gets out of Gatun Lake, depending on the traffic, and then another ten hours to get through the canal. I want to get home. You and I are driving across the isthmus. Besides, neither Benton nor Jinks can take another day aboard ship. They've had it a lot worse than you, believe me." He shoved a coffee cup in her hand. "Drink this, get up, get dressed, and get packed so the steward can take your luggage to the cargo gate."

"I need some cream," Gabrielle told him after she peered into her cup.

"Well, get your fanny out of that bed and get it yourself," he said, shaking his head in exasperation. "You're already entirely too spoiled for your own good, so don't expect me to contribute to the problem."

Gabrielle's defense mechanisms dropped into place. She jutted her chin, squared her shoulders. "I'm not spoiled. Why do you keep saying that?"

"Because you're much too used to an adoring public catering to you. I'm only an audience of one. I don't have time for all the ego boosting and stroking you seem to crave."

"Crave? I don't crave anything. What you say isn't true!"

"It is true. You can't seem to separate yourself from the fantasy of all those roles you dance—Cinderella, Sleeping Beauty, then there's the Sugar Plum Fairy and the Snow Queen. Fantasy love, every one of them. What happened this morning is real, Gabrielle. You behave as though it were a performance—a quite good one, I admit"—he bowed his head, an insufferable mocking gesture—"but certainly nothing worthy of applause."

Gabrielle felt weak and, even though clothed, naked. She had given him her all this morning, held nothing back—she hadn't wanted to. She had been a fool; now she was fragmented, shattered, paying the piper for her foolish thoughts and actions.

"You're an animal," she hissed, "insensitive, arrogant. Who—what—gives you the right to judge me?"

"No one and nothing," he drawled. "I'm taking it."

"Like you do everything you fancy?"

"I didn't take you, Gabrielle, if that's what you're inferring. You offered. Do you think I didn't notice you had changed out of those pajamas into a, shall we say, provocative gown? I just accepted a sample. That's what it is, isn't it? A tantalizing sample?"

"Get out of here, you—you—"

"Worm. I believe that's the word you're looking for."
He saluted her, a mocking gesture, with his cup.

Gabrielle skewered him with her fury. "Yes, worm!"
Anger made her voice waver, anger aimed at herself, as
much as Micah, but she attempted a tone of sweetness.
"There's a little biological fact about worms I'd like to
share with you." Micah's expressive eyebrows lifted with
insolent question.

"I'd like to hear it."

"Did you know one end of the worm is female and the
opposite end is male? They come together like this"—she
made a perfect circle with her thumb and forefinger—"to
propagate. So, Mr. Davidson, why don't you go off somewhere and propagate?"

Micah stared at her for several long seconds as her words
registered their meaning. Then he threw his head back and
roared with laughter. He was still chuckling as he walked
into his cabin. A second later he stuck his head around her
door once again.

"Ninth-grade biology, right after snails," he said,
laughing still. "When I was in the ninth grade, I was more
interested in fishing with the damn things than their sex
life." He blew her a kiss and pulled the door closed.

Gabrielle jumped up, ran to the door, and locked it,
then went into the bath and locked the adjoining door
there too. The click sounded loud in the small space.
Micah rapped on the door.

"Don't use that damn fruity bubble bath, Gabrielle. I
can't stand the smell." She used the entire vial and deliberately dripped a drop of the oil into his shaving kit.

Gabrielle spent most of the day in her cabin. She took
her meals there and only opened the door to the steward to
collect her luggage, and again for the cabin boy. While he
cleaned the cabin, she went on deck, where she kept a wary
eye out for Micah. She needn't have worried. She learned
from a talkative steward that he was closeted with Captain
Dressler. Benton and Jinks were not recuperated, but
stayed in their cabins along with Helen, who was sleeping
after having been up most of the night caring for her two

patients. Later she worked on the contracts with as much determined dedication as she had put into the ballet.

After dinner Gabrielle heard Micah stirring around in the bath. He sang in the shower. She turned the music off in her room so she could listen and tiptoed nearer the door, making sure it was locked carefully from her side. She was completely absorbed in listening to him, turning the shower off, still humming—off-key—the whirring of his electric razor. Then, startlingly, there was a rap on the door. Surprised, she backed off a few steps.

"Gabrielle, are you in there?"

"No, I'm not," she called back with velvet smoothness.

She heard him laugh. "I see. Does that mean you're still pouting?"

Yes. Yes. Yes. "No, I'm not. I've been working on contracts."

He rattled the doorknob. "Open up."

"No."

There was silence for a few seconds. The only sounds were the low hum of the great diesel engines and the slap of amber waves as the ship plowed through the south Atlantic. "Want to have dinner with me and then take a stroll around the deck?" Micah murmured, his voice kind, persuasive. Gabrielle almost said yes.

"No, thank you," she replied coolly. "I've already eaten and I'm tired. I'm going to bed."

Micah pondered that. "Want some company?" he asked so quietly Gabrielle had to put her ear to the door to hear him. His unmitigated gall and colossal ego infuriated her.

Another long silence stretched between them. Gabrielle heard her own breathing, her heart pounding, the engines, the waves.

Then Micah said, "Does that mean no?"

She thought he was coarse, barbaric, remorseless; she had made love to him only this morning like a wanton peri, a fallen angel, abandoning all her principles, her self-imposed rules, and now he was teasing her. She put her mouth right up to the door so that he could hear every syllable. "Micah, when you take that stroll on deck, why don't you try out some of that invincibility you're so *certain* you're endowed with—try walking on water!'' Then she stepped away from the door and refused to answer any more of his pleas.

It was only after she was in bed that night that images of Micah began to sabotage her resolution against thinking about him. She loved him...she didn't love him...he was tender...he was savage. She plotted ways to make him fall in love with her, plotted ways to bring him to his knees. She wanted to marry him, and then didn't, sure that there was no room in her life for domestic bondage.

She kept remembering his mouth fastened on hers, the touch of his fingers as they explored her body, the solid hardness that made her mouth go dry. Her pulse began to race as she became saturated with emotion and sensation, and unable to conquer the demands of her body, she forced herself to recall all the things she hated about Micah. These thoughts coupled with the gentle rocking of the ship; the seas splashing against the hull like soft whispers were like a narcotic and they lulled her into a dreamless sleep.

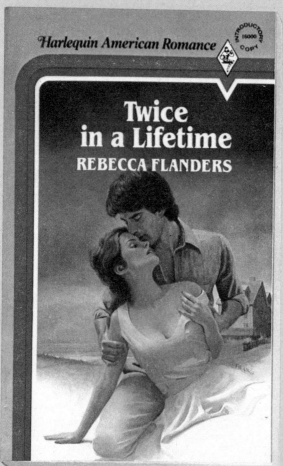

TWICE IN A LIFETIME

Rebecca Flanders

CHAPTER ONE

BARBARA sat in the crowded airport lounge, waiting for her flight to be called, and fingered the letter of invitation from her sister somewhat uncertainly. Barbara was twenty-six years old, self-sufficient, and mature, and she had been managing her own life since the first day she had left home for the independence of the state university. But, sitting alone amid the bustle and confusion of excited travelers, she felt somewhat like a lost and frightened child. She had felt that way a lot since Daniel had died.

She had been widowed a little over a year, and she knew her sister, via long-distance conferences with their mother, was worried about her. Perhaps with good cause, Barbara had to admit uneasily, for although most of the time Barbara managed to convince herself she was getting along just fine, there were still feelings of bitterness and periods of black depression she did not seem to be able to control. Of course it was a tragedy to be widowed so young, and everyone commiserated, everyone claimed to understand what she was going through. The real tragedy was that no one understood. No one could understand what it was to lose the one and only love of her life, not just a husband, but a lover and a friend... Most people would go their entire lives without ever finding what she and Daniel had shared, and to have their life together severed so abruptly and so cruelly was more than unfair, it was incomprehensible...

But Barbara wasn't meant to be alone for long.
Follow her as she rediscovers the beauty of love.
Read the rest of "Twice in a Lifetime" FREE.

Now you can share the joys and sorrows of real-life love in Harlequin's new *American Romances*.

Find out what happens next. Send for the rest of "Twice in a Lifetime" FREE as your introduction to Harlequin's new **American Romances**. Romance novels that understand how North American women feel about love.

GET THIS BOOK FREE!

Mail to: Harlequin Reader Service
1440 South Priest Drive, Tempe, AZ 85281

YES! I want to be one of the first to discover Harlequin's **new** *American Romances*. Send me FREE and without obligation, "Twice in a Lifetime." If you do not hear from me after I have examined my FREE book, please send me the 4 new *American Romances* each month as soon as they come off the presses. I understand that I will be billed only $2.25 per book (total $9.00). There are no shipping or handling charges. There is no minimum number of books that I have to purchase. In fact, I may cancel this arrangement at any time. "Twice in a Lifetime" is mine to keep as a FREE gift, even if I do not buy any additional books.

154-CIA-NAAC

Name	(please print)	

Address		Apt. No.

City	State/Prov.	Zip/Postal Code

Signature (If under 18, parent or guardian must sign.)

This offer is limited to one order per household and not valid to current American Romance subscribers. We reserve the right to exercise discretion in granting membership. If price changes are necessary, you will be notified. Offer expires July 31, 1983.

PRINTED IN CANADA

Introducing Harlequin's new *American Romances...*

with this special introductory FREE book offer.

◀ SEE EXCITING
DETAILS INSIDE

Send no money. Mail this card and receive this new, full-length Harlequin **American Romance** novel absolutely FREE.

Chapter Eleven

Grinding hawsers, clanking chains, and shouting men woke Gabrielle. A pungent smell of bananas filled the cabin. She lay in bed with her eyes closed, trying to place the unfamiliar sounds. Something was missing and it took her only a collective few seconds to discover what it was: The steady, throbbing dullness of the ship's engines was quiet. They had docked! They were in Panama. God! How could she have overslept today, of all days?

She stretched languorously with a peculiar sense of contentment, of harmony that was at odds with the misery she had felt when she had finally fallen asleep last night. Her hand swept across the bed; it was cold. She had the persistent feeling that Micah had been with her last night, but that was impossible. She had locked the doors adjoining their cabins, and the door to the corridor too. Yet, there was a deep indentation in the pillow next to hers. She buried her face in it and inhaled Micah's scent. So, she hadn't been dreaming. He *had* come to her bed, he *had* pulled her to him, curving his long length against hers. He was the owner of the ship. Why hadn't she remembered that? He probably had a key to every cabin and locker on the *Upsure*. Gabrielle got up and cautiously looked into Micah's suite. It was deserted, and his shaving kit was gone from the bath too. Only a vague whiff of his cologne hinted he had showered earlier. Damn! If he had stolen into her bed like a thief in the night, the least he could have done was awakened her so she wouldn't miss a single minute of what promised to be an exciting first day on the isthmus.

She ordered coffee brought to her cabin and sipped on it as she bathed and dressed with an alacrity that would have made even her old wardrobe mistress applaud. She had chosen a toast-colored crepe wraparound blouse that knotted at the waist, and wore it above a full-circled brown skirt; a simple ensemble, yet elegant, for her introduction to Panama, the link between continents. And later that afternoon as she strolled along Avenida Central in bustling Panama City, exactly fifty-one miles from where she stood at this very minute, shopkeepers lounging outside their stores as they were prone to do would hiss and signal one another to draw attention to the stunning American woman accompanied by a tall dark man, who never allowed her very far from the protective circle of his arm. The shopkeepers admired and envied the man as he smiled with infinite patience while the beautiful woman darted from one shop to another, one lottery stand to the next; the man would scowl at them when he discovered them staring overlong at the exquisite creature that was certainly his.

But that was later, and right now Gabrielle was wondering what to do with her swag of curls. They had long since outgrown the couturier cut she had had in London four months ago. She needed something chic, but manageable for the day that stretched like a delightful gift before her. She decided on a braid and with deft fingers pulled the dark mass to the back of her head and wove a single French plait from crown to nape, tucking the loose ends under and locking them with a single pin. Wispy tendrils escaped, but Gabrielle paid them no heed.

Five minutes later the few belongings left in her cabin had been shoved into her faithful tote. She gave the cabin a quick once-over on her way out. Her eyes lingered for a solitary moment on the bed where she had come to know Micah, but she pushed those thoughts into the far recess of her mind and made her way to the deck.

A cloudless blue sky reigned over the harbor crowded with ships of every size and color; brown foam-flecked water lapped against the sides of the ships. Farther out to sea the water was blue-green, shimmering in the sun. Gabrielle gasped and sighed, delighted. She twirled around on her toes, trying to see everything in one fast glimpse. A line of flags caught her eye; they fluttered far above the buildings lining the piers like a wash of tattered rags hung out to dry. She counted twenty-one and recognized only two—the red, white, and blue of the United States and England.

As she walked around the deck slowly, trying to absorb the sounds, the flavor, and the color of this new, exciting experience, the smell of bananas became so strong she imagined she tasted them on her tongue. Her gaze swept the docks and she saw why.

Banana-laden trucks lined up on the wharves, their high wooden sides groaning and splayed with their yellow-green burden. Cinnamon-colored workers, gaily dressed and gesturing wildly, unloaded the stalks into crates being hauled aboard a vessel docked opposite the *Upsure*. Gabrielle watched the crates being winched aboard and hoisted over the rail only to disappear in less than a minute into the bowels of the ship.

Backed up to the wharves was another sea, one of red-tiled roofs. It was all she could see of the steaming, decaying, thriving, and exotic city of Colon; huge barns and warehouses on the concrete jetty blocked all else from her view.

As Gabrielle neared the gangplank, she saw Helen, elbows firmly planted on the rail, herself watching the activities on the jetty. Helen was dressed neatly in khaki slacks and a white blouse. A straw hat protected her fair, freckled complexion from the brilliant sun. Gabrielle noted with her dancer's eye that unlike so many women Helen's age, Helen was still trim, firm, and fit.

"Where is everybody?" Gabrielle asked, joining her at the rail. Helen's head shot up.

"Heavens! You startled ten years off my life."

"Sorry," Gabrielle said and smiled, adding, "Why didn't somebody wake me up?"

"Oh, Micah said to let you sleep," Helen answered, returning her elbows to the rail. "He's got a big day planned for you." Helen looked at Gabrielle with a mixture of envy and chagrin. "Lucky you, a tour on your first day here."

"A tour? I thought we were just driving across the isthmus. Micah didn't say anything about sight-seeing."

"Well, he probably just decided or he forgot to tell you," Helen said.

Gabrielle thought it unlikely that Micah had forgotten. Perhaps he had decided to apologize for his harsh words, and the tour was his way of going about softening her up. If that was true, she would accept his apology gracefully. She didn't want anything to spoil her first day in this exciting tropical paradise.

"Where is everybody?" she asked Helen. "The ship seems deserted."

Helen grunted, disgust showing plain on her face. "Well," she drawled, "the two who were *so* sick got dressed the minute the gangplank was hoisted into place. That was at three o'clock this morning. They went into Colon and I haven't seen them since. Captain Dressler is arranging for a cargo and his passage through the canal. Micah got his car unloaded, walked it through customs, and has gone to find Jinks and Benton. Max is waiting for us on the helipad at Fort Gulick, and has been" —she glanced at her watch— "for more than an hour."

"Sounds like things are really jumping."

Helen snorted. "Things are always jumping in this place." She glanced at Gabrielle. "Are you ready for Chepo?"

"I suppose. I'm a little nervous."

"Well, don't be. You'll stay busy. And there are *chivas* that go into town every day from the village, which is only a mile or so from the house. So if you get bored, you can always go into Panama City for the day."

"Oh, I doubt that I'll be bored. There's too much work for that," Gabrielle said, speaking her thoughts aloud.

"It's really the same with us in Coco Solito, but to tell you the truth, I love a break. Did Micah mention Toboga to you?" Helen asked.

"No," Gabrielle answered slowly and wondered what else Micah had in store for her that he had seemed to conveniently fail to mention.

"He's made arrangements for all of us to spend New Year's on Toboga. It's a small island about ten miles off the coast of Balboa. Quite a few of the expatriated Americans go over to old man Wu's for a party. We'll be joining them this year. Three whole days," Helen said wistfully.

"I can hardly wait." Something along the pier caught Helen's attention. "Oh, my God!" she groaned. "Look at that." Gabrielle looked.

Two streaks of color exploded out of the milieu on the pier: the striking burgundy of Micah's new sports car, and the garish chartreuse-green Jinks wore. As the car drew near, Gabrielle saw that Jinks had somehow crammed his rolls of fat into a one-piece leisure suit. He sat poised on the boot of the car, each hand curved over the headrest of the seats in front of him, with his knees squeezed between Benton's and Micah's shoulders. Jinks swayed precariously as Micah stopped the car at the foot of the gangplank.

Gabrielle laughed at the spectacle, but choked it back when she saw the dismay in Helen's face.

"Uh-oh," Helen muttered under her breath as they watched Jinks produce a flask, unscrew the top, and take a swig before passing it on to Benton with a pudgy hand. She sighed. "I'd better get down there and get those two to Fort Gulick. I can see right now I'm going to have my hands full." There was a long-suffering tone in Helen's voice that drew a word of sympathetic understanding from Gabrielle.

"If Jinks wasn't such a good doctor," Helen said with a snicker, "sometimes I think I wouldn't even keep him around for decoration—his clothes are too outlandish!" She turned and gave Gabrielle a quick hug. "I'll see you Friday. Take care and don't let Micah run roughshod over you," she warned, then half ran, half walked down the gangplank. Gabrielle watched, a smile on her face, as Helen's gestures indicated she was reading the riot act to both Benton and Jinks.

Micah got out of his car and walked around it. He patted the fender, kicked at a spoked wheel, wiped off a headlight, then propped one foot on the running board. He was behaving like royalty, Gabrielle thought, inspecting a new jewel. He looked like the owner of the classic car, though. He wore tan slacks belted low on his hips, a beige pleated-down-the-front sport shirt, and a straw hat similar to the one Helen wore. The brim on Micah's hat was folded rakishly over his forehead to shade his eyes from the sun. He bent his head up and angled the briefest of glances at Gabrielle, then lifted a hand in a cursory wave. Gabrielle realized his inspection of the car had been for her benefit—offstage theatrics to get her attention. Suddenly a feeling of excitement shivered through her, evoking a thrill of secretive pleasure, a thrill of *knowing;* she knew his dark mahogany body intimately, every little crevice of his face, the feel of his mouth, the taste and smell of him. This knowledge was persuasive, seductive, so much so, that Gabrielle, for a short time, completely forgot Micah's angry, harsh words.

A checkered cab negotiated slowly around the banana trucks and came to a stop a few yards from Micah's car. Helen, with Jinks and Benton in tow, started toward it and appeared surprised when the back door opened and an elegant, attractive bronze woman stepped out. The woman skirted the threesome to reach Micah. She threw her arms around his neck and as Micah embraced the woman, Gabrielle felt something clutch savagely at her throat. She closed her eyes to shut out the sight.

Gabrielle had ignored the possibility that Micah had other women, let those thoughts, those doubts, slip conveniently from her mind, even after Helen had told her about the banker's daughter. *Stupid, foolish woman,* she told herself. She should have realized theirs had been a classic shipboard romance. Romance? Not even that. Lust, sex—two bodies coming together because they had been thrown together, confined in the space of the ship for the past four days. A sensual interlude, not unusual in a contemporary woman's life. So, why did she feel so wretched?

Micah disengaged himself from the eager woman and led her back to the taxi. She climbed in behind Helen and Jinks. Micah watched the taxi move down the pier until it turned out of sight, a sideways tilt of his head suggesting something on his mind. When he turned and started up the gangplank, Gabrielle retreated and made her way swiftly to the dining room.

He found her there a short time later. "So this is where you disappeared to. Are you ready to go?" He smiled at her, his voice pleasant, but Gabrielle felt bruised, violated, and there was a note of peevishness in her voice when she answered.

"Yes, but why couldn't I have gone with the others?" She waited for him to offer some explanation about the white-suited woman who had greeted him on the pier. He made no mention of it.

"Because I want to drive you across the isthmus in my new car. What do you think of it?"

"It looks just like any other sports car to me," Gabrielle said, staring out the porthole at the black hulk of another ship docked alongside the *Upsure*.

"There's nothing very interesting out that window," Micah said, noting her haughtiness.

"I like the view."

"View or no view," he said impatiently, "I'm ready to get on the road. Let's get your bag. I've still got to get you through customs, and remember, you're here on a tourist visa as my guest, not as an employee."

"Where's the rest of my things?" Gabrielle asked in an icy tone as they made their way off the ship into the huge barn that housed customs.

"They've already been sent through customs and are aboard the helicopter. Max will drop them off at Chepo on his way to Coco Solito."

"I don't understand why I couldn't have gone ahead with Max, then," Gabrielle continued stubbornly, barely nodding civilly to the customs agent while he flipped through her passport, visa, and tote.

"Because I *thought* I wanted the pleasure of your company," Micah muttered. "I'm beginning to think it was a mistake, myself."

"I'll just bet you are," she answered, mentally accusing Micah of preferring to be with his "welcoming committee" rather than with her. Gabrielle offered her thanks to the customs agent as an aside when he smiled and handed her back her documents.

"Did you pay attention to what the man said? You have to get your visa renewed every thirty days. Don't forget."

"I heard, but I hope I won't need to," she answered, provoking an ominous silence while Micah handed her into the car. The seats were smooth and luxurious. Gabrielle gave the chrome appointments and burgundy leather a brief sweeping glance. The car was impressive, but she bit her tongue to keep from making a comment. Micah opened the boot and tossed her tote in before coming around and getting into the driver's seat. The car purred into motion. Gabrielle pretended interest in the sights, but after a few minutes she leaned her head back on the headrest and closed her eyes.

Micah slammed on brakes. Her eyes flew open.

"What's wrong?" she asked, alarmed.

"You tell me," he said between clenched teeth. The line of his jaw remained rigid as he glared at her. "I'm a busy man, Gabrielle. I've been away from this project for more than three months, work has piled up, but I thought I'd make time to take you into Panama City, have a drink and dinner before we go home. If you'd rather go straight to Chepo, just say the word. I don't have valuable time to waste catering to one of your sullen moods."

"If you feel that way, why didn't you just go off with your welcoming committee?" she said icily.

"What welcoming committee?"

To Gabrielle's amazement Micah seemed genuinely puzzled. She enlightened him. "The one in the white suit," she answered and, at the look of surprise on Micah's face, wished she had held back the words.

He looked at her a long minute, then his lips curved in an ironic smile. "Well, well, well," he drawled. "I do believe there's a little green devil sitting alongside that chip on your shoulder this morning."

"There is not, and there's no chip on my shoulder."

"You're right about that. It's a whole damn log. Maybe I can chip it down to size, though," he said, suddenly moving his hand behind her neck and drawing her head close to his. "Something tells me I should have done this, and earlier," he said, kissing her thoroughly. A horn honked behind them. Micah ignored it until Gabrielle twisted her mouth away from his.

"Stop it. Everyone is staring."

"So they are," he said. "Must be my new car." He

glanced at her out of the corner of his eye as he put the car back into motion. "Happy now?"

"God, but you're arrogant!" She tossed him a dark look. "Are you going to tell me who she is?"

"No," he said, amused, but there was a tone of finality in the single word. Gabrielle sighed and watched the countryside roll by. Micah put his hand on her knee.

"You're not listening to a word I said."

"Yes. I heard you. You said this was the Boyd-Roosevelt Highway," she repeated as they drove under a canopy of greenery. The atmosphere under the towering trees was hushed, as though they had entered a dark, quiet cathedral, except they were moving through it and the jungle was closing in on both sides. She put his hand back on the steering column.

"Sorry, no more samples," she said.

Micah pursed his lips thoughtfully before he answered. "That's fine with me. A sample wouldn't do me now. I want it all."

In spite of herself, Gabrielle felt a sweep of excitement. There was a wild, animal sensuality about Micah and she felt drawn to it, but she refrained from any further provocative remarks. During the next several hours Micah didn't say one word at which Gabrielle could take offense. The disquieted feeling that bothered her was pushed aside as Micah became a gay, attentive host. Gabrielle got caught up in the gaiety and discovered she was enjoying herself.

Panama City was far more spectacular and exotic than Gabrielle could have imagined. Shops selling fabrics, boots, hats, jewels, perfumes, clothes, and whiskey lined Avenida Central, and nestled among the shops were restaurants, bars, and cantinas. Throngs of people seemed to move in waves out of the shops, spilling onto the sidewalks already crowded and edged with easels filled with fluttering bits of paper. Beside each easel a gaily dressed Panamanian hawked to the crowd.

"What are they selling?" Gabrielle asked, her curiosity aroused, unable to make out the words the hawkers were yelling into the din.

Micah smiled. "Tickets for the National Lottery. Are you a gambler?"

"Do you have to ask? I thought you said you know everything about me."

He chuckled. "I know you don't play bingo."

"Very funny," she said dryly. "How much are the lottery tickets?"

"Two for fifty-five cents. But hold your horses. I'll park and we can walk around. Would you like that?"

"I'd love it. But if I win the lottery, how will I know?"

Micah laughed outright. "You have a one-track mind. Just listen to the radio every Wednesday and Sunday morning. The numbers are announced. If you happen to get lucky, I'll bring you downtown to collect."

"Do you ever play?"

"Once in a while. I won thirty-two dollars once. I gave the ticket to Maria, though."

"Maria?" she said stiffly. "Is that another of your women?"

Micah groaned. "What do I need other women for, when I have you?"

"But you don't have me!"

He lifted an eyebrow in certain disbelief. "Too bad for me," he teased. "Maria is my cook and housekeeper."

Micah found a parking spot in a narrow side street and to Gabrielle's delight she found the top of every alley and the side streets were filled with fruit sellers hawking their wares. Other vendors sold tamales, fried plantain, and *carne en palitos,* which were spicy bits of meat skewered on a bamboo sliver and grilled over hot coals. She had to try them all.

"Only one more," she said to Micah and stopped in front of an old woman tending a brazier.

"This is the very last one, or you won't eat supper," Micah said indulgently. He grinned at her as she drew the tiny bits of meat off the stick with her tongue. "You're the first person I ever saw take to lizard so fast."

"Lizard? What do you mean?"

"You don't suppose they can afford to sell that stuff for twenty centavos a stick, do you, if it was anything else?"

"Whatever it is, it's delicious," Gabrielle decided aloud, sure that Micah was joking.

"Let's head back to the car," he said suddenly. "It's going to rain." Gabrielle shot a glance up to the sky and saw nothing but blue sky and protested against cutting her tour short.

"Give it two minutes," Micah said, hurrying her through the crowds. It did rain, a veritable deluge. Gabrielle took refuge in an entranceway of a building with a group of Panamanians while Micah scrambled to raise the roof on his new car. By the time he had the canvas locked in place, the rain had stopped. She hid a smile when he muttered a few oaths under his breath and motioned for her to get into the car. He flicked his shirt away from his neck where it clung, damp and sticky.

"Dinner in Panama City is out," he said glumly. "We might as well head on to the mountains and stop in at Harry Horton's on the way."

Gabrielle knew the moment she stepped inside Harry's that it was one of the cantinas Helen had warned her about. The mirror behind the bar, if there had ever been one, was obscured by dusty football pennants, bent license plates from every state, and pinups, their edges curled and torn. A recent photograph of an elegant Miss Piggy was tacked near the ceiling next to a faded sepia poster of Marilyn Monroe. Micah led her to a table, its linoleum edges faded and patina-smooth from countless elbows. Her chair rocked on the uneven wooden floor. A thin man, his wiry arms and legs moving swiftly in misguided rhythm, rushed from behind the bar to greet Micah.

"Davidson! Man, it's good to see you. When we heard about the crash, we thought you were a goner for sure." He stared at Micah's neck. "Ugh, looks nasty," he said and pounded Micah on the back. Gabrielle winced in sympathy when she saw Micah grimace. Harry looked at Gabrielle with undisguised approval. "What for you, young lady? I know what this old cuss drinks."

"She's staying with Coca-Cola in this place, Harry," Micah told him. "We'll take two of whatever you're serving for supper tonight."

After Harry had deposited a bottle of Jack Daniel's and her Coke on the table, Gabrielle asked hesitantly, "Is it safe to eat the food here?"

Micah laughed. "A hell of a lot safer than buying off street peddlers like you did today."

Gabrielle leaned back in her chair. She was exhausted and her leg was beginning to throb. She propped her foot on the rung of her chair and made herself as comfortable as she could manage. There was a lot going on in the dimly lit cantina and it soon drew her mind away from the ache in her leg. Men, singly or in small groups, left the bar and came over to speak to Micah, to say hello. They treated him with respectful deference, smiled shyly at Gabrielle, then went back to the bar or disappeared out the back of the building, where a cockfight was in progress. No one disturbed them while they ate though, and the food was delicious. Harry brought them wooden bowls filled with stew thick with chicken and spices, side dishes of fried rice and fried plantain sprinkled with cinnamon and sugar. After they had finished eating, Micah lit a cigarette and inhaled deeply. He smiled at Gabrielle through the smoke. He had a look of contentment about him and Gabrielle realized she had never seen him so relaxed. She returned his smile.

Harry came over to remove the dishes.

"The chicken stew was delicious, Harry," Gabrielle told him. A look of pride creased Harry's thin face.

"I'm glad you liked it, miss, but it tweren't no chicken. That was iguana. Caught the rascal myself this morning."

"Iguana?" Gabrielle phrased the question silently to Micah.

"Lizard," he said succinctly.

Gabrielle felt her stomach lurch.

"Harry!" Micah called the man back. "Bring the lady a brandy and be quick about it." To Gabrielle, he warned, "Don't go getting sick on me now."

"I thought you were just joking," she said. The few sips of brandy that Gabrielle managed to swallow did more than calm her stomach, it made her drowsy.

A half hour after the sun went down, they were back on

the Pan American Highway heading into the mountains. Gabrielle closed her eyes and this time Micah didn't object. Her mind lazily recorded the day, filing it away for pleasant memory later until she visualized the white-suited woman. . . Micah's arms around her, their heads together. Had they made love? Had Micah asked her to meet him at the pier, then sent her away again to wait for him?

"Who was she, Micah?" she said aloud, unable to contain her curiosity a moment longer. "The woman in the white suit, the one on the pier this morning."

"Are we back to that again?"

"Tell me," she insisted, sure she wouldn't like the answer. She didn't.

"Vanessa Thomas."

Gabrielle sat up straight, all thoughts of sleep erased from her mind. Helen had mentioned a woman named Vanessa. Micah had planned to marry her. "Is Vanessa the banker's daughter?" she asked.

"The one and same," he said, cutting a sharp glance at her. "Looks like you've been doing a little investigating of your own."

"Someone volunteered the information. I certainly didn't ask."

"You just did," he said pointedly.

"You used to be engaged to her," Gabrielle said, and to her own ears the statement sounded like an accusation.

"It's none of your business," he said curtly.

"Luke Bryant isn't any of *your* business!"

"Quit playing these little games. We had a good time today. Why are you trying to spoil it with an argument now?"

"It's no game," Gabrielle informed him. "I'm here to work and let my leg heal, nothing more." She spoke the words to convince herself as much as she tried to convince Micah, but somehow, with all that had passed between them, the words sounded aloof and foreign and meaningless. She watched his mouth twist into a sardonic curve in the dim glow from the instrument panel.

"What worries you the most, Gabrielle? That I will or I won't have you in my bed tonight?"

Gabrielle gasped, furious at his arrogant and perverse manner and annoyed at herself, because she *had* wondered where the day would end, especially when she had been sitting across from him at Harry Horton's.

"You're disgusting," she said. "No wonder Vanessa Thomas refused to marry you!"

"That was a long time ago," he said smoothly. "She's changed her mind now."

Gabrielle recoiled at his words as though she had been struck with a hammer. Did he mean that he had asked Vanessa to marry him again? Something Helen had said haunted her with vivid recall. "After an accident like Micah's, a man thinks twice about his destiny, building a dynasty, and perhaps an heir or two."

They rode the rest of the way to Chepo in silence. The jungle rolled by in darkness. Strange shapes of trees, huge fronds, an occasional house, with nothing to illuminate them, no shape recognizable for what it was.

Micah put the car in low gear to negotiate a steep incline, then inched across a narrow wooden bridge. A few yards later he parked under a thatched shelter separate from the house. Light from behind shutters drafted a striated pattern on the porch. Flowering hibiscus and jasmine, barely discernible in the dark, spilled their fragrance into the air. Gabrielle stood by the side of the car and waited for Micah to retrieve her tote from the trunk.

She saw the white streak fly at her, but before she could make a sound or move out of the way, she was knocked to the ground. Only then did she shriek a warning to Micah.

"Shadow!" There was a warm, caressing tone in Micah's voice as he hugged the animal. "Sit!" he commanded to stop the dog from weaving in and out between his legs. The dog obeyed instantly.

"Are you all right?" Micah helped her up, brushing debris from her skirt. There was undisguised concern in his voice as his hands traveled the length of her. "Nothing's broken, thank goodness," he said with obvious relief. "I'm sorry about that. I guess Shadow has missed me."

"It's okay, I'm fine," Gabrielle assured him, still shaken. Suddenly a terrible scream of agony split the air.

Gabrielle started, her eyes widened with fear as the sound grew and another voice joined the first until the air seemed to vibrate with throaty shrieks.

Micah began to laugh, but stopped when he saw her face. "It's just howler monkeys. There's a tribe of them close by. They're harmless. Your scream probably stirred them up." He called the dog to heel, then took Gabrielle's arm. "Come on, let's get you into the house.

"Do you need a drink?" he asked, putting the briefcase and her tote on the end of the sofa.

"No, thank you," she answered calmly and looked around the room she stood in. It was spacious, cool, and tastefully decorated. She liked it. There was a subtle aura of welcome and warmth in the way the two immense sofas faced one another, the indirect lighting that gave off a soft glow yet illuminated the entire room. Gabrielle looked at Micah. "A bath and some sleep will do me."

"You have a shower; the bathtub is in my room. You're welcome to it."

"I'll manage with a shower." She didn't want a repeat of the incident aboard the *Upsure*; she was too emotionally drained and physically exhausted to trade insults with him anymore tonight.

There was an uncomfortable silence between them. Gabrielle felt her limbs begin to tremble as the moment grew awkward. Micah started toward her and she stiffened, but all he did was take her arm.

"Come on, then, I'll show you to your room. You'll feel better after a good night's sleep."

The room he took her to was softly lit by a tall lamp, and an overhead fan, identical to the ones in the living room, rotated slowly. The carved bed was entirely surrounded by a swath of mosquito netting hung from the beamed ceiling. Gabrielle swept the room with a quick glance. Her suitcases were nowhere to be seen. She groaned audibly.

"Didn't my things get here?"

Micah walked over to a dresser and pulled out a drawer. He lifted a handful of lace. "All here. Maria has unpacked for you."

"Thank you. Good night," she said firmly.

Micah took a step in her direction, but changed his mind in midstride and walked out the door with a nod of his head.

Gabrielle searched among the drawers for clean pajamas, took a quick shower, and crawled into the bed. It felt marvelous. She massaged her aching leg and waited half expectantly, half fearfully, for Micah to join her. He didn't.

Thoughts of him crowded her mind. Why did they seem so star-crossed? He seemed to have some magical power over her, even though she recognized it for what it was—a pervading sexuality that engulfed her, making her incapable of resistance. And for that, she couldn't decide whether to love him or loathe him.

Chapter Twelve

The following morning Micah, bathed and dressed in his desert tans, sat at his desk and waited impatiently for Gabrielle to join him. Three times he sent Maria into her room with the instruction not to wake her, but if she was up, to tell her to join him for coffee. And three times the housekeeper returned to say Gabrielle was still fast asleep. Usually he was a notably patient man, but where Gabrielle was concerned, his patience dangled on a short string. Unable to endure waiting another moment, he left his desk, strode through the courtyard, ordered Maria to prepare a tray, and carried it himself into Gabrielle's room, which was still shuttered against the brilliant tropical sun. He set the tray on the bedside table and parted the netting.

Gabrielle lay sprawled on her stomach, her face toward him. Her long dark lashes lay on her cheek, her provocative lips parted slightly. A feeling of protectiveness overwhelmed him and he fought the urge to gather her up into his arms. He stared for a long time at her comely shape, thinking she was vivacious even in her sleep. His chest tightened curiously. The emotions she evoked in him were intoxicating. He sat down on the bed and, unable to keep his hands from her, began to knead her back. Gabrielle woke almost immediately, turned over, and brought the sheet up over her face.

"Get out of here," she murmured sleepily.

"Are you always this nasty in the morning?" he asked, sounding indulgent.

Gabrielle let the sheet slide from her face. Her eyes were bright with humor. "Didn't your investigators tell you I don't like to be disturbed before nine?"

"No, and if any had, I would have throttled him for getting to know you too well. Besides, it's after nine." He lifted a damask napkin off the tray. "Maria's made your coffee. I'll be leaving within the hour for Coco Solito. I need to show you a few things before I go and I want your passport and visa.''

Gabrielle sat up and accepted the cup from Micah's outstretched hand. She peered into the cup. ''Cream?'' Micah poured a dollop from a sterling silver decanter without a single word. Gabrielle lifted an eyebrow, surprised that he performed the small service without a disparaging remark, but if Micah noticed her expression, he kept it to himself. ''What do you need my passport for?''

''So I can put them in my safe. I don't want them lost.'' He looked at her while she sipped her coffee. ''If your disposition was as fine as you look in the morning, we'd get along a hell of a lot better.''

Gabrielle laughed, enjoying his teasing, the repartee, the tantalizing eye contact. ''You know, Micah, you have more gall than a chicken gizzard. *You* are the one with the black moods and the sour disposition, not me.'' He grinned and the devilish gleam in his dark eyes told her his mood was far from stormy this morning. Her chest and neck began to grow warm. ''Get off my bed,'' she ordered. He lifted an eyebrow at her unexpected command, but stood up and moved away. He looked well rested and entirely masculine, she noticed. His dark skin gleamed against khakis that hugged his muscular frame. His pants were tucked into polished leather boots. He reminded her of pictures she had seen of big game hunters: hands perched arrogantly on hips, one boot-clad foot propped on their kill, smiling visages that promised there was more to come. Gabrielle felt like she was the quarry. As she watched, Micah began to unbutton his bush jacket.

''Don't!'' she said, instinctively aware of his intentions.

He grinned wickedly. ''If you're not getting out of that bed, I'm getting in.'' He glanced pointedly at his watch. ''We have time.''

The excitement Gabrielle felt cut to the quick. She circumvented it by setting her cup on the table and scrambling out of bed. ''No, we don't,'' she stated emphatically. Micah's hand shot out, grabbing her wrist. He tugged her into an encompassing embrace. He let out a moan of sweet pleasure. "We do have time for this," he told her as his hands moved under her pajamas, down her back, below her waist, and cupped velvety bare flesh. He pressed her into him so hard Gabrielle felt his belt buckle bite into her skin.

"Don't do this, please," she said, pleading softly and enjoying every pleasurable sensation his fingers were arousing.

"Dear Gabrielle," he whispered, "I can't help myself." His lips were in her hair, at her temple, on her mouth. Gabrielle leaned into him, captivated with the potent warmth of his body. Her arms slid around his waist. His lips occupied hers tantalizingly, forcing her to breathe through her nose, and the clean, soapy smell of him mingled with his cologne, an aphrodisiac well remembered. When his tongue began to explore her mouth with an urgency born in his loins, her own tongue darted out to meet his.

As their lips and hands lingered on one another, caressing, touching, and exploring, Gabrielle, with an inexplicable flash of clarity, understood they were sharing more than a shallow burst of passion stimulated by lust. No single person had absorbed her attention as Micah had done, as he was doing now. Not ever. Only the ballet had reached into her very core. She buried the thought close to her soul and brooded on it.

He pushed her away with a guttural sigh formed deep in his throat. "I could kick myself for not coming for you last night," he said huskily.

Gabrielle kept prudently silent. She would not admit that she had waited for him, that her desire had raced through her veins as strident as his own. A peculiar, unfamiliar look creased his powerful mahogany features. It was gone in an instant, veiled behind the dark mask.

"Time or no time," he told her, breathing shallowly. "If you don't get dressed, Max is going to be waiting on me till noon." His hands came out of her pajamas slowly, reluctantly, then he moved to sit in a heavy carved chair. Gabrielle searched through the drawers until she found yellow shorts and its matching cotton top. She turned to Micah, the clothes dangling from her hand.

"If you'll be kind enough to get out of here, I can be

dressed in two minutes.'' Micah smiled, his twisted little smile.

"I want to watch."

"Voyeur!" she snapped and went in the bath, slamming and locking the door behind her. He was still sitting in the chair when she emerged a few minutes later. Raw hunger glittered in his eyes as he looked her up and down slowly. Gabrielle averted her face, pretending not to notice, grabbed her sandals, and walked out into the early-morning sun that beat down in the courtyard. She sensed Micah right behind her, felt his hands grasp her waist. His fingers splayed, locking her against him, and traveled as slowly as his eyes had up the yellow fabric until they cupped her breasts.

She stiffened. "No more, Micah. Stop it. I'm here to work, not—not to satisfy your sex drives."

"Why do you fight it, Gabrielle? Just go with it, enjoy it," he whispered.

She had to fight it, she thought. In the sun, on the veranda, away from the bedroom, she regained her perspective and yesterday's events careened into her mind. The specter of Vanessa Thomas loomed large, casting a pall as dark as storm clouds over her unordered emotions.

"I'm not fighting anything. I don't have to," she lied. "I'm just convenient. If another woman was here, you'd behave the same."

His hands released her, pushed her forward to the living room. "God! You'd try the patience of Job," he said to her back.

"I would if he was lusting after me like a bull."

"Is that so?" he said, his voice silken with sarcasm. "You think that's what I am, a rutting bull?"

"Oh, no," she said sweetly. "You're a worm. Don't you remember?"

Micah grunted. "Ninth-grade biology really made an impression on you, didn't it?" he muttered unhappily. "Step in here a minute." He indicated a small tidy room near the niche that held his desk.

"The radio. It's our only communication system with Coco Solito on the Mamoni River. Don't touch the dials, just press this button on the speaker. You'll hear a buzzer if I'm trying to reach you. Then just flip this switch. Got it?'' She nodded. "I've written Benton's number down and put it by the phone. Now, where's your passport and visa?''

Gabrielle walked over to the sofa where she had left her purse last night. She removed the documents and handed them to Micah.

"Won't I need these if I go into Panama City?''

"No, not until you leave.''

"Well, suppose I do want to leave, I mean, sooner than—''

"You agreed to stay for ninety days," he reminded her coolly.

"Suppose it doesn't take me ninety days? Suppose I get the contracts completed?''

A muscle jerked in Micah's jaw. "You signed on for ninety days and you stay for ninety days.'' He swung back a carved panel, one of three decorating the wall, opened the safe, and put her documents inside. Gabrielle felt a twinge of loss. She no longer controlled her life. With her travel documents in Micah's possession, she was no longer free to leave... to escape. And she wondered why *escape* had leaped into her mind. The sound of a helicopter's rotors beating the air began to seep into the room. Micah flipped the shutters and looked out.

"Max will be here in a couple of minutes.'' He handed Gabrielle an envelope and some keys. "There's the rest of your salary, some expense money, and the keys to my car. Don't wreck it.''

Gabrielle glanced into the envelope. She saw several one hundred dollar bills along with a check. "I won't come near needing this much for expenses," she told him.

"You will if you drive the car. Gas here is two twenty-five a gallon, and that little number really eats it up.'' The noise from the helicopter got louder. Micah walked to the courtyard door and let out a short whistle. Shadow came bounding up. "One more thing," he said to Gabrielle. "We're going to Toboga for New Year's. I'll be back Friday, noon. Pack enough for three days, a swimsuit and something dressy.''

"I'd rather just stay here and work. After all, I'm just an employee," she said. Her chin lifted, challenging him to counter the remark. She wanted him to say she was more than an employee, more than just a passing fancy. She wanted him to say Vanessa Thomas meant nothing to him. But he didn't. His fingers bit into her arm; he brought his face inches from hers.

"Damn you, Gabrielle, stop being so stubborn. I hope your mood has improved by Friday, but if not, and you want misery, I can dish it out," he warned, releasing her arm. He signaled the dog, who followed at his heels. Gabrielle watched Micah board the aircraft and Shadow leap in behind him. She rubbed her arm where his fingers had pressed into tender skin as she silently called him a string of names, none of which sounded so mild as grubby old worm. After the helicopter disappeared over the trees, she turned to go introduce herself to Maria before she began work.

Chapter Thirteen

In the hours after Micah left, Gabrielle established the routine that would carry her through the long days of her stay at Chepo. She rose each morning, awakened by the stillness and silence that preceded the dawn as the howler monkeys, frogs, and other jungle creatures sought out their lairs to sleep through the heat of the tropical days.

After coffee and perhaps a mango, plucked from the tree in the garden, she worked on contracts, typing those she had translated the night before. Maria prepared an early lunch and went off with her husband, Garcia, each afternoon. She returned in the evening to prepare dinner. Gabrielle learned Maria had several children who stayed with Garcia in the village, but Micah had insisted that while Gabrielle was at Chepo, Maria must stay the night. Once Gabrielle had grown accustomed to the night sounds, she insisted Maria spend her evenings with her family. By silent agreement neither mentioned it to Micah.

Garcia accompanied Maria to Chepo every morning. He spent most of his time hacking away at the jungle that seemed to creep up overnight to cover the manicured lawns and the log-floored helipad. He saw to it that the gas-powered generators that provided electricity for the house were kept fueled and running.

After a siesta Gabrielle donned her pointe shoes and leotards to practice simple pliés, jetés, and battements, using the banister on the veranda surrounding the inner courtyard for her barre. When her injured leg tired and began to ache, she bathed, luxuriating in Micah's huge porcelain tub.

For dinner she dressed in simple cottons and sat alone, served by Maria at the magnificent triangular table in the dining room. She often worked there afterward until nightfall, and when her concentration lagged, she read, choosing books from the shelves that lined the walls in Micah's room. When the howler monkeys began their bull-throated song accompanied by thousands of tree frogs, she made ready for bed.

Micah was never very far from her mind. When she brushed her teeth each morning, she wondered if he was doing the same at that very minute. When she sat down to dinner, she wondered if he was eating, and when she poured cream in her coffee, she wondered if he was having coffee too. She wondered if he thought of her at all.

On Thursday afternoon Gabrielle was exercising in the courtyard so she didn't hear the Jeep as it struggled in low gear over the edge of the mountain. A horn honked twice, startling her. She grabbed her terry robe to cover her leotards, wiped the sweat from her face on a corner, and went to answer the door.

A blond giant of a man stood on the other side of the screen. A straw hat shaded his eyes and all she could see of his face was a wild, bushy blond beard. He wore shorts that had probably once been khaki, but now were faded cream beneath the dirt. A tattered shirt, its sleeves ripped out, exposed tanned, muscular arms. A machete, hung at his waist, flopped against his knee. Olive-green socks fell over the tops of mud-spattered boots. Gabrielle thought she had never seen a more disreputable character. He stared at her through the screen. Gabrielle clutched the robe around her and noticed with dismay that the latch on the door hung loose. A tiny coil of fear held her speechless. The man saw her hesitation.

"Hello," he said, and the sound of his voice was low, and mellow, unexpected for such a large man. "You must be Gabrielle Hensley. Helen told me you would be here. I'm Father Chardin."

"The priest?" she said, surprised, and more than a little relieved.

"I didn't know my fame preceded me," he chuckled. "May I come in?"

"Oh, yes, I'm sorry," she almost stuttered. "It's just— I've only been here a few days. Maria isn't here at the moment and I wasn't expecting company." She stood aside, feeling somewhat awkward. In the future, she told herself, when Maria wasn't here, she would latch the doors.

Father Chardin whipped off his hat and offered his hand. Gabrielle noted vivid blue eyes. "Miss Hensley," he said and nodded formally as she automatically put out her hand to clasp his. Father Chardin lifted his other hand, displaying a gunnysack, knotted at the top.

"I brought dinner," he volunteered with a wide smile. The sack seemed to move.

"What is it?" Gabrielle asked, at first suspicious and then certain that whatever was in the sack was alive right this minute.

"Iguana. Maria transforms it into the most agreeable delicacy," he told her.

"I'm not hungry," Gabrielle said quickly, almost rudely, positive she would never put another piece of the animal in her mouth, especially after seeing a picture of the prehistoric-looking lizard in a book only last night.

Father Chardin laughed. "Don't tell me you're one of those whose stomach doesn't agree with his palate."

"I'm afraid so," Gabrielle admitted.

"Have I interrupted your nap?" he said, eyeing her robe.

"Oh, no. I was just doing some exercises." Then, remembering that she was probably expected to perform the duties of a hostess with Maria not here, she offered Father Chardin some refreshment.

He swept a deprecating look at his clothes. "I've been in the jungle for a couple of weeks. I'd like to clean up first. Micah is kind enough to allow me the use of his home to wash away this muck before I return to Panama City."

"Oh," she said, realizing that Father Chardin was probably as familiar with the house as she had become. Hesitantly she asked, "Did you see Micah? I haven't heard from him since he went to the logging camp."

"No, I didn't. He wasn't in Coco Solito when I passed through. Helen said he was out with his crews marking trees to be cut." He smiled. "If you will excuse me?"

"Oh, certainly," Gabrielle said, embarrassed that she had kept him standing in the room when he was eager to bathe. She watched him from the room. He stopped by the kitchen and tossed the sack through the door, then with sure familiarity he went into one of the bedrooms along the back of the courtyard.

Gabrielle wondered that Micah would have a priest as a friend, but then she didn't really know him very well. Anyway, Father Chardin was a welcome diversion and she hurried to bathe and dress. Maria waved to her from the kitchen door.

"Father Chardin is here, Maria. He's having supper with us."

"*Sí, señorita,* I know," she said with a smile. "I am cooking his favorite."

"Don't put any of that lizard on my plate, Maria," Gabrielle said adamantly. Maria looked crestfallen, and Gabrielle relented. "Well, just a small portion, no more."

Delightful aromas were coming from the kitchen when Gabrielle stepped refreshed and dressed from her room an hour later. She hurried across the courtyard to the front of the house. Father Chardin stood behind the bar, built with the infamous manchineel, one hand resting lightly on the wood that Gabrielle could not bring herself to touch. He turned at the sound of her footsteps.

"Ah, Miss Hensley! I was just trying to decide which of Micah's devil's brews to sample to quench this powerful thirst I have."

Gabrielle laughed and noticed that he looked every inch a priest in his dark suit, Roman collar, and clean-shaven face. His strong chin had an unexpected dimple. She joined him at the bar, gingerly resting her elbows on the polished wood.

"Micah keeps the best private stock between here and the presidential palace," the priest mused, finally deciding on Tanqueray and tonic. He plopped ice into two glasses, poured the gin, and splashed some tonic. "No lime," he said, "but I pulled one of these bitter oranges from a tree in the garden. It has enough bite, I believe." He swirled a sliver of peel round the crystal rims and handed a glass to Gabrielle.

She tasted the drink and found it delicious. Curious

about the priest's relationship with Micah, she said, "You seem to be at home here."

He chuckled. "Actually it's Micah's tub that draws me here, and if one bathes in the devil's backyard, one is more likely to know what he's about."

"Devil?" Gabrielle repeated, trying not to bristle; after all, Micah was a man she felt drawn to, had made love to. He had his faults and he deserved some of the names she had called him, but "devil," coming from a priest, sounded ominous. Father Chardin noticed the slight upward movement of Gabrielle's chin and laughed.

"I'm sorry. I didn't mean to shock you. It's a private joke. But there are others who would call him that and more." He smiled. "Micah seems to create an intensity of feeling wherever he goes. Either you like him or you don't. Which is it with you, Miss Hensley?"

Gabrielle was taken aback. "I haven't decided," she said quickly.

Father Chardin's mellow laughter echoed in the room. "You are charming, Miss Hensley, and tactful. Come, let's sit down.

"Before Micah allowed me the use of his home as a way station," he began after settling his large frame comfortably on one of the sofas, "I had to use the tin shack at Harry Horton's. The bishop frowned on that, I'm afraid."

"I can imagine," Gabrielle exclaimed, recalling the attractive women who table-hopped and the sounds of a cockfight that made conversation almost impossible at times when she and Micah had been there.

"Oh, you know Harry's already?" the priest said, surprised.

"Yes, Micah took me there. Is that so unusual?"

"Well, no, but it's not a place I would take a lady, although with Micah I'm sure you were treated as royalty."

"I wouldn't say that"— Gabrielle smiled— "but Harry seemed to like Micah pretty well."

"Yes, I'm sure he does," the priest said dryly. "When Micah opens up Coco Solito, Harry wants to be the first one in with his cockfights and loose women."

"Oh," Gabrielle uttered, embarrassed by his bluntness. Father Chardin laughed at the look on her face.

"Call me Amand, and I assure you I mellow down after a couple of these." He shook his glass. "It's just that I see what modern men—if you can call them that—are doing to the Indians, even as far down as the Darien and it makes me mad."

"Why? Are you an environmentalist? Besides being a priest, I mean."

"I'm an archaeologist, but my anger isn't an entirely noble gesture. I need a refill. You?" Gabrielle declined. "Much to my chagrin," Amand said, arranging his thick frame comfortably once again, his drink refreshed, "I find I want the jungles and the Indians to remain pristine and unaffected for a selfish reason of my own. For the past ten years I have been working my way down the Pacific Coast, beginning in Oregon, searching for clues—anything to try to prove my claim that the Chinese influenced the early cultures on this continent. Right now I'm attempting to scout out and establish perimeters, sort of mapping out the best areas to concentrate my search. If I find nothing in the Darien jungles, I'll focus more on the Mayan culture in Mexico where there seems to be the strongest evidence." The priest eyed Gabrielle with his vivid blue eyes. "Stop me if I'm boring you," he said. "The Chinese are my favorite subject—after God, that is," he said, rolling his eyes upward as if to ward off a bolt of lightning.

Gabrielle laughed. "I'm not in the least bored. Helen mentioned you to me and said it was a lifelong quest. I think it's fascinating, although I admit I've never heard it mentioned that the Chinese traveled over the Pacific."

"Oh, they did, they did," Father Chardin said, warming to his subject. "I think when the Vikings were landing on the Atlantic Coast, the Chinese were setting foot on the Pacific. You see," he said, leaning forward and becoming more intense, "about a thousand years ago a serene and sophisticated era lasting about six hundred years emerged in the Mexican culture. The Mayans established all their deities either just before or at the beginning of this era: the Rain God, *Tlaloc;* the Moon God, *Xipe;* and the God of

Happiness among many others. The God of Happiness intrigues me, he is the one most resembling a Chinese, with high collars, flowing robes, and distinctly Oriental features.

"About the time Micah began building Coco Solito, I heard a rumor of a *nele,* a tribal medicine man who uses a peculiar stone idol or doll to make very strong medicine. The description of this medicine doll sounds remarkably like the Chinese God of Happiness." A faraway, wistful look came over Amand's face. "I would give my eyeteeth to get a look at the doll and learn how the *nele* came to have it."

"Well," said Gabrielle, considering his problem, "you could always get sick in some faraway jungle village and then maybe he would come to treat you." Amand laughed.

"I've considered that many times, unfortunately I'm healthy as a horse and besides, I've done my work too well—the Indians think my God is so powerful He protects me from all earthly evils. I would like to have a tangible clue, though, to take to China with me."

"You're going to China?" Gabrielle asked, recalling the class in Chinese folk ballet she had taken while in the Fine Arts Academy. The classic moves of the dancers had been handed down generation to generation and spanned centuries.

"My Superior General has granted me permission. It's up to the Chinese now. They welcome visitors, but allowing a foreigner to study their archives in Peking . . . well, that is another matter."

Maria appeared in the door to announce dinner and hours later, after Amand had left for Panama City, Gabrielle decided she liked the priest immensely. He was an interesting conversationalist and an excellent listener. He had skillfully drawn her out and seemed genuinely interested in her. His laughter was infectious and when Gabrielle had got up enough courage to ask him why he had become a priest, his eyes had twinkled with merriment. "Besides my calling, you mean? I was the only boy among nine sisters." He had laughed. "The peace and quiet of the monastery was like a haven to me."

Chapter Fourteen

It seemed to Gabrielle that Friday noon was never going to arrive. As the hands on her watch moved closer to the magic hour when Micah would be home, she found it more and more difficult to concentrate on the contracts. Eventually she gave up and sat on the sofa, trying to rationalize her feelings toward him. She tried to tell herself that it was simply because he had offered her a job when she needed one so desperately. That was true, but Gabrielle knew it was something more than that. It was something she could not explain, even to herself. It was a feeling she had never had before, an attraction she had never felt for any other man. She tried to tell herself it was just the chemistry of sex. She wanted Micah and she wanted the ballet. She wondered if she could have them both. She wondered about Vanessa Thomas. Micah's words, "She's changed her mind," kept haunting her.

When the helicopter arrived, an agonizing twenty minutes late, Gabrielle was standing on the front porch. Shadow was the first one out and he came bounding up to her. She scratched his ears and let him in the house. Helen and Jinks followed along with J.T. Coats, the logger boss. J.T. was a barrel-shaped man, a widower, with shy, melancholy eyes. Max was black, handsome in a rough sort of way. He wore a beat-up army fatigue hat low over his eyes and aviator glasses with cocky sureness. Micah, without seeming to, made sure Max kept his distance from Gabrielle.

After a quick greeting Helen preempted Micah's bath, while Gabrielle acted as hostess, serving the men drinks, until one by one they too disappeared into rooms to bathe and dress for the launch trip to the island of Toboga.

Micah's eyes followed Gabrielle around the room as she gathered up the dirty glasses. For some unearthly reason she felt suddenly shy in his presence.

"Leave those damn things for Maria, and come sit by me," he told her. Gabrielle began to tremble as she made her way across the room. She sat down opposite him, which was as close as she dared. Now that they had the room to themselves, the air seemed charged with electricity.

"Have you heard from Benton?" he asked.

"Yes, he called yesterday. He said to bring the contracts I've finished with me today and that he'll meet us at Tocumen with a bus to take us to Balboa," she answered, surprised at how even her voice sounded. Micah nodded, silent for a minute.

"Miss me?" he said, and the question was like a caress, sending tiny stabs of desire, flickering little fires, coursing through Gabrielle's veins.

"No, why should I?"

Micah smiled and the disbelief showed plain on his face. Helen joined them just then and Micah listened, amused as the two women chatted about this and that, small innocuous everyday occurrences. Gabrielle discovered herself talking too rapidly, avoiding Micah's eyes and the ironic smile that lifted the corners of his mouth, and sighed unknowingly when he got up without a word and went to bathe and pack.

The twenty-minute ride to Tocumen was Gabrielle's first flight in a helicopter. The inside of the aircraft was far more spacious than she had imagined, but it was a no-frill business machine. She sat next to Helen on a metal bench, twisted so she could look out the windows. Conversation was impossible with the noise from the rotors thick over their heads. The panoramic views of tiny jungle-locked villages were breathtaking and it seemed to Gabrielle that as they skimmed the tops of the trees the dark green terrain behind became enclosed in a white mist.

Benton was waiting for them at Tocumen. He had hired one of the quaint *chivas* to take them to Balboa, Pier Eighteen, where a launch waited to ferry them to Toboga. Jinks produced his flask and the party became more raucous as the little bus maneuvered through the crowded narrow streets.

Another dozen or so passengers boarded the launch with them for the forty-five-minute trip to the island. Jinks recognized two army doctors, who were with their wives. The doctors were stationed at Fort Amador. Jinks introduced them around and Micah invited them to join their party, an invitation they happily accepted.

Micah worked his way over to where Gabrielle sat in the lee of the small cabin to avoid the salt spray the boat was kicking up. The woman next to Gabrielle shifted on the bench to make room for Micah so that Gabrielle felt bound to scoot a little forward. Even so, it was a tight squeeze when he sat down between them. He draped an arm around Gabrielle's shoulder.

"I'm not sure this was such a good idea," he said.

Surprised, Gabrielle said, "Why? I'm having a good time."

"I see that," he said wryly. "I was hoping to have you to myself for a while."

"Really? Why?"

"You have to ask?" He bent his lips near her ear, whispering, "Shall I make love to you right here and give all these idiots something to talk about?"

"No, I can wait...I mean—"

"I can't. I've been crazy thinking about you," he murmured.

His fingers traced a feathery pattern on her arm. Gabrielle shivered, sure that she wanted what his evocative words and caressing eyes promised, and just as sure he was using her for his own ends. She tried to quell a mounting hunger for him, but it kept on building and she had to bear it.

"Tell me about Toboga," she demanded breathlessly, determined to change the subject.

"Won't work," he teased, enjoying the response he was provoking.

Gabrielle twisted to face the prow, ignoring both Micah and the salt spray that licked at her as the ferry chugged through the end of the canal under the soaring arch of the Bridge of the Americas. She paid gratuitous attention to several silvery white gulls that appeared to think the best fishing was immediately in front of the ferry. They squawked and cried as the small craft sliced through their feeding grounds. Micah shifted, bent low, and began talking into her ear.

"Toboga," he said in a monotone, "is a resort favorite with mainlanders, especially me. It's called the island of flowers because its footpaths are lined with hibiscus, oleander, and jasmine. No automobiles are allowed on the island. The only way to get around is on foot or in a water taxi—that's a *pangas*. We," he emphasized, "are going to go fishing, make love, go swimming, make love, go dancing, and make love—want to hear more?"

"You idiot," she said, laughing. "Are you the same dark, moody Micah Davidson I met in Houston?" He didn't answer, but squeezed her shoulder, and the small intimate gesture sent happiness winging through her and chased away all the doubts that had been haunting her the past week. Gabrielle leaned back against him, content with his pleasant, gay mood and, for the moment, her own.

Excited shouts and whistles erupted from the men aboard the launch as they sailed near a sleek yacht moored in the bay. A topless sunbather on its deck jumped up and frantically began searching among some deck debris. Gabrielle felt sympathy for the women, but she had to laugh too. "Did you see that?" she asked Micah.

"Ah, no. I missed her," he said.

His voice carried such a lilt of wistfulness that Gabrielle turned to look at him and found his eyes twinkling with merriment. "You liar!" He laughed and then joined in the good-natured abuse that was being bandied about; most of the wives were chastising their husbands for catcalling.

There was near pandemonium on the small wharf as several launches from the mainland disgorged their passengers on the island at the same time. Gabrielle, watching Micah, saw him exchange a signal glance with Jinks and nod toward Benton, who had already sorted his luggage from the pile on the wharf and was heading toward Wu's hotel.

"Benton," Micah called, "where're you headed? We're taking *pangas* from here to the cottages."

"I'm staying at Wu's," Benton called back, "where the action is."

"Oh, come on," Micah coaxed. "I've got us places right on the beach, and we're going surf fishing this afternoon. You can get over to Wu's later." Benton hesitated.

"Okay," he agreed. "Won't be much going on for a few hours anyway." He handed his luggage to a native porter with instructions to carry it to the hotel. Micah engaged two of the water taxis to take them around the island to a cluster of cottages shaded by monkey plum trees, flowering hibiscus, and graceful coconut trees. Gabrielle was enchanted, but her enchantment slipped when she discovered she and Micah were to share one of the cottages. He had not consulted her—that was the first thing that got under her skin—nor did she like him taking her for granted. She resented his assumption that she would share the coziness of just the two of them in the small house. It was one thing for him to deposit her at Chepo; she had agreed to that with Benton before she had met Micah, but this was entirely different. And, she told herself, she had no coy illusions about the morality of the situation. Simply stated, she wanted to be asked!

She was agitated. "You have your nerve," she told him after he dumped her luggage in the living room.

Micah expelled a heavy sigh. "Be practical. You could hardly room with Benton or Max and I didn't want you to impose on Helen and Jinks. We have separate bedrooms—that should suit your proprieties."

"There's no lock on the door," she answered after making a quick inspection.

"Is that so?" he said, amused, as though he were dealing with a recalcitrant child. Gabrielle fumed and stood in the middle of the room while he separated their luggage and carried hers into one of the bedrooms. He was back in less than a minute, made a quick inspection of the tiny kitchenette, then telephoned for ice, soft drinks, beer, and a few other items he thought essential. When he hung up, he gazed at Gabrielle for a reflective moment. "Loosen up," he said softly. "You know I want you, I've made no bones about that, but if you say no, it's no. I have never forced myself on a woman and I'm not about to start with you.''

Gabrielle was beginning to feel foolish in the wake of Micah's declaration. The problem, she admitted to herself, was that she didn't want to say no. Micah walked past her, went to the door, looked out over the golden beach with the waves lapping at the sand. ''Why don't you get into your swimsuit and let's both take advantage of this beautiful weather. I'll be back in a minute.'' Gabrielle shrugged wordlessly and watched him until he disappeared around the corner of the cottage.

Standing on the porch in the flower-scented air, shaded from the sun, she felt the tension begin to ease. Toboga was beautiful. It measured up to every travel poster she had ever seen of a tropical island: sun, sand, swaying palms, sloops and sailboats moored offshore, the water taxis plying back and forth among the small jetties. *Stop behaving like a harridan,* she told herself with a twinge of conscience. Wasn't everything going her way? Didn't she have a good job to see her through the spring until she could begin dancing again? And wasn't she fortunate to be here at this very minute? Benton had mentioned that the States was gearing up for the worst winter of the century and here she, Gabrielle Hensley, was, recuperating on a tropical island and getting paid for it to boot. Now that she had worked out this understanding with herself, Gabrielle felt marvelous; the happy feeling she had felt earlier returned and she began to anticipate the effect her swimsuit would have on Micah.

The swimwear she had brought with her was a simple, straight piece of lined peach-colored fabric with a drawstring at each end. The shorter length of string locked the suit top around her neck. The silk then draped her front and curved up between her legs to lift over her rear and was held there by the other drawstring looped around her waist. The suit had no back and no sides and now that she had it on, Gabrielle thought it might just be entirely too daring. Impossible, she decided; after all they *were* on a tropical island.

She scooped up a bottle of Shade, her sunglasses, and a

towel from the bath. Each of the cottages had a thatched-roof porch and she stood barefoot on the warm boards and looked up and down the beach. Several other swimmers were in the surf and on the sparkling white sands. Helen came out of the cottage next to hers and waved.

"Come on, let's go find us a good spot," she called to Gabrielle. They were just a few yards along the beach when guttural shrieks sounded from Helen's cottage. Helen took Gabrielle's arm and pushed her rapidly across the warm sand.

"What's that?" she asked, sure that someone was in pain or being attacked.

"Ignore it," Helen ordered in a curt voice.

"I can't," Gabrielle said, turning to go up to the cottage.

Helen caught her arm. "It's just Benton. Jinks is giving him some antibiotics. He had a lung infection and won't take his medicine."

"God! It sounds like Jinks is killing him."

Helen snickered. "He's not. Micah's holding him down. Benton is scared to death of needles." Gabrielle sympathized silently, recalling her bruised hips from all the injections she had to take when she had been in the hospital.

Micah emerged from the cottage, Jinks right behind him, walking fast on his chubby legs. A bamboo chair came flying out the door, missing them both by inches. It landed with a soft thud in the sand. Micah and Jinks grinned at each other.

"You're mean," Gabrielle told Micah as he neared her, but Micah didn't seem to hear the accusation. His eyes traveled slowly over Gabrielle.

"What happens to that when it gets wet?" he asked, slipping a finger under her suit at her neck.

Gabrielle smiled, feigning insouciance, then said, "It clings."

"Don't go near the water," he ordered, "until I get back." He left on a run to their cottage.

Jinks laughed and eyed Helen's diminutive frame inside her one-piece suit. "What happens to yours when it gets wet?" he asked, not to be outdone by Micah.

"Nothing you can do anything about," she countered dryly.

"In that case, I'm going into the village," he announced, a pained expression on his face.

GABRIELLE sat in the shallow surf, letting the warm waves wash over her legs to lap at her thighs. Helen sat next to her, while Micah reclined on the sand nearby, a towel over his shoulders to protect his scars from the tropical sun.

The three of them had spent more than two hours snorkeling and exploring a sandbar that connected Toboga to El Morro, an island about one hundred yards offshore. They had frolicked in the water like seals, and Micah had behaved with an ordinate innocence so that Gabrielle suspected it was a ploy to lower her guard. If he only knew, she thought, how exhilarated she felt by just being near him.

"This is grand," Helen said lazily, "but if I'm going to last into the wee hours of the new year, I'd better go take a nap." She turned to Micah. "How are we getting over to Wu's? *Panga* or by foot?"

"We'll walk," he told her absentmindedly while watching Gabrielle pin up her sea-damp curls without benefit of a mirror. The effect was stunning. He thought, *She's everything a man could want or ask for in a woman.* She was beautiful, but it went deeper than that. There was an honesty about Gabrielle that wasn't abrasive. She had spirit and intelligence. He liked those qualities in a woman. He liked Gabrielle. And the thought made him apprehensive. Did she like him? He determined to have the answer.

Helen was smiling, following his gaze. "See you two later," she said, picking up her beach bag. Neither Gabrielle nor Micah paid her any attention. Both were aware that in less than a minute they would be alone on the deserted beach, separated by a few scant yards of damp yellow sand.

Gabrielle turned onto her stomach in the shallow water and propped her chin in her hands. Her gaze wandered over the line of cottages set picturesquely in lush greenery. The green appeared more vibrant, the pink and purple hibiscus more vivid, and their scent, entwined with that of the jasmine, was intoxicating. Lazy waves with crystal foam twirled around her breasts, caressed her thighs, and met the incoming surf at the back of her knees. It was a warm, sensuous feeling—a feeling she welcomed, enjoyed. *Just go with it,* she told herself, recalling Micah's words to loosen up, *and don't worry about what happens next.* Her gaze left the line of cottages and fell on Micah. She watched him watching her. His swimsuit was as revealing as her own and she had difficulty keeping her eyes above his waist. She wanted him, and she couldn't think beyond that.

He dropped the towel from his shoulders and joined her at the water's edge, building a little mound of damp sand to pillow his head. "Having a good time?" he asked, stretching out on his back beside her.

"Yes, it's marvelous. The island is lovely."

"So are you," he said, his voice husky. Gabrielle's heart began to thud against her ribs, pounding all the air from her lungs. Micah's hand slid through the inch of water, found the opening at the side of her swimsuit, and cupped her breast. His thumb brushed over her nipple until it began to swell as desire mounted in Gabrielle causing an electrifying ache that demanded attention, stabbing little jolts of want that demanded surfeit.

"Don't you think you've taunted me enough?" he said, his voice low and caught with urgent longing. Gabrielle's throat constricted, making it impossible for her to answer. Her face said all he wanted to know. In the next instant Micah was scooping her up in his arms, carrying her to their cottage. Gabrielle clung to him, her arms tight around his neck. Micah's steps faltered as he approached the porch, then stopped altogether. He looked beyond Gabrielle's head. Gabrielle didn't understand what was happening; she turned her head to follow his gaze. Vanessa Thomas stood on the porch. *Their* porch, hers and Micah's. Micah let Gabrielle's feet slide slowly to the floor.

"What are you doing here, Vanessa?" he asked in a brusque tone, feeling his heart plummet into some stony crevasse he hadn't known existed until this very minute.

"You invited me," she answered, smiling at Micah in one instant and giving Gabrielle a venomous glance in the next.

"I did what?" Micah said, disbelief warring with the anger in his voice. He was mortified. Vanessa was lying. She made a habit of it—"Never tell the truth when a lie would do" was her motto. Up until this precise moment he had always had a special place in his heart for Vanessa, his first love. Because he could no longer be hurt by her, he had tolerated her, overlooked much of her behavior. Right now he regretted that tolerance more than any single thing in his life.

"Yes, darling, don't you remember? When you were in the hospital, you invited me to Wu's and the New Year's celebration. We were too busy," she said coyly, "to discuss it when I was in Houston, but you did mean this year, didn't you?" Vanessa smiled deprecatingly, as though she was forgiving him for being so tactless to forget their date, and turned her attention to Gabrielle. "Who have we here, darling? Someone to take the edge off?"

Gabrielle gasped. There was no mistaking the vulgar innuendo in Vanessa's tone. She glared at Vanessa, then Micah, and the look she bestowed on him chilled Micah to the bone.

"Vanessa Thomas, Gabrielle Hensley," he said stiffly.

"Ah, yes, the lame ballerina," Vanessa said, her malignant-filled smile illuminating the naked hatred spewing from her eyes. Gabrielle recoiled, but recovered instantly and pushed past Vanessa into the cottage, her mind a whirlwind of mixed emotions and anger.

Lame ballerina! Micah had discussed her with Vanessa. How could he? And yet, when she had questioned him about Vanessa, he had told her to mind her own business. Good! Gabrielle decided she didn't want Vanessa to be her business, and neither would Gabrielle be Micah's.

While she showered, washing away the golden sand and salt water, Gabrielle was first angry, then indifferent. When she emerged from the stinging spray, she heard the murmur of angry voices coming from the other room. She lay on the bed listening, not hearing the words, just the voices, and she began to get mad, until her own anger was utterly absolute, leaving her with an ice-cold calm.

She would fight Vanessa, not because of Micah, but because she was Gabrielle. Vanessa might be Micah's date for this evening, but it wouldn't matter—he would have eyes only for Gabrielle. And, Gabrielle decided, she would not go near Micah all evening. Intuition told her she could torment Micah. Vanessa could sit there and watch, helpless, because Vanessa had no control over Gabrielle. None at all.

She got off the bed and moved a chair under the doorknob. There would be no interruptions, no angry words with Micah—not yet. Gabrielle laid out the pleated silk culottes and the devastating, alluring tunic. Then she began to create her arsenal, creaming her body with Chloé, touching her pulse spots with 20 Carats, not forgetting her ankles nor the backs of her knees. A thought came to her, so she put on her short terry robe, removed the chair, and glided through the living room, ignoring the two sitting on the sofa. Their immediate silence as two pairs of eyes followed her was deafening.

Gabrielle went outside and plucked a vine of blooming jasmine, stopped in the small kitchenette for a soft drink, and reentered her room. She replaced the chair. She gave herself a pedicure, then a manicure, and rested while her nails dried. Then she began to apply her makeup, skillfully using bases, blushes, both liquid and powder, to enhance the delicate structure of her features. She took particular care with her eyes, redoing them several times until just by lowering her lashes she could go from a look of innocence to one of mystery and promise. She worked on her lips, outlining them, shaping them, coloring them, until they were ripe and full. She practiced a slight moue. She wasn't disappointed with the effect.

Only her curls seemed to rebel at her determination, but she brushed them until they behaved and lay low on her neck; she plaited the vine and wove the jasmine around the soft chignon. The fragrant blooms were her only adornment.

Micah rapped on the door and rattled the knob. "Gabrielle, I want to talk to you." He sounded frustrated and angry. *Too bad.*

Gabrielle inhaled and called casually, "I'm getting dressed, Micah. Can't it wait?" He muttered something she didn't understand and after a few minutes Gabrielle heard the shower running in his room. She finished dressing quickly, circling the tunic with the copper belt at her waist, and scooped up her slim-heeled sandals. She would have to carry them until she was outside Wu's; the quarter-mile walk on the footpaths in heels was still too much for her leg.

Vanessa wasn't in the living room and Gabrielle noticed something she hadn't seen earlier—Vanessa's luggage piled next to Micah's bedroom door. Her composure slipped, but she recovered immediately. She would not stay in this cottage with Micah and Vanessa. She would ask Helen if she could stay the night in the cottage next door. Hopefully Helen would understand without asking too many prying questions. There was a rap at the front door. Gabrielle answered it. Max stood there and stared.

"My God," he muttered under his breath. Gabrielle gave him a brilliant smile.

"Max, I'm glad you're here. Will you walk me over to Wu's? Micah's still dressing and I promised to be there early to hold our table."

"Sure," he said, behaving as though he could not believe his good fortune. Gabrielle tucked her arm through his. They had walked only a few yards when he stopped abruptly.

"Er, Miss Hensley—Gabrielle," he almost stammered, his demeanor anything but cocky, "you're sure this is okay? I mean, the minute I stepped into the house at Chepo, the boss made it clear...you know, you're off limits. I mean" —his voice got stronger— "you got Davidson stamped all over you."

Gabrielle started to make an angry retort, but stopped herself. It wasn't Max's fault, nor hers either. Instead, she said evenly, "I don't belong to Micah Davidson. You must have misunderstood. He was probably just being protective because he used to be a student of my father's."

"Oh." He seemed unconvinced. "Look," he explained, "I like my job, and there's a hundred other guys out there waiting for me to slip up. And the boss—well, if he caught me fooling with his woman, he'd tear me into pieces so tiny you couldn't use 'em for postage stamps."

Gabrielle laughed at Max's fears. "Max," she said with just the right amount of empathy in her voice, "Vanessa Thomas is here at Micah's invitation. She's his woman, not me. That's why I had to leave the cottage early," she said, lowering her voice. "They wanted some privacy. So you don't have to worry. I mean nothing to Micah, not *that* way."

Max looked at her with more assurance, but voiced another doubt, pushing for certainty. "I've heard of the Thomas woman, but I got the impression that the boss doesn't like her too well."

"Oh?" Now it was Gabrielle's turn to grasp at straws. "What makes you say that?"

"It was something Father Chardin said. He mentioned that he had to give her a lift from Chepo to Tocumen Airport. He said Micah ran her off. He also said her tongue was so vile he thought she was a direct descendant of the original serpent. That's why I remember. Father Chardin doesn't usually have a whole lot to say, not about women."

"Vanessa was at Chepo? When? Do you remember?"

"I sure do." Max grimaced. "It was the day the chopper went down."

"Oh, Max," Gabrielle said airily, "that was months ago. She visited him in the hospital and was his guest for several days in Houston before we sailed. Does that sound like he doesn't like her?"

"I guess not," he agreed, tucking her arm in his once again. "You want me to carry your shoes?" he asked, smiling.

CHINESE lanterns hanging from ceiling beams cast multicolored glows in the dark-paneled clubhouse that jutted over the edge of the island. A mariachi band was in full swing and couples spilled from the dance floor onto the deck outside; they seemed more interested in the silvery path cast by the full moon than the music and gaiety inside. Gabrielle felt a twinge of melancholy. She realized she had been looking forward to this evening, had anticipated spending it with Micah—face the truth, she told herself—in his arms. She tried to dispel the feeling as Max guided her to a table set for twelve.

Benton was already there, picking at a plate piled high with food. He greeted Gabrielle and Max, seeming unconcerned that the others hadn't arrived. "You better hit the buffet," he told them. "Old man Wu has already replenished it twice. This crowd is inhaling the stuff."

Gabrielle followed Benton's suggestion and found a place in line. The buffet stretched across an entire wall, beckoning the revelers to help themselves from mounds of pink shrimp and delicately seasoned chicken—at least Gabrielle hoped it was chicken and not iguana. She passed it up. Wooden bowls of *seviche,* raw fish cooked in lime and bitter orange, sat next to great platters of golden-brown *empanadas,* tiny fried meat pies. Golden papayas, mangoes, and melons hugged the foot of the towering centerpiece: island-grown pineapples cleverly strung together to resemble graceful palms. There were so many cheeses and salads, Gabrielle held up the line behind her trying to decide which to choose. Impatient and hungry, the guests finally worked around her. She filled two plates.

"You hungry?" Benton teased when she returned to the table. He bent his head to her ear. "I know you know this already, Gabby, but you look ravishing tonight."

"Thank you," she said demurely. "Are you flirting with me, Benton?"

"And ruin a good friendship? I should say not," he wheezed. "I just thought you might need a little moral support since Vanessa crashed the party."

Gabrielle's fork stopped in midair. Were her feelings for Micah that obvious? How could they be? She didn't even know what they were herself. But Benton's declaration of friendship and subtle suggestion that he was an ally revived her spirits and blunted her melancholy. She entered into the gaiety of celebration as the empty seats around the table began to fill. Seeing the new year in on a tropical island, she told herself, would be an experience to remember. She thought about some resolutions and decided she had only one—rejoin the ballet company as a prima ballerina. She decided against making any resolutions that included Micah.

A half an hour later only two places remained empty at the table. Those of Micah and Vanessa. Jinks, Helen, the two army doctors and their wives, and J.T. chatted and joked among themselves. No one seemed to notice the absence of Micah except Gabrielle, and against her will she was becoming a mass of tangled nerves.

Her eyes swept the room occasionally, watching, but she would have missed Micah's entrance altogether if it hadn't been for Max. He stopped talking to her in midsentence and raised his eyes as someone approached. He seemed to stiffen and the smile slid off his face. Gabrielle turned and saw Micah threading his way through the crowd. She couldn't miss him; he towered over almost every man in his path. He didn't look happy. Vanessa clung to his arm and she didn't look happy either. In a way Gabrielle couldn't blame Vanessa for wanting Micah. He was dressed tonight like most of the other men—silk beige slacks and the pleated *guayavera* shirt worn over the hips—yet he was far more elegant, far more attractive than those around him.

Vanessa's gown was tight across her hips and the décolletage on her too-red dress spilled its contents, leaving nothing to the imagination. Vanessa had applied her makeup with a clumsy hand, Gabrielle noted; not only was there too much of it, but her lipstick ran out at the corners. Tsk, tsk, Gabrielle thought with the glee a woman can't help feeling when she knows her adversary is at a disadvantage.

Micah's eyes met Gabrielle's and held as he neared the table. His mouth was grim. Gabrielle smiled.

"I hope you don't mind," she said, just loud enough for her voice to carry over the clamor around them, "I asked Max to walk me over. You were busy in your room. I didn't think I should disturb you—or wait." She let her glance slide disdainfully to Vanessa.

"Did I hear my name?" Max injected, pretending that

he hadn't heard every word Gabrielle said. She gave him a dazzling smile.

"I was just letting Micah know you got me here safe and sound." She leaned provocatively close and whispered to Max, "They look like they've had a lovers' quarrel. Let's you and I dance." She stood up and put out her hand so that there was no way Max could refuse without being rude. He got to his feet.

"That's a mambo. Can you do it?" he asked, carefully avoiding looking at Micah.

"You'll have to show me the steps." Gabrielle laughed. She wondered if her voice sounded as hollow to the others as it did to her. Max demonstrated the simple steps.

"It's all in the knees," he said, undulating his hips suggestively. "Keep your shoulders straight."

"You mean like this?" Gabrielle asked, miming his moves precisely. Max watched with blatant approval. "Exactly!" he said and pulled her to him. Gabrielle glanced surreptitiously at Micah over Max's shoulder. His eyes were fastened on her, watchful, his face impassive, yet saying much by revealing nothing.

Suddenly Gabrielle knew she had to halt the secret game she was playing or Max would become an innocent victim, and she didn't want to be responsible for Max losing his job. Benton had mentioned that it had been Max's skill as a pilot that had saved both his and Micah's lives. She could have gladly clawed Vanessa's eyes out and she wanted to hurt Micah as she felt hurt, but it was unfair to use Max as an unwitting pawn. Without seeming to, she disengaged herself from Max's arms and danced more circumspectly. When the mambo ended, she pleaded thirst and sent Max to the bar for a glass of champagne. While he was gone, she asked Benton to exchange places with her so that she sat safely between him and Helen. Micah watched and so did Vanessa. From the look on Vanessa's face Gabrielle was sure Vanessa thought it was just a ploy Gabrielle was using to get closer to Micah. Micah had no such illusions, but the harsh line around his mouth relaxed and after that Gabrielle carefully avoided looking at either of them the rest of the evening.

The mariachi band retired, replaced on the low stage by a group whose specialty was old and familiar American nostalgia tunes, like "Stardust," "Sentimental Journey," and "Smoke Gets in Your Eyes." Homesick and expatriated American couples jammed the dance floor. Gabrielle declined all invitations. Micah didn't leave his chair, although over the voices nearest her Gabrielle could hear Vanessa pleading with him to dance. Vanessa was as miserable as she was. The thought gave Gabrielle little satisfaction.

The bandleader announced the last dance before midnight and couples began moving to the dance floor in waves. Helen and Jinks were the first to leave their table, then the doctors and their wives. Gabrielle panicked. Soon there would be no one sitting between her and Micah. She grabbed Benton's hand.

"Come on, you promised me one dance, Benton. This is it."

"I did?" he said, surprised.

"Benton!" she ground out insistently. He looked at her face, saw her look of desperation, and stood up.

Aloud, he said, "Okay, if it means that much to you, but I can't dance." As soon as they were out of earshot of Micah and Vanessa, he asked, "What's going on?"

"Nothing. I just want to dance the last dance."

"Sure could've fooled me," he mumbled. Gabrielle realized Benton had told the truth. He couldn't dance and she had to lead them to the outer edge of the writhing mass of bodies and out on deck to keep from being crushed, elbowed, and stepped on. Micah materialized behind Benton.

"I'm cutting in," he said tersely.

"My pleasure," Benton returned, relieved, and handed Gabrielle over to Micah with an apologetic smile. "Told you I couldn't dance."

Feigning a resigned air, Gabrielle let Micah take her in his arms. He was a skillful dancer and too late she realized his intentions. He maneuvered her off the deck onto the nearly deserted pier. Only one other couple was there and they seemed to be inspecting the *pangas* tied up bow to stern on either side. Micah spoke first, his voice quiet.

"I just wanted to wish you a happy new year."

"Thank you, same to you," she replied, trying to inject some warmth into her tone. She failed disastrously. Neither of them tried to speak above the roar that came from inside the clubhouse when the bandleader began the ten-second countdown to midnight. The crowd chanted the seconds away. Micah held Gabrielle lightly, looking down at her, until noisy pandemonium told them both the new year had arrived. The band struck up "Auld Lang Syne" and for all the noise, the song was poignant as hundreds of voices carried the tune across the island.

Without warning, Micah kissed her. When she didn't respond, his kiss became savage, his tongue darting and hard, trying to provoke the response he wanted. Gabrielle forced herself to remain aloof, warring against the strident sensual signal that winged along every nerve in her body. Micah withdrew his lips, but kept her pressed against his body, forcing her awareness of his hard, physical need. As if she could ignore it, she thought.

"I thought we'd better have that talk," he murmured.

"I'm not interested in your sex life," she told him.

He laughed, a bitter sound. "I hardly have one, do I? You keep saying no."

"I'm not interested in being part of a ménage à trois." She backed out of his arms and gave him a sweet, yet icy, smile. "What do you need me for? Vanessa gives the impression that *she* says yes. And there's another thing, I don't appreciate you discussing me with her. I am not any of her business."

Micah clenched and unclenched his fists. Gabrielle watched them tighten, pulling skin taut over knuckles. She wondered where his leather brace was. He hadn't worn it all day.

"I haven't discussed you with Vanessa. She spent a week at the Galleria. She could have heard about your leg from Benton, Helen, or Jinks, or read about it in the paper. You made the gossip columns, as I recall, the night you attended the ballet with your friend Val."

Gabrielle forced another smile. "That's true," she conceded. "I guess that takes care of everything but the sex."

"Vanessa doesn't interest me," he said, grinding out the words like a proclamation.

"Since when? Last September at Chepo? Or when you were in the hospital? Or maybe since that week in Houston you just spoke of?" Gabrielle paused for effect. "Or did you lose interest last week when she met the *Upsure* in Colon, or hasn't she interested you since maybe fifteen minutes ago? Vanessa's on red alert, Micah. A woman doesn't get that way over a casual acquaintance or a ten-year-old broken engagement. You've been sleeping with her. It shows."

A deceptive calm came over Micah's face, betrayed only by the pulse pounding in his temple. Gabrielle waited for him to deny his affair with Vanessa. He didn't, and her mind throbbed with the pain of his silence.

"I want to go back to the cottage now and get my things. I can move in with Helen and Jinks."

"No," he said softly, "the party will be breaking up soon. We'll all go together. You stay in the cottage with me. I won't touch you," he said bluntly.

What kind of twisted honor was he falling back on at this late date? Gabrielle wondered. "I didn't expect that you would, with Vanessa so readily available. I just don't want to be under the same roof with the both of you."

"You won't. She's staying at the Hotel Toboga."

"How inconvenient for you."

"You're treading deep water, Gabrielle. Stop while you're ahead," he warned. His words were meaningless to her. She felt like she had already drowned, felt ther ache tug at her throat, and knew she no longer had to ask the reason why.

Chapter Fifteen

Gabrielle stepped onto the porch. The weather was perfect. A stormy, overcast day would have matched her mood rather than the picturesque scene that lay before her. Blue-green water lapped gently against the sand, driven by a warm zephyr that whipped her skirt around her knees.

The island seemed deserted, probably because everyone was sleeping off the effects of the seemingly endless flow of liquor they had consumed the night before. Micah, though, wasn't in his room. She had looked. He was undoubtedly with Vanessa. Gabrielle wanted to believe he wasn't interested in Vanessa, but everything so far said otherwise. Now she had to contend with an ache that went far deeper than the surface, an ache that stretched beyond sexuality, an ache that left a gaping hole where her heart used to be.

"Hey, Gabby," Helen called from her cottage, "want to walk to the village with me? I need coffee."

"Me too." Gabrielle smiled and went to get her purse.

"The men left hours ago to go deep-sea fishing," Helen told her as they met on the footpath. Gabrielle felt a twinge of guilt for her earlier thoughts of Micah's whereabouts. "We have the day to ourselves," Helen continued. "Let's have coffee first, shop a while, and then eat brunch at the hotel."

Gabrielle agreed and the two of them spent a leisurely morning. Gabrielle bought and wrote postcards to her parents and Val. She posted them in the tiny island mail station and was assured the cards would get a Toboga cancellation. That done, she and Helen wandered over to Wu's for brunch. Many of the other island visitors had the same idea, and the hotel dining room was full.

"Oh, look! There's Benton." Helen pointed to a table by the windows that faced Panama Bay. "Let's join him," she said.

Benton looked up at them as they sat down, his eyes bleary and heavy lidded behind his glasses.

"Why didn't you go fishing?" Helen asked and at the same time signaled a waiter.

"Whoever heard of getting up at the ungodly hour of five A.M. on New Year's Day?"

"You sound better today," Helen said, eyeing Benton closely.

"I feel lousy," he informed her.

Helen laughed, Benton winced. "Yes, well, that's from spirits of the bottle, not the body," she told him.

After breakfast Helen and Gabrielle persuaded Benton to return to the cottages with them and spend some time sunbathing on the beach. They took a *panga* back to the other side of the island, since Benton insisted his legs were too rubbery for the walk.

Gabrielle and Helen snorkeled and swam while Benton waded in the surf, his pants rolled above his knees. Gabrielle paddled over to him in the shallow water.

"Why don't you put on your swimsuit and come in the water, Benton?" she encouraged, smiling. "Can't you swim?"

"I can swim a little, but one drop of salt water in my lungs would be all the excuse Jinks need to start poking me again. He's a sadist with his needles, you know," Benton said seriously.

"Oh," Gabrielle said, letting her mouth go under the water to hide her smile. Later, while Helen beachcombed for shells, she and Benton lounged in the shade on the front porch of her cottage.

"Will you tell me something?" Gabrielle asked, watching him out of the corner of her eye.

"If I can," he said lazily. "What?"

"Is Vanessa still on the island?"

"No."

The single word was a balm to Gabrielle and she felt the cavity where her heart should be begin to fill and crowd her chest. Perhaps Micah hadn't lied to her after all. Another question preyed on her mind and she asked it too.

"Micah and Vanessa—why didn't they get married?"

Benton grimaced. "You're spoiling my day, you know, not that it started out all that good. I'm not a fan of Vanessa's."

"Why not?"

"She's spiteful, malicious, spoiled, to start with. Her father raised her by himself and he didn't do a very good job. Vanessa thinks that she should have what she wants, when she wants it, regardless of those around her."

No worse than Micah, Gabrielle thought. "It sounds to me like she and Micah were made for each other."

Benton laughed and choked back a wheeze. "Well, not quite," he said, and then surprised himself by adding, "Micah has a few saving graces, although they're not always visible, but Vanessa caught him off guard, I guess, because he sure didn't see through her. They say love is blind, and I'd say ten years ago Micah could have used a pair of glasses twice as strong as mine. You sure you want to hear this?"

"I'm sure," Gabrielle said adamantly.

"Well, Micah and Vanessa had been engaged about three months by the night of the rehearsal dinner. I was hosting that since Micah's parents were dead, and it was the first time I met Vanessa. By that time Micah had known her for about three years, but I had been sick and stayed on Micah's farm during the years he worked for Vanessa's father.

"In the few days between the rehearsal dinner and the wedding Micah was asked to run for mayor of Atlanta. He said he'd think about it. Vanessa was thrilled. She saw herself as the darling of society and pressured Micah to accept. Micah decided he wasn't a political animal and refused the invitation. Vanessa was furious. She told him if he didn't run for mayor she wouldn't marry him. Micah put her attitude down to nerves, but Vanessa was serious, and she didn't show up at the church. Well, she did, but more than forty-five minutes late—by that time Micah and I were on our way back to south Georgia. We stayed on the farm a while, then came to Panama. End of love story."

"You mean that's all?" Gabrielle said, incredulous. "Vanessa refused to marry Micah simply because he wouldn't run for mayor?"

"It was enough for her, but I think at the last minute she realized she was cutting off her nose to spite her face. Micah waited at the church—we all did—for thirty minutes. He called Vanessa and she reiterated her terms. Either he run for mayor or no marriage. She underestimated Micah and she certainly overestimated the power she thought she had over him. We left. The gossip columnists had a field day. We read that Vanessa said her limousine had been involved in a minor accident on the way to the church, and that was why she was late. It wasn't true, of course, but there were over five hundred people packed in pews and she said the first thing that came into her mind. She regretted it later, because then the newspapers had it that Micah left her at the altar, not the other way around. A few months later she married the loan officer in her father's bank."

Gabrielle started. "Vanessa is married?"

Benton snorted. "Vanessa's hobby is getting married, but between them she turns up on Micah's doorstep."

"Oh," Gabrielle said thoughtfully. "He seems to tolerate her well enough."

"You're wrong about that," Benton said firmly.

"I am?" Gabrielle felt exhilaration sweeping up her spine. She should have believed Micah. She owed him an apology about Vanessa—nothing more, she amended.

"Yes," Benton concluded. "He's punishing her."

Gabrielle changed her mind about the apology.

THAT night there was a fish fry on the beach. Wu lent a cook from the hotel kitchen and with the help of several island women, he cooked and served the fish the men had caught that day.

The evening was cool, millions of stars twinkled and glowed in a clear night sky, and a full pumpkin-colored moon provided them with light to eat by. There were a half-dozen strangers, Americans that Jinks and Micah invited that had been on the fishing boat with them. Everyone was gay, the food superb, and Gabrielle was happy. Micah was friendly toward her in a reserved sort of way, but spent most of his time with the men, recounting their fishing exploits. When the party finally broke up long after midnight, Micah sat on the porch, smoking a cigar. Gabrielle passed him with a casual good-night. When she was putting the chair under the doorknob, it slipped out of her hands and crashed to the floor.

Micah called through the cottage, "Forget about the chair, Gabrielle. You won't need it." She replaced the chair against the wall and couldn't decide if she was disappointed or not.

It seemed to Gabrielle that she had just fallen asleep when Micah stuck his head in her room. "You awake?"

"I am now," she said, wishing it weren't so.

"You want to see some jungle?" he asked pleasantly and stepped farther into the room. Gabrielle opened her eyes. The sun was shining through the blinds.

"On the island?"

"No. Near Coco Solito. We've got a problem and we have to get back to camp. Do you want to go?"

Gabrielle considered the invitation a minute. "Why are you being so nice to me? I'm not sick."

He grinned. "Maybe I'm trying to woo you."

"Phooey," she said, sounding every bit like her mother.

"Can you be ready to go in fifteen minutes? That will give us time to have breakfast at Wu's before the launch leaves for Balboa."

"Yes. But I didn't bring any heavy-duty clothes with me. Are we stopping at Chepo?"

"No, again," he said. "You can borrow some from Helen. Fifteen minutes," he said, closing the door.

"Wait!" she called after him. He poked his head back through the door. .

"Do you want a good-morning kiss?" he asked with mock lechery.

"No, I do not. I just remembered today is Sunday. I was wondering if I can listen to the radio to see if my lottery tickets won."

"Christ!" he said and slammed the door. Gabrielle shrugged. Sure didn't take much to get him back to normal, she thought.

Listening to the men talk at breakfast, Gabrielle learned

why their holiday on Toboga had to be cut short. More than a month ago a census taker had gone down the Bayano River to count heads in the Indian villages along the river. On his way back in the height of the dry season, the Bayano had fallen to a trickle of what it had been a month ago. The government official had tired of trying to push his *piranga* through the gelatinous mud and had taken off across the jungle. By chance he passed through sector eighteen, where trees had been pegged and numbered for cutting. He discovered the five-acre tract to be overrun with sloths.

The arboreal mammals were a protected species. The census taker had informed the Ministry of Interior and now that official was in Coco Solito. No trees could be topped out and cut until every sloth had been tagged and moved. Fourteen of the animals had been spotted in the section, an exceedingly high number for so small an area in the jungle. If the Interior official found that the area was a breeding and mating habitat, he might not allow the section to be cut at all.

J.T. didn't relish sending his men up into the trees to get the sloths. It was dangerous. The animals clung to anything that got in their path with the tenacity of a steel vise. And they often hung for months on a single branch, moving only inches a week to feed on leaves and new shoots as they sprouted through the bark.

Besides that, the sloths were hosts to dozens of bugs and parasites that made their home generation after generation in the wiry strawlike fur. All in all it promised to be a nasty job. Gabrielle thought it sounded exciting and forgot entirely about her lottery tickets.

They had no more than arrived in Coco Solito when Jinks had an emergency. One of the natives had been clearing heavy brush from around his hut when his machete slipped. He had a nasty cut across the top of his instep. Micah and J.T. disappeared into the Quonset hut that served as operation headquarters. Gabrielle followed Helen through the clinic where Jinks took his patient. Behind the spacious room were living quarters, and Helen led her to a small bedroom. She lent Gabrielle a set of well-washed khakis—two sizes too big in the waist—a long-sleeved undershirt, and a pair of boots. Gabrielle had to wear two pairs of socks and lace the boots tightly to keep them on her feet.

After she had changed, she wandered back toward the front of the house and stood outside the clinic door watching Helen and Jinks, an interested spectator.

The native was stoic about his injury, but his wife and children were wailing and causing confusion. Helen coaxed them outside, while Jinks prepared his patient. Gabrielle noticed Jinks was no longer the recalcitrant husband wanting to be babied, but an efficient and skilled physician. Helen deferred to him respectfully as he issued quiet instructions.

Benton had not come with them to Coco Solito. When the launch had landed in Balboa, he had gone on to Panama City. He avoided the heavy, breathless humidity in the jungle camp as much as business would allow. Gabrielle wished this time, though, that he had come with them. She would have enjoyed his company; at least, she wouldn't feel so left out. Everyone was busy and had no time for her. She thought about knocking on the door to the Quonset hut, but changed her mind and sighed. She might as well look around the village. It was too small for her to get lost in, and Micah could find her easily. He had said he wanted her to go with him when he inspected sector eighteen—wherever that was.

Coco Solito was filled with houses built on stilts that held the small wooden shelters several feet above ground. Thatched-roof huts were bunched together in an orderly group, while pigs, dogs, and naked children cluttered the packed-earth street. The men, having the day off, lounged about the logging camp in small groups, while their wives were busy around cook fires. Several young girls were bunched around an old-fashioned hand pump. They smiled shyly at Gabrielle as she passed them.

A woman dressed in splashy colors came around a corner of one of the houses balancing a basket on her head. It was filled to the brim with monkey plums harvested from a tree not far from the village. Later Gabrielle learned she would put them into small paper sacks and take them into Panama City to sell, joining other street vendors that crowded the sidewalks.

Separated from the village was a group of tin barns filled with heavy equipment. Some of it was enormous; it was used to haul and stack cut timber at the river's edge. When the river rose during the rainy season, it would lift the log rafts and carry them into the bay to be hoisted aboard barges that would take them to the *Upsure*. To Gabrielle it seemed like too much work, but then she recalled the contracts she had translated. A single log of mahogany could bring as much as two thousand dollars. If this project was successful, Micah was going to be far richer at the end of the rainy season than he was today.

Mules and horses were corralled and sheltered opposite the huge tin barns. Gabrielle leaned on the rough wood rails, watching a small colt try to nurse its mother. The mare nipped at her offspring.

"Shame on you," Gabrielle said to the mare, laughing at the colt's unsuccessful antics.

"I wondered where you had wandered off to," Micah said, walking up behind her.

Gabrielle turned and smiled. "Jinks and Helen are busy with a patient. I've just been looking around the village." Micah had changed into the inevitable khakis, and Gabrielle wished he wasn't so damned good-looking.

"Don't wander beyond the clearing—ever," Micah warned. "It looks peaceful enough, but this is just a small patch of civilization and that's still dangerous jungle out there." He pulled her away from the corral and looked her up and down, then smiled at the gathers at her waist. "I see Helen found you some clothes, fit okay?"

"I'll manage," Gabrielle said stiffly, slightly embarrassed at how she looked in the ill-fitting garments.

"I know you will," Micah said, observing the tilt of her chin. "I'm just teasing. You can take it, can't you?"

"I can handle anything you dish out, Micah Davidson," she retorted. "Is that why you brought me here? To make a pest of yourself?"

"You don't think much of me, do you?" he said, leaning nonchalantly against the fence.

Gabrielle smiled. "You're so perceptive, it's no wonder you own all of this," she said, making a large sweeping motion with her hand. Suddenly Gabrielle found herself wrapped in his arms, steel bands locking her tight. She didn't struggle.

"Is this what turns you on? Forcing me?"

"Forcing you! I don't force you. You want me, for all your denials," he said. "And I want you. What's there to force?"

"You've got me mixed up with Vanessa, haven't you?" she asked, feeling his arms loosen somewhat. She backed away and looked at him. His eyes narrowed to slits, his smile derisive.

"You're the one with Vanessa on the brain. Why do you keep throwing up these barricades? I'm a patient man, but not that patient."

Gabrielle ignored the blood pounding through her veins, the trembling his nearness caused. She was annoyed because he always seemed to be picking on her, tearing at her, and she never seemed to have time to recover so she could think things out.

"It'll be a cold day in hell before I come crawling in bed with you! Try that on for patience!" she told him, furious.

Micah sighed heavily, then took possession of her, destroying her cool control with his lips. Gabrielle's senses reeled under the pressure of desire that welled up in her. His lips hungrily drained her of all resistance and she returned his kisses driven by a hunger that matched his own. Micah broke off the kiss and murmured, "How's that for snow in this hellhole?"

"What are you trying to prove?" Gabrielle whispered.

"Only that when I want you in my bed again, you'll be there. I thought you needed a reminder that my patience with you has run dry."

Micah's effrontery was beyond any she had ever experienced. Gabrielle's skin burned dark and hot at his words. "Did it ever occur to you that a woman likes to be made love to with tenderness, with love, without having to parry a bunch of off-color gibes from a sex maniac?''

Micah was taken aback. "What is this? You're giving lessons now? I didn't realize you had *those* qualifications." He gave her a gentle shove in the direction of the clinic. "Go ask Helen for a hat, you'll need one where we're going."

"Apologize to me for that remark," Gabrielle insisted.

"About the hat?"

"The one before that!"

"I don't think I've said anything that requires an apology," he said. "If anything, you owe me one. Now, go get the damn hat."

Gabrielle stood her ground. "That's another thing I don't like about you. You never say please or thank you...you just order people about like you own them. I don't want to go anywhere with you. Take me back to Chepo."

Micah groaned. "Suit yourself," he said. "Max will fly you back tomorrow." He turned on his heel and headed toward the Quonset hut where a group of men waited. Gabrielle felt the hot angry flush of humiliation crawl to her scalp. They had probably witnessed the entire scene between her and Micah. *Oh, damn him...damn him... damn him.*

Chapter Sixteen

Gabrielle sat across from Helen in the gazebo-type screened enclosure at the back of the clinic. Helen called it a porch, but in reality it served as kitchen and dining room. A wood-burning stove occupied one corner. It was being stoked and brought to life by Louisa, a logger's wife who helped Helen with housework, cooking, and cleaning the clinic.

"Don't look so glum, Gabby," Helen said. "You're not at the end of the world, and besides, no one would dare breathe a word of gossip where Micah can hear."

Gabrielle sighed and continued to fret. She had told Helen about her confrontation with Micah, not what had been said, only that he had kissed her and that she thought they had been seen by some of Micah's men. She didn't want Helen to hear about it secondhand.

Helen continued. "What you and Micah do is your business anyway, so don't worry about it."

"I wish I had never taken this job now," Gabrielle said. "I could have managed something until I can get back to the ballet." Gabrielle sounded more wistful than irritated, and the longing in her voice brought a sharp glance from Helen.

"Gabby," Helen began casually, "have you ever thought about what you'd do if you couldn't dance?"

"Couldn't dance?" Gabrielle repeated. The thought was incomprehensible. "But I can dance, Helen. It's just a matter of time until the bones in my leg knit strong enough to take the strain. Dancing isn't easy, you know."

"I'm aware of that. But don't you want to get married? Have kids? I mean the way you and Micah go at each other's throats, one would think you already—"

"Helen!" Gabrielle exclaimed, annoyed. "Micah has nothing to do with the way I feel, and marriage and babies would just get in the way right now. I only asked you about

Micah on the *Upsure* because I was curious about him. That's all."

"Oh," Helen answered, then returned her attention to the task in front of her: trimming the wick of a kerosene lamp. The house and clinic were wired for electricity, but Helen liked the smell of kerosene. It reminded her of Oregon and the camping trips she and Jinks used to take. She struck a match to the wick. The glow circled a surprisingly large area, but beyond the porch everything was in dusky gloom. A shadow fell across the table.

"Am I interrupting something?" Micah asked pleasantly, noting the strained look on Gabrielle's face.

Helen answered. "No, not a thing. We're just going to get supper started." Helen got up and moved to join Louisa near the stove.

"Where's Jinks?" Micah asked the question of Helen, but kept his eyes fastened on Gabrielle.

"Over at Luis's. Chica is near her time and he's gone to see if he can coax her to come to the clinic, but I personally think it's a lost cause. She's frightened to death—all those old wives' tales." Helen snorted. Micah nodded; he was used to hearing this complaint from Helen. He spoke to Gabrielle.

"Did you have a pleasant afternoon?"

His insolent mocking tone was not lost on Gabrielle. "Very, thank you," she said icily, refusing to meet his eyes.

"You changed clothes, I see," he said, slipping a finger under the thin strap of her yellow sun dress. Gabrielle pushed his hand away.

"I wish you'd have the decency to keep your hands to yourself in public," she hissed, remembering her humiliation earlier in the day.

Micah bent to her ear. "Does that mean I can have the privilege in private?" Gabrielle glared at him.

"No, and you know it." She stood up. "Excuse me, I need to see if I can help Helen with supper." Micah's hand shot out and grabbed her wrist. He held it loosely.

"Keep your seat and talk to me for a few minutes—without grinding your teeth and running off like a scared rabbit."

"You're the one who grinds his teeth, not me, and I'm not scared of you." She sat down. "So what do you have to say?"

"Why, nothing in particular. I'd just like to see a smile on your face for a change."

"I smile a lot, when you're not around," she told him, allowing hauteur to seep into her voice.

Micah grimaced. "Look, let's start all over. How about staying over a few days? I won't bother you. I just want you around. As soon as we move those damned sloths, we start cutting timber and I won't be able to get back to Chepo for weeks. What do you say?"

"No."

"In that case, I'll take what I can, while I can," he said determinedly, this time grabbing her wrist with firm pressure and pulling her behind him toward the house. He called to Helen, "We'll be back in a few minutes." He looked at Gabrielle with a bitter gleam in his eyes. "Maybe," he muttered quietly.

Father Chardin pushed the door open as Micah reached it with Gabrielle in tow. "Micah! Gabrielle! I didn't expect to find you here at Coco Solito," he said, surprised.

Gabrielle heard Micah's suppressed groan. She smiled brilliantly at Amand and threw up a torrent of words. "I'm just here for the night. We came in from Toboga today." She pulled her hand from Micah's grasp and moved back into the gazebo. "Helen and I were just starting supper. Will you join us?" Gabrielle cut a glance to Micah to see how he was taking all this. He met her gaze with one of his own and the slightly cynical look on his face said he would deal with her later. But later she wouldn't be here. And Helen had already told her that Micah slept in the bunkhouse with the single men. All she needed to do was avoid him, stay close to Helen and in the house. He wouldn't dare try anything with the priest around. Once back at Chepo she would have the breathing space she needed to think everything through sensibly and put her emotions back on an even keel. Gabrielle hurried over to the stove and began taking plates out of the warmer.

"May I borrow your lamp later, Helen?" Amand asked.

"The villagers want me to say Mass tonight. They're setting up a temporary altar under the trees at the south end of the village. But I'll need more than candles for light."

"Sure, but after supper," she answered. "And I second Gabby's invitation. Will you have supper with us?"

"I'd better." He laughed. "Frenchie tells me they've been making beer all weekend and there's to be a celebration with dancing and music tonight." Amand joined Micah who had seated himself in one of several wicker chairs facing toward the village. Helen shooed Gabrielle away from the stove, telling her she and Louisa could manage. Gabrielle felt she had no choice but to join Micah and Amand. Anything else would appear rude to the priest. Louisa brought a tray with cups of fresh perked coffee. Micah took thê role of host. He handed Amand a cup, then Gabrielle.

"Let's see, the first time I served you coffee, I believe you said you took cream," he said, smiling blandly. The startled look on Gabrielle's face told him the remark had hit home, reminding her of the morning aboard the *Upsure*, the morning they had made love. He poured cream into her cup from a wooden pitcher. "Say when."

"That's enough, thank you," she said, glowering at him. If he thought she was going to put up with this, he was sadly mistaken, she told herself. His behavior was becoming boringly predictable and beyond her emotional tolerance. Right now she would give anything to be in the thick of things backstage at the ballet; petty grievances, infighting, snide jealous remarks. What she was learning in the civilian world, Gabrielle thought, would make it easy for her to breeze through backstage infighting without blinking an eye.

"Would you, Gabby?" Amand was talking to her.

Gabrielle started. "I'm sorry, I was a million miles away. What did you say?"

"I asked if you would like to go to Mass tonight. You'd have to bring your own chair."

"Oh, no, thank you anyway. I'm Baptist," she said, declining.

Amand laughed. "I won't try to convert you. But the children have been practicing their music and afterward there will be the bonfire and dancing and more music—not spiritual. You'll enjoy it. I'm using lots of incense tonight," he said with a twinkle in his eye. "I notice the wind is coming up from the stables."

Gabrielle laughed and looked at Micah. "Are you going?"

"No, I have work to do."

"Well, I guess I will, then, Amand," she said, smiling. "What's the celebration? New Year's?"

"There's that, but mostly because Micah here cuts his first tree tomorrow, at least he was supposed to. I heard about the sloths," he said to Micah. "By the way, I stopped by Harry's on my way in and he said to tell you there's been quite a few Americans through his place looking for work. He mentioned that the Jari River project has been cut drastically and a lot of loggers and engineers are up from Brazil."

Amand explained to Gabrielle. "The Jari is a project of an American billionaire named Ludwig in the Amazon. Micah's logging here in Panama isn't on the same scale, but we did learn one thing about our environment: If you cut down and burn millions of tons of virgin jungle, it upsets the delicate balance of nature. Scientists say the Jari River project provoked thunderstorms miles away. Micah doesn't plan to mill his lumber here, but he's not sure either whether the logs will make it down the Mamoni and Bayano rivers."

"Amand," Micah said patiently, "why is it you think I'm going to destroy the jungle? I'm not. I'm only removing selected trees, and those only with the agreement of the government of Panama. And the log rafts will make it down the river. Look at all the other debris that gets shunted into the bay during the rainy season. We'll get our logs to the barges."

"And if you don't?"

Micah laughed. "I'm going to do the same as Ludwig: cut my losses and get out. Thanks for the message from Harry. Gabrielle, will you tell Benton to go see Harry? He'll know what to do." Gabrielle nodded.

By now delectable aromas were coming from the stove and Jinks bustled in and joined them. "What are you fine folks drinking?" He grimaced when they chorused "Coffee." "I think I need a little something stronger than that," he said and disappeared back into the house. He returned with a bottle of whiskey. He held up the bottle.

"Amand, what about you? I know Micah will."

Amand declined. "Save me a sip for after Mass, I'm going to be very thirsty then."

Jinks chuckled. "Gabby, may I fix you a drink?"

Helen walked up and took the bottle from Jinks. "I'll fix the drinks, my friend. You are too heavy-handed. Supper's on the table," she announced to the rest of them.

Two hours later Gabrielle stood next to Helen and watched the celebration begin. After dinner she and Helen had followed Father Chardin to the clearing under the trees where he said Mass. He had graciously carried their metal fold-up chairs, and true to his word, the altar boys sprayed the air generously with incense. The fragrance had been delightful and the service, in Spanish and Latin, had been strangely moving.

Almost immediately after Mass the villagers had carried their chairs and benches some distance from the corrals and lighted the bonfire. Someone pressed a thin cup of the *chicha* beer into Gabrielle's hand. She sipped it, found it mild, cool, and frothy. All along the narrow village streets women bent over their cook fires, roasting *carne en palitos,* whole chickens, and pig ribs; each fire held its own pot of black beans and rice.

Someone began to strum a guitar, soon joined by tambourines, mariachis, and drums. Gabrielle watched, delighted, as a group began to dance the *tamborito,* a folk dance choreographed with mincing, stiff steps, yet the flow was elegant and appealing. Her feet itched to join them.

Helen laughed as Gabrielle tapped her feet to the music. "There's Jinks. I think he's fixing to do what you've been thinking you'd like to." But Jinks cut through the dancers and approached Helen, a serious countenance on his face.

"I think I'm going to need your help," he told her quietly. "Chica has gone into labor and she won't come to the clinic. Luis is frantic. We'll have to do what we can there."

Helen turned to Gabrielle. "I'm sorry, but duty calls. Will you be okay?"

"Yes, but is there anything I can do to help?"

"No, not a thing. This is Chica's first baby and she's just frightened. All the old wives' tales have her confused. She does what Jinks tells her to do one day and the next follows the advice of the *nele*. He's out like a light, though, thank goodness." She pointed to an old man propped up against one of the trees, an empty bucket on its side next to him. "That's what *chicha* beer does to you, so take it easy." Gabrielle promised she would and watched the pair hurry off toward one of the small houses.

Amand left a group he had been talking to and walked up to her. "Looks like I'll have a baptism on my hands soon," he said, smiling.

"I guess you will. Helen and Jinks just left to—to see to it."

Amand chuckled at her choice of words. "I think we'll have to let Chica and Luis take a little of the credit. Listen, do you want to make the food circuit with me?"

"Food circuit? Amand, we had dinner less than two hours ago."

"I know, I know, but who can resist those delectable aromas? Besides, it's my holy duty to bless each pot."

"Before or after you sample the cooking?"

Amand laughed. "Why, before, of course. If it's bad, that makes it good. Haven't you ever heard of the power of the Lord?"

"Yes, and you're being sacrilegious, but I'll come with you. I'd like to see if this miracle of the blessing really works. I can't cook." Amand chuckled and took her arm, leading her from one cook fire to the next. He said a blessing over each, then he and Gabrielle, out of courtesy, ate a small portion of whatever meat was being served and a helping of beans and rice. *Chicha* beer flowed freely. After about the dozenth stop, Gabrielle pulled Amand aside.

"I can't possibly eat another bite of beans and rice, or swallow another drop of beer. My stomach is rebelling and my head is woozy." Instantly concerned, Amand guided her over to the nearest house and sat her down on the steps. Several children, some naked, some dressed in their holiday finery, stood in a circle around them, smiling shyly and watching with huge brown eyes.

"Are you going to throw up?" he asked with not the least bit of subtlety.

"Heavens no. I'm just stuffed and everybody wants me to eat second helpings. You should have warned me."

Amand had the grace to look contrite. "Well, they don't often get a beautiful American lady to visit and each of them wants you to stay at her house the longest so her prestige in the village will be the greatest. You can't stop now, the others will be offended."

Gabrielle moaned softly and stood up. "You should have told me I was on display. I'll go with you, but I can't possibly face another bowl of beans."

Amand laughed sheepishly. "All right, just fake it then. Do most of the talking, then they won't notice you haven't eaten. And take it easy on the beer."

"Tell me, Amand," Gabrielle said as they neared the next cook fire, "have you been blessing the beer too?"

"Only if it's close to the cook pot. Why?"

"I'm just wondering who I'll have to blame for the headache I'm sure to have in the morning. You or a much more heavenly spirit."

An hour later they had worked their way back to the bonfire. Gabrielle looked at the medicine man, still sound asleep, and envied him his bliss. For the past few minutes her head had been reeling, her vision blurry, and she knew she was beginning to weave. She leaned heavily on the priest for support. "Listen, Amand," she said, clutching his arm, "I think I had better get back to the clinic."

"You do look a bit done in," he agreed. "I'll walk you back." They had only managed to negotiate a few yards when Micah loomed in front of them. At least to Gabrielle he seemed to loom. He spoke a few words to Amand, words that Gabrielle couldn't hear.

"I'll go right away," the priest said. "Will you see Gabrielle back to Helen's for me? The *chicha* has done her in, I'm afraid." Micah took one look at Gabrielle and scooped her up into his arms. Gabrielle began a weak protest, but gave it up. It was so much easier to be carried than to try to force her feet to move, knees straight, and somehow keep the top of her body from toppling over. She rested her head on Micah's shoulder.

"Thank you," she murmured and closed her eyes against the vertigo that washed over her. The sounds of laughter, strumming guitars, and throbbing drums mingled and faded as Gabrielle slipped into a *chicha*-induced stupor. She didn't feel the gentle hands as they undressed her nor the trembling fingers when they tried several times without success to get her nightgown over her head. She didn't hear Micah's ragged sigh as he adjusted the mosquito netting expertly around her bed.

When she woke the next morning, she discovered she was wrapped cocoonlike in muslin sheets, but that was the least of her worries. Her head pounded and she thought that somehow the drums from the night before had managed to invade her head. Gabrielle was sure she could pinpoint the route of every ounce of blood as it pulsed through her body. Her nerves seemed to absorb every tiny sound and she groaned achingly when she heard the door open to her room. Rattling dishes and the soft swishing of the net being pulled back crashed like cymbals in her head.

"How's the inebriate today?" Micah asked, peering down at her.

Gabrielle moaned. "She died."

Micah buried a chuckle in his throat. "I have something here that might bring her back to life: a pitcher of freshly squeezed orange juice, a pitcher of iced water, and a little something from St. Joseph."

Gabrielle opened her eyes. Micah's teeth gleamed in a Cheshire cat grin. He looked fresh, clean, and pain-free— all the things she was not.

"You mean Father Chardin?" she said, confused.

"Aspirin," Micah said, handing her a glass and the tablets. She swallowed the aspirin and the water and held out the glass for a refill. *Chicha* beer left one god-awful thirsty, she discovered.

"Thank you," she said. "Now be nice to me just this once," she pleaded, "and go away. I need some sleep."

"No, what you need is some fresh air. Louisa is heating you some water to bathe. I promised to show you some jungle and I thought I'd take you for a ride. We have a very gentle mare in the corral. Frenchie is saddling her for you."

"Me? Get on a horse? Micah, you must be crazy. My head would fall off." He laughed and Gabrielle held her head.

"No, you won't, we're just going around the perimeter of the village, maybe a little way down the river's edge. Show you some alligators in the wild," he said, still smiling.

Gabrielle shuddered. The closest she ever wanted to come to an alligator was on somebody's belt. She kept the thought to herself however and instead asked, "Are Helen and Jinks riding too?"

"No, they're still asleep, but with good reason. They were up all night with Chica."

"Oh, did she have her baby? Was everything all right?" The last thing Gabrielle remembered from the night before was Micah whispering in Amand's ear and Amand hurrying off toward the village.

"Yes, but it was touch and go for several hours. She had a boy." He paused. "Are you interested in children?"

Gabrielle pulled herself up on the pillow, gazing steadily at Micah. "What kind of a question is that?"

"No kind, I was just asking, that's all," he said blandly. "I thought you might like to see the baby. By now half the village has been to see him and I'm sure Chica has heard of you from all the women. She would be honored for you to visit. Amand mentioned you were a big hit with the villagers last night."

"Amand!" Gabrielle sputtered. "I sure have a thing or two I'd like to tell him. It was his fault—"

Micah laughed. "He's gone, but you can tell him when you see him." Gabrielle silently hoped that the priest's halo got so heavy he'd suffer with a headache as great as her own. Her bedroom door swung open again.

"Here's Louisa with your bathwater," Micah said. "Wear those khakis you had on yesterday," he instructed, then smiled wickedly. "Considering your condition, I'll wait thirty minutes." He turned to leave.

"Wait!" Gabrielle said. Micah folded the mosquito netting back once more and looked at her questioningly. "Say please," she ordered.

Micah opened his mouth to protest, then spit the word out sharply. "Please!"

"A *nice* please," Gabrielle suggested, looking directly at him.

Micah sighed in exasperation. "Please," he said softly. "Please, please, please, with honey and spice, lots of chocolate, mounds of whipped cream, ten pounds of sugar—please. Will that do?"

"Very nicely," Gabrielle said, smiling up at him. "Next we'll work on thank you." As painful as it was, the smile stayed on Gabrielle's lips as she struggled slowly through the next several minutes.

Her nightgown lay in a crumpled heap next to her bed. She mentally berated herself for her overindulgence. She had drunk alcohol before, but never to the point where she couldn't remember dressing and undressing, and obviously last night she hadn't even managed to pull a simple shift over her head. Never again, she told herself with fervor.

It took more than the thirty minutes Micah had allotted her to meet him at the stables. To Gabrielle's keen eyes her skin looked taut and drawn and the ill-fitting khakis were no help. She pulled the straw hat down over her eyes and adjusted it to a rakish angle to blot out the sun's glare as she walked to the corral, but she was sure she would have a permanent squint before the day was over.

She rode a roan mare and it plodded serenely alongside the rust-colored stallion Micah rode. Gabrielle imitated Micah's relaxed slouch and found it much more simple than she had thought to meet the rhythm of the horse. She needn't have worried about the sun. Away from the village and under the canopy of trees it was as though they were in a wild, green amphitheater where the sun seldom penetrated.

For the most part they rode in companionable silence. Gabrielle let her mind drift and only brought it back to the present when Micah pointed out the alligators. The ugly prehistoric-looking creatures sunned on the banks of the river, yawning occasionally to display row upon row of razor-sharp teeth.

Micah signaled her to stop and Gabrielle reined in her horse, pausing in the shade of a towering tree. Without speaking, Micah pointed out a female alligator guarding her nest of eggs high on the mud bank of the river. They watched as the alligator left her nest and wandered down to the river to feed. Almost instantly a small capuchin dropped out of an overhanging branch and began to despoil the nest, frantically searching for the eggs. It found one, leaped back to its protective perch, and began to eat. Gabrielle watched, fascinated, as the monkey broke the egg, licked out its contents, discarded the shell, and raced back to the nest for another. A second monkey joined the first and they made so much chattering noise they drew the attention of the nest's owner. The mother hurried back to her nest, wide jaws agape in a roar of disapproval.

Gabrielle shuddered and rooted for the tiny thieves as the monkeys scampered to safety, each hugging his prize. She silently chastised the mother alligator for leaving her nest unguarded, but laughed aloud as the monkeys sat on the limb over her head, enjoying their repast.

As Gabrielle turned her horse back onto the path, she discovered Micah staring intently at her, his look unmistakable. Like an emotional jolt, she felt again the erotic compulsion that vibrated between them. She told herself she was imagining things and forced her mind back to the incident at the corral yesterday—his arrogant behavior, her humiliation. But the scene wasn't strong enough to overpower the feeling she had, the desire she held in check. With unerring feminine instinct, she knew only the specter of Vanessa kept her out of his bed, and that was the thought that Gabrielle clung to as Micah reined his horse closer to hers.

"We'd better head back now. Two hours in the saddle is quite enough for one day," he told her. "As it is, in the morning you'll probably discover a multitude of muscles you didn't know existed. Sure I can't talk you into staying over? I give excellent massages," he added.

"No, I won't stay over and I won't need a massage either," she said flippantly. "I assure you I'm in excellent physical condition. I practice routines for two hours every day without the slightest ache."

Micah reined in his horse and stopped. "What do you mean? Practice routines?"

"I work out every day in the courtyard. It helps pass the time."

"You're not supposed to do that," he said casually and flicked his horse into motion next to hers. "As I recall, Dr. Baker said for you to see him before you begin dancing again."

"It's hardly what you could call dancing. Just simple pliés, jetés, and a few easy leaps—simple stuff, to keep in shape." Gabrielle thought for several seconds, then asked, "How do you know what Dr. Baker said? I've never mentioned him to you."

"You said yourself," he countered, "my investigators were thorough."

Gabrielle's antennae swirled into motion. "No, I don't believe you. Dr. Baker has been our family physician for years. He wouldn't tell you or anyone else a thing, not about me or any of his patients, unless he had permission to and I know I haven't given anyone permission to pry into my affairs."

"Well, you must have mentioned it to Helen and she told me," he said, brushing her remarks aside. "But no exercises—period. You understand?"

The path they were following was becoming too narrow for both horses, but Gabrielle stubbornly continued to ride abreast with Micah. "No, I don't understand. I'm fine, my leg is fine. What's all this concern over a broken bone that's virtually healed? Unless—" Gabrielle couldn't voice the question. A prickling sensation of alarm raised the fine hairs on her neck and her arms and a chill licked at her spine. Was there something more wrong with her than a broken leg? Yesterday Helen had asked what she would do if she couldn't dance. Gabrielle had not considered the question worth answering and Helen hadn't pursued it. She thought back to her last conversation with Dr. Baker. He had said nothing to alarm her. "Take your calcium tablets every day, eat lots of protein.... Give the bones all the time they need to knit." There had not been a single out-of-the-ordinary thing happen. Micah was just using the issue of her dancing to chip away at her independence, to break her spirit. It was the classic male chauvinist maneuver. She would make him admit it. She repeated her question.

"Why all the concern about a broken leg, Micah?"

He evaded answering. "You're an adult, Gabrielle, can't you follow a simple direction from your doctor?" He was angry.

"Yes. But I know how I feel and I feel fine. My leg is well. If I weren't here, I'd already be back in rehearsals. What's wrong with you? You've had this hang-up about my being a dancer since we met. What's it to you as long as I do the job you hired me to do?"

"Christ!" he muttered, and that was all the answer she got. He swung his horse ahead of hers onto the narrow path that led into the village and the single file precluded any further conversation.

GABRIELLE went with Helen to see Chica's new baby, and after telling the new parents how beautiful their son was, Helen walked with her over to the helipad, a duplicate of the one at Chepo, where Max was warming up the motor. The rotors began to pick up speed, swirling gray dust into the air.

Gabrielle thanked Helen for her hospitality and watched warily as Micah tossed her luggage into the bowels of the aircraft. She had a moment of anxiety when she thought he was going to kiss her so she stuck out her hand. Surprised, Micah took it, then laughed and whispered in her ear.

"Don't get the idea you can outfox a fox all the time, Gabrielle," he warned with an amused gleam in his eyes. "Remember, my patience with you has reached its limit."

Then Micah boosted her into the helicopter and his taunting smile faded into a frown as he saw her take the observer's seat next to Max. Gabrielle gave Micah an impish grin and lifted her hand to her brow in a casual, but triumphant, salute.

Chapter Seventeen

On Tuesday Vanessa began to telephone Chepo. The first time she called, Gabrielle answered the phone.

"Oh, this must be the lame ballerina," Vanessa said, oozing venom.

"My name is Gabrielle Hensley," Gabrielle told her, positive she would tolerate no further verbal abuse from Vanessa.

"Well, Gabrielle Hensley," Vanessa said, "you needn't think Micah will keep you around for long; he'll tire of you soon. He always does with the things he picks up here and there, and he *always* comes running back to me."

Gabrielle laughed into the telephone. "Oh, really? I heard it was the other way around, Vanessa; that you ran to him between your other, er—what do you call all your marriages? A hobby?" At that Vanessa became vitriolic and Gabrielle held the receiver away from her ear.

"He's going to marry me!" Vanessa screamed. "You just wait and see. I know what he wants and I can give it to him."

"Oh?" Gabrielle retorted coolly. "I wasn't aware that Micah went in for second- and thirdhand goods. Perhaps you'd be better off giving to charity, Vanessa. I'm sure you would be more appreciated."

Vanessa hung up.

Even though Gabrielle felt she had bested the woman in the verbal exchange, there was something frightening about Vanessa. There was something poisonous and unhealthy about the other woman's spiteful jealous rage. And that she was jealous, Gabrielle had no doubt. Vanessa had made little attempt to hide her feelings when they were on Toboga and it looked as though Micah was just using Vanessa as a pawn in the game he was playing. But even through the anger Gabrielle could detect a thread of con-

fidence in Vanessa's voice. The woman was certain that
Micah would marry her. Why? Gabrielle had no answer.

After that single call Gabrielle never answered the telephone. She gave up the task to Maria. And Vanessa called
each day. Maria had no trouble recognizing the husky
voice of the one guest of Señor Davidson to whom she had
taken an instant dislike. She remembered the woman's visit
three months before. She had prepared Miss Thomas's
breakfast at the woman's request. Miss Thomas had re-
jected the food, swept it off the table with disdain and
vulgar language. Maria had cleaned up the mess and
cooked another omelet. Again Miss Thomas refused the
food and a dozen eggs later Miss Thomas finally speared
the eggs with her fork, waved it in the air, and threw the
fork at Maria. Mr. Benton had finally spoken to the horrible woman and she had gone off without any breakfast at
all. Now when Miss Thomas called, Maria pretended she
spoke no English. Vanessa finally stopped calling.

AFTER some hesitation to drive Micah's new car, but en-
couraged by Benton, Gabrielle began to drive into Panama
City twice a week. At Benton's office in the Tivoli Hotel,
Gabrielle and Benton reviewed the contract translations.
She met his secretary, Rosa, a shy, attractive Panamanian
who looked after Benton like an adoring niece.

One particular morning their work carried them to noon
and Gabrielle and Benton lunched together. Thereafter
they lunched together every time Gabrielle was in the city.
Once, when Gabrielle mentioned she was going to see the
Golden Altar of San Jose, Benton accompanied her. After
that, when he had the time, he took her to see various
points of interest: banana plantations in Puerto Armuelles
and Changuinola, and the resort at Maria Chiquita Beach
where volcanic sand, soft as velvet, looked astonishingly
like fresh ground pepper. Benton and Gabrielle became
good friends, and the twice-weekly trips into the city were
always full of excitement so that Gabrielle was never bored
and always sighed with tired relief when she negotiated the
wooden bridge that signaled she was once again safely
back at Chepo.

Gabrielle had not seen Micah for three weeks. Today, out of the blue, Helen had called on the radio to tell her Micah was on his way to Chepo, to be dressed, that he was going to take her into Panama City to renew her visa.

As Gabrielle dressed—she had decided on the Mikado print—she debated whether she should mention Vanessa's phone calls to Micah. She decided against it, unless Micah himself brought up Vanessa's name, and that would be unlikely. Gabrielle smoothed the silk sheath down over her hips, the dress molded to her figure and enhanced the delicate brown of her skin. The mandarin collar circled her neck like an accolade, so she swept her curls to the back of her head and locked them in place in keeping with the classic Chinese look of the dress.

When Micah arrived, she was shocked to see how tired and worn he looked. He was making no pretense of wearing his leather brace anymore and the scars on his neck appeared healed.

"You look good enough to eat," he said, and the smile he bestowed on her seemed to wash away the tiredness she had noticed only moments earlier.

Gabrielle laughed. As a matter of fact, she was bubbling over with happiness. She felt as giddy as a schoolgirl on her first date. She had missed Micah more than she cared to admit.

"Oh?" she teased. "I didn't know you liked Chinese food."

Micah grinned and came within a foot of her. "If I wasn't so dirty, and so pressed for time, I'd show you just how much I *dearly* love it." He fixed himself a drink and carried it with him into his room. While he bathed and dressed, Gabrielle waited impatiently. Somehow she had the feeling that today they would get along just fine.

By the time they got into Panama City, Gabrielle was having difficulty keeping the butterflies in her stomach from fluttering their wings. Micah did little more than inquire of her health, but he did ask pointedly how she spent her free time and how her work was going. He seemed pleased that she and Benton were getting on so well. She made no mention of her dancing and Micah was satisfied with her answers, but he was preoccupied and in no mood for casual chitchat. They had her visa stamped, lunched with Benton, stopped by Harry Horton's for a drink, and returned to Chepo. Max was waiting, lounging on the veranda with Shadow.

She and Micah had not argued, but neither had he made any advances toward her, so that when Gabrielle stood on the porch to say good-bye, she had been taken completely by surprise when he kissed her—a kiss so full of hunger and longing that just the memory of it distracted her.

GABRIELLE shrugged and flipped the Off switch on the electric typewriter. No more work today, she declared. She looked at Shadow lounging near the desk.

"Shadow, did you know today is my birthday?" His ears perked up, then lay flat again. Gabrielle laughed. "That's what everyone else thinks about it too," she said aloud, setting aside the delightful birthday greeting she had received from home. Even Hattie had added her signature to the card after her parents. Gabrielle felt a twinge of homesickness, then sighed.

Ordinarily she would have gone into Panama City, rounded up Benton, and asked him to celebrate this auspicious day with her. But she hadn't seen or heard from him in a week. She had seen Micah only once in the past seven weeks and that had been the day he took her to get her visa stamped.

She wished she knew where Benton was keeping himself. Even Rosa didn't know and said so when Gabrielle had called earlier. But the girl hadn't seemed alarmed; Benton often had work to do that took him out of Panama a few days at a time. Gabrielle didn't want to spend her twenty-fifth birthday alone, but since it looked like that was what she'd have to do she went about her day as usual.

"Come on, Shadow, you can keep me company while I exercise," she told the dog. He got up and followed her placidly to the courtyard. He stirred up the parakeets in the lower branches of the mango tree, then curled up in its shade while Gabrielle changed into leotards. It was much too warm for tights and Gabrielle dusted herself with baby powder to stave off some of the sweat she always generated during these sessions. She put her hand on the banister, took a deep breath, and closed her eyes. It always helped to empty her mind so that she could concentrate on her work. When she opened them a moment later, Shadow was bounding up to Micah, who stood in the doorway to the living room.

"Micah!" Gabrielle exclaimed, letting her arm fall to her side in a graceful arc. "I didn't know you were coming home. I didn't even hear the helicopter arrive."

"I thought we agreed you wouldn't do these exercises until after you saw Dr. Baker," he said, straining to keep the harshness out of his voice.

"You ordered. I didn't agree," she told him.

Micah walked around the veranda and Gabrielle felt herself being yanked away from the railing. The jerky movement caused a cloud of powder to swirl and float in the air between them.

"You're not supposed to be doing this, Gabrielle. Now stop."

She jerked her arm out of his grasp. "What do you mean—stop? You can't order me about like this! I've done your work—the contracts are almost finished—and these routines, simple as they are, help build up my leg. Besides," she said, trying to appeal to his practicality, "I need to stay flexible, otherwise I'll be weeks getting into shape for rehearsals."

"You're just kidding yourself. You are *never* going to dance again. Why can't you believe that?" he asked, glaring at her.

So, they were back to that again. "You are wrong. I am a dancer. I will dance. Why can't *you* face that? What's it to you, anyway, Micah?" Her eyes searched his face; it was devoid of expression now. "You said the same thing when I was in Coco Solito. This time I want an answer."

He held her robe. "Put this on and come into the front room. We need to talk."

"I don't need to discuss my career with you. I'm not giving it up," she said, following him. He went to the bar and poured brandy into two bell-shaped snifters.

"I don't need this either," Gabrielle told him, refusing the drink.

"Sit down," he said quietly, so quietly, almost compassionately, that Gabrielle felt the hairs stiffen on her neck. She changed her mind about the drink, brought the glass to her lips, and took a long swallow. It burned her throat.

"You may not have given up dancing," Micah began, "but dancing has given you up."

"What—what do you mean? *Is this some trick?*"

Micah emitted a heavy sigh. He didn't like doing this. He wished he had never made that telephone call to Nate Hensley. Nate had at first been cautious about Gabrielle's condition, but then he had seemed to throw caution to the wind and confided in him. Gabrielle's health was at stake. Micah felt squeezed between a rock and a hard place. There was no easy way to do this, he thought. "I mean that when you broke your leg the orthopedic surgeons discovered you have a bone problem," he said bluntly. "It's called osteoporosis and it's rare, very rare, in a woman your age. Why do you think they decided against steel pins for support in a break as bad as the one you suffered? Because your bones wouldn't support them. They used glue, Gabrielle, simple, ordinary *Krazy* glue to put your bones back together."

Gabrielle looked at him in horror. "You're lying! You're lying!" She wanted to scream the words, but her throat was closing, so the sounds only rasped out. "Dr. Baker would have told me if what you say is true, or my parents—"

"No, Dr. Baker said you were too emotionally distraught. He thought it better to wait until your depression lifted. He expected you to follow his advice—no exercises. He was going to tell you when you see him in April."

"It's not true," she said into the air in front of her. Micah had spoken calmly and his words had the unmistakable ring of truth. Gabrielle couldn't shrug off the sinking feeling in her stomach. Her world was crashing down....
Chicken Little...Chicken Little....

"I don't believe you," she said again, as if not believing would make it less true, but even to her ears her voice carried no conviction.

Micah sipped his brandy, watching her from under his lashes. He wanted to smile, tried to offer her some consolation. He wanted to gather her up in his arms and tell her it didn't matter, that he loved her anyway. He loved her? The idea unnerved him, rocked him to his very core. His knees went weak and he had to sit down. Gabrielle was watching him and it was all he could do to placate his inner turmoil to recompose a suave exterior. "I didn't want to be the one to tell you," he said. "At times you seem to hate me enough already and the bearer of bad tidings...well, you know the old saying...."

"Oh, I do, I do," Gabrielle said, hating him passionately, wishing she could hurt him as he had hurt her. Her eyes glittered, almost feverishly, dazed. "But you can't stop me, Micah, not you, not the doctors, not anyone. I will dance again. I will!" She wrenched the words out.

"No, I can't stop you," Micah said softly. "You have to stop yourself. Your leg will never be strong enough to take the punishment. Your body just doesn't convert calcium properly, Gabrielle; that's why you have to take the pills. Your bones have a tendency to shed their outer layer. That is why your leg will never be strong. It's not the end of the world, you can teach, have your own studio—"

"No! I'm a prima ballerina," she said, as if she could will it, recall it, undo the accident, undo the whole horrible nightmare. All her anger, her fury, the sense of being cheated, she directed to Micah.

"I hate you, Micah Davidson."

He lifted his brandy snifter in mock salute. "Fine, marry me and make me miserable."

Gabrielle looked at him, his serious countenance, watched him watch her. "You are stark raving mad... I despise you—" The words caught in her throat.

"I won't ask you twice," he said. His mask dropped into place, his face impassive, detached, self-assured, as though he hadn't just ground her life into shattered pieces.

"Good!" she spit at him. "Marry Vanessa. You two deserve each other." Gabrielle got up and was at the door before he spoke again.

"Change clothes, Gabrielle. I want you to go with me

into Panama. I have to check on Benton. He had an appointment with me he didn't keep. I have to find out what's wrong."

"No, I want to be alone," she told him. *To cry, to scream.* She felt as though she had been physically beaten, she needed time to sort out the pieces of her life, rearrange the jigsaw, make it work, somehow.

"Not tonight," Micah said tonelessly. "Get dressed or I'll dress you myself."

Gabrielle needed something, anything, to empty her mind of Micah's words, but there was nothing...just nothing. She bathed and dressed like a robot, in a vacuum of shock. It was her birthday, she remembered. Micah had chosen the cruelest of presents.

BENTON had not returned or called his office. Micah began to comb the city, working in a grid with bleak determination, every restaurant, every hotel, every cantina. When the search in those places proved fruitless they stopped at cockfights and cantinas near the ruins, and farther out, near the banana plantations. No one had seen Benton, some not for days, some not for weeks.

They stopped to eat. It was late. Gabrielle picked at her food, not hungry and not understanding why Micah seemed so desperate to find Benton. He left her to make several more phone calls and still no one had seen Benton.

It occured to Gabrielle that Benton might have quit, just left, without telling Micah, but she said nothing. It was after three in the morning when they returned to Chepo.

Gabrielle was weary, weary and numb. Micah seemed even more so, his mood strange. They had not said more than a dozen words to one another all night. Gabrielle was less inclined to worry about Benton. Working for Micah Davidson would put a strain on anyone. Benton was probably taking a well-deserved vacation. She had her own worries.

Shadow was waiting for them on the front porch. He seemed to sense the undercurrent of anxiety that emanated from both Micah and Gabrielle. He whined and, when let in the house, curled up on his rug. Gabrielle hurried across the room ahead of Micah.

"Wait a minute, I want to talk to you," Micah said, his voice tired, but still demanding.

"Haven't you talked enough? Or do you enjoy seeing people suffer?"

"I don't want you to suffer. I just want to make sure you won't go against Dr. Baker's instructions again, or do anything else foolish. I want you to call your parents in the morning. It's direct dial. Talk to them and Dr. Baker too. I wish I could stay here with you or take you with me, but I can't. We're camping in each sector as we cut it and it's too primitive and dangerous for you."

"Will there be anything else?" she asked, her voice heavy with as much sarcasm as she could muster.

Micah acknowledged her tone of voice by lifting one expressive eyebrow. "If you hear from Benton, tell him to leave a message with Helen in Coco Solito. She'll get it to me."

Gabrielle went through the motions of getting ready for bed in the bathroom. She took off her clothes, put on a gown, brushed her teeth, washed her face. Why didn't she look different? How could the outside of her body look the same when inside it was crumbled and torn?

Moonlight filtered in through the wooden shutters as Gabrielle padded barefoot across her room. It was all the light she needed to find the gap in the mosquito netting that draped her bed. The minute her head hit the pillow, hands reached for her and pulled her into solid warmth.

"How can you be so arrogant?" she asked Micah. "You can't possibly believe that I want you? Not after today? Get out of my bed!" Gabrielle lay still, expecting her words to undo Micah's arms.

"No," he said. "You need someone tonight, Gabrielle. All I'm going to do is hold you."

"You're the last person I want to hold me."

"So you say," he murmured softly, curving his body comfortably around hers. "But I'm the only one here. Now, go to sleep...please," he added.

Gabrielle was certain she wouldn't sleep, she was too

aware of his arm across her waist, his leg locked over hers, his breath warm on her neck. She hated him. But after only a short while, wrapped in a way in Micah, not merely in his arms, she slept

In the next two days Gabrielle finished the last of the contracts. If only Micah would release her, she could go home. She eyed the safe. Next time he came to Chepo, she would insist he return her passport and visa.

She called her parents. When she asked her mother to deny what Micah had told her, Emily began to cry and handed the phone to her father. Nate told her he had wanted to tell her before she left for Panama, but Emily and Dr. Baker had convinced him not to. "I have faith in you, Gab," he said. "I just wish saying that you're young, you'll get over it in time would help, but I know how devastated you must be. I wish it were different."

Gabrielle began to cry then, until there were no more tears and her eyes felt raspy and dry. Maria clucked around her like a mother hen, seeing to it Gabrielle had cool damp cloths for her swollen eyes, cooking special little tidbits to entice Gabrielle to eat, offering bowls of monkey plums, Gabrielle's favorite after mangoes. Seeing Gabrielle's distress, Maria refused to go home nights and, for the first time in weeks, slept at Chepo.

Shadow gave up his spot on his rug and came to lie by the sofa. His gold-flecked brown eyes looked as sad as Gabrielle felt. She laughed at him, and the sound was foreign to her ears.

"You're outdoing me, Shadow," she told him. "Come on, I'll take you for a walk."

Gabrielle didn't know it then, but she began to accept in those few minutes that her dreams of being a prima ballerina had to be discarded, and her soul began to heal itself, taking its cue from a lifted spirit, a squared shoulder, a tilted chin, and a tinkling laugh—challenging the future, not sure what it held, but sure that there was one.

When Gabrielle and Shadow returned to the house, Maria excitedly showed Gabrielle a telegram for Micah delivered by the local *chivas* driver. Gabrielle tapped it thoughtfully. It must be from Benton. Should she or should she not open it? Yes, she decided, then she could call Helen and leave a message for Micah. She tore it open. Her eyes scanned the yellow paper and the blood drained from her head. She felt as if it were draining from her whole body: her legs were weak and she put out her hand and supported herself against the sofa. The telegram was from Vanessa.

> Dearest darling,
>   I have the most exciting news. I'm pregnant. I've gone home to get best medical care possible for our little bundle of joy. We shall have to marry quickly. Come home soon.
>
>   With all my love, Vanessa

Gabrielle folded the telegram and slid it back into its envelope. She had torn it open. There was no way she could pretend she hadn't seen it. She put it on Micah's desk.

It didn't matter, she told herself. She felt nothing for Micah, simply nothing; she didn't even hate him anymore. She felt like a moth caught in amber, a moth destined never to flutter its wings, never to dance, never to love, never to tempt the flickering flame of a candle. And that was a good thing, she decided. She could never be hurt again. Gabrielle felt like it was the day after never.

SHE heard the straining and growling motor as the Jeep came into view over the sharp rise. Gabrielle walked out onto the porch and watched as the Jeep slowly and carefully negotiated the bridge over the chasm, then the headlights wobbled from one side of the narrow road to the other. She sucked in her breath as the twin beams of light skimmed the very edge of the precipice. Whoever was driving had to be drunk.

The Jeep snarled into the drive, missing entirely the thatched-roof carport, and abruptly jerked to a halt in the jasmine. The crushed petals spilled their fragrance into the air.

"Benton!" Gabrielle shouted and watched him climb out of the Jeep. He waved a bone-thin hand, forcing himself to a steady walk. He stopped in front of her, his feet firmly locked to the ground. The rest of his bony frame swayed precariously.

"Hello, Gabby," he said, and his wide smile pulled thin lips far back into the hollows of his cheeks.

"Benton, you're drunk!" Her arm circled his waist, helping him up the steps. His thin body was hot; his arm felt papery with fever. A corkscrew of fear gripped Gabrielle's stomach.

"I am, a little," Benton agreed in a clear voice, free of all wheezing. Gabrielle started at his clear nasal twang.

"Where have you been? Micah looked all over Panama City for you last week."

"On Toboga. Swimming, drinking, eating"— he paused, a smile on his once handsome face— "and other things you're too much of a lady to hear about." Benton stumbled. Gabrielle grabbed a swath of his shirt and lowered him to the sofa. "A little brandy would be nice," he told her.

Her hands shook, splashing the golden liquid. Benton took the snifter, swirling its contents against the fragile glass expertly, and held it under his long nose, inhaling deeply. "Marvelous stuff, brandy, especially Micah's... truly fit for the gods." Gabrielle waited breathlessly for a wheeze. None came. He looked different.

"Benton, are you all right?" Utter dread dripped ice-cold in her veins at his smile. Now she realized why he looked so changed. "Where are your glasses?"

"Lost 'em swimming." He laughed, a twangy, gay sound. A boyish grin pulled his pale, taut skin over his hollowed-out face. His eyes glittered, the lines bracketing them, smoothed.

"Benton, just sit right there, I'll be right back," Gabrielle said and walked as fast as she could without running to the radio. She flipped the switch. "Mamoni—" Her voice cracked with fear. "Mamoni, come in, please." There were several long seconds of silence, then static.

"This is Mamoni." Helen's clear voice jumped from the receiver.

"Helen! Benton is here. He's sick, very sick. Tell Micah and Jinks. Tell them to hurry," Gabrielle rattled, near hysteria and feeling totally helpless.

"Gabby, slow down." Helen's voice crackled. "Say again."

"Benton is ill, he's burning up with fever, he's drunk, he's—he's— Helen!" Gabrielle's voice lifted in panic. "Tell Micah!"

"They're not here, Gabby. They've gone into the interior. I don't expect them back until tomorrow."

"Send Max after them!" Gabrielle almost screamed.

"He's in Panama City, picking up supplies. Gabby, calm down. Tell me exactly, how high is Benton's fever? How does he look?"

"I don't know. He looks. . . I can see the veins through his skin. He's—he's parched, he's been eating everything, he lost his glasses, he's not wheezing, his voice— Helen, for God's sake!" Gabrielle cried. "He's sick. You've got to come."

"I can't, Gabby. I've got a logger with a burst appendix. Gabby? Did you hear me?"

"Yes," she whispered. Gabrielle flipped the machine off and hurried back into the living room. "Benton!"

"I'm awake. I was just resting my eyes." He smiled sheepishly. Relief washed over Gabrielle and she sank down on the ottoman at his feet. Benton stared at her a long moment.

"You," he began, "you've got to remember to look around Micah's anger. He's been hurt, seen too much. We both have, but in Micah everything got twisted. That's why he's so angry all the time—he's never held out for hope and there's always a tiny thread of hope, isn't there? Micah doesn't believe there can be anything pure or innocent left in this godforsaken world." Benton started. "Better not tell Amand I said that." His chuckle was bell clear. "Aw, don't cry, Gabby." His eyes twinkled in merriment. "I'll tell you a secret. Do you remember our interview?"

"Yes." She smiled through her tears.

"I was going to hire you whether you could do the work or not. I made up my mind to do it myself if I had to." He laughed. "You did work, though, too well and too fast. I keep having to look for ways to slow you down, have 'accidents' with the contracts."

"I know you do. I saw you 'accidentally' pour coffee on one. Why, Benton?"

"Because Micah needs you. He will more than ever soon. If you don't stay, he'll be lost. . .just plain lost." His voice faded; his chin fell forward on his chest.

"Benton!" Gabrielle thought she screamed, but it was only a whisper.

His head jerked up. "I'm so tired, Gabby."

"Wait a while, Benton. Please, talk to me." *Wait a while for what?* she asked herself. Gabrielle was afraid of the answer.

He straightened the snifter and lifted it carefully to his lips. He looked at her over the rim. "You love him, don't you?" A thread of desperation sounded in his nasal twang.

"Yes" —she nodded— "I do."

"Then everything will work out. You'll see to it?"

A deep sob, which had hung like a tight knot in her throat, broke sharply from Gabrielle's lips. She choked it back. "I'll try."

"I wish you'd stop crying." He smiled. "You know what I have a taste for?"

"No, tell me. I'll make it for you."

"Peanut butter cookies."

"Peanut but—" Gabrielle laughed, stifling her sobs.

"Yes, warm from the oven. . . . My mother used to—" his voice faltered.

"Come in the kitchen with me." She helped him up, not daring to leave him alone.

Benton sat at the table, talking while she sifted, stirred, and mixed. He dipped a spoon in the peanut butter, savoring the taste. "Did I never tell you I was raised in Kansas, Gabby?"

"No, you never did."

"Western Kansas. It's flat, rolling land; you can see for miles—not like here, where you can't even see around the next leaf." He closed his eyes, remembering. "There's nothing more beautiful than a section of new wheat, Gabby. When the wind blows and ruffles the blades, you imagine a wide, green, bottomless sea. And during harvest you can chew a handful of the grain—it's sweet like chewing gum, only better. And snow! Lordy, the snow! So cool." His head bobbed on his folded arms.

"Benton, wake up," Gabrielle pleaded. "You were telling me about the snow," she prompted.

To Gabrielle's immense relief, he raised his head. "One winter" —he laughed— "it snowed and snowed, dry, powdery snow, and one morning we woke up freezing. The water in my fishbowl froze, cracking the glass. The fish looked like little golden chips. They lived, though," he said with awe. "When the ice melted, they flopped around. Mother let me put them in a cup until we could get into Dodge City and buy another bowl." Benton rested his chin in his hands, his eyes closed, immobile.

"Benton," Gabrielle whispered as she forked the imprint on each little mound of dough on the pan.

"I'm tired, Gabby." He didn't open his eyes.

"I'm baking cookies for you, remember?" she pleaded.

"I'll wait," he said slowly. "I wanted to tell you about my son."

"Your son?" Gabrielle froze.

"Yes, you see, I once knew a girl like you, Anh Loan, but that's— Never mind." He fumbled for his wallet and drew out a faded photograph. Gabrielle wiped sticky dough from her hands. A chubby sloe-eyed, black-haired infant looked out of the picture. A wide, happy grin creased his fat brown cheeks.

"His name is Thuen." Benton took the snapshot and placed it carefully back in his tattered wallet. "Micah took him to the mountains when I was in the hospital. It was safer there." He was silent, tears trickling down his face. "We tried to get him out after we got home, but the village was overrun. The old woman who had him disappeared," he said sadly. The aroma of baking cookies wafted in the still kitchen. "Smells just like home, Gabby."

"They'll be ready in a few minutes, Benton."

"I'm tired. Just let me rest a minute," he said and bent his head on his folded arms. Gabrielle listened for his breathing. It was quiet and steady, free of the wrenching wheezing. She cleaned the table around him and rinsed the dishes. She took the cookies from the oven.

"They're ready, Benton," she said, sliding the hot pan on the table. "Benton?" Only the soft swishing of the old-fashioned ceiling fan turning lazily above their head sounded in the room.

"No!" she moaned, her hands flying to his neck. No pulse. Then his wrists. "Benton!" she screamed.

Maria's plump bulk filled the doorway. "Gabby! *Qúe? Qúe?*" Maria's voice rose in fear. *"Madre de Dios!"* She crossed herself and moved swiftly to catch Gabrielle as she folded slowly in a faint.

Chapter Eighteen

Someone was calling her name. Gabrielle raised her swollen lids. A shaft of moonlight slipped through the shutters, ruffling a pattern of cold light through the net across the bed.

"Gabrielle!"

"Amand, I hear you," she said. Her throat felt so dry. "Benton—" She dreaded to say the words.

"Yes," the priest murmured compassionately. He sat next to her on the bed. "Are you all right?"

Gabrielle nodded, but the tears welled up, her body racked with sobs, and she couldn't speak. He let her cry, waiting patiently, sure the tears would ease her grief. Finally the dry sobs choked and stopped.

"Micah?" she asked.

"He's on his way. Max is flying them here."

"So soon? I thought—"

"You slept all day," Amand informed her. "Maria called me. Luckily I was at St. Joseph's." Gabrielle moved sluggishly. She felt disintegrated.

"Are you okay now?" Amand moved to the door.

"I'm fine, Amand. At least, as fine as I can be. I just need to bathe." She gathered her things, dreading to see Micah. What could she say?

Gabrielle refreshed the cloth for her swollen eyes. She was drowsy, spent with emotion, and almost slept again as the bathwater cooled. The cloth flew off her eyes. Micah stood over her. Beard stubble, days old, shadowed his square jaw, pulled taut. A muscle leaped as he held his jaw rigid. His fists clenched and water dripped from the cloth he held in his hand. His eyes.... Gabrielle lowered hers, unable to look at the pain etched in Micah's eyes.

"What happened?" His voice was ragged, and he gave her no chance to gather her wits, no chance to answer him.

"Answer me!" he said and sat on the edge of the tub and grasped her shoulders violently, lifting her with such force she had to fold her knees under her to keep from hanging in midair. Water shed from her silken body.

"Micah, he went swimming... he—he lost his glasses... he wanted some peanut butter cookies. We were sitting in the kitchen." She inhaled deeply, the thudding of her heart pirating the air from her lungs. "He said he was tired... I...he...."

"You were there when—"

"Yes, every minute."

Micah pulled her to him, gripping her wet body. Her arms circled him, her lips against the scars in the hollow of his neck. His khaki shirt was rough against her breasts and her salty tears mingled with the water that imprinted her body on his shirt.

"He talked about you," she told him, her voice muffled against the taut cords of his neck. "He told me about Thuen." She felt the muscles in his back ripple and shudder. His arms crushed her so tightly she couldn't breathe. A while later she heard him draw a ragged breath, filling his lungs with air as he regained his composure.

"What's going to happen now?" she asked quietly as he untangled her arms from his neck.

"Jinks is flying with Benton, home to Kansas. Amand is saying Mass here tonight."

"He was a good friend, Micah." Tears began to flow again. He draped a towel over her shoulders, covering her nakedness.

"Yes, he was," he said softly. "Now, stop crying and get dressed." He pressed his lips gently to hers. "Maria is fixing something to eat for later. Then Max is taking Jinks and—and Benton to Panama City. Amand is driving Helen back to Coco Solito."

GABRIELLE heard the roar of the helicopter as it lifted from its peeled log pad. Max and Jinks, with Benton, were the last to leave. She shook the dishwater from her hands.

"You go on to bed, Maria. I'll finish these and turn out the lights."

"Yes, I think so. I am very tired." Maria's straw slippers swished on the wooden floor as she made her way to the back of the house.

Gabrielle stepped into the courtyard. Rain clouds were scudding across the mountain, blocking out the stars, and with them came the rain. Gabrielle moved under the veranda as the rain came down, a near impenetrable curtain of water. It wouldn't last long, she knew; these tropical deluges, she had learned, seldom did.

A lamp threw a mottled glow on the rain-washed tile through the living room screen.

"Micah?" Gabrielle called out, seeing no one in the long room. He raised his hand in the shadows from one of the long sofas, then folded his elbow over his eyes without saying a word. His long length, cloaked in an Egyptian cotton caftan, filled the sofa. Gabrielle pushed the ottoman out of the way and knelt down on the smooth, cool floor. She put her hand on his heart and felt its steady rhythm.

"Micah, talk to me," she whispered. When he didn't answer, she drew her fingertips down the bare arm he had crooked over his eyes. The muscles and tendons were rope tight.

"You need to relax. Why don't you cry or scream or something?" Her voice was barely a whisper. Micah refused to answer, so she let her fingers wander and explore the scars on his neck, the smooth muscular chest. She held her hand over his heart and felt it flutter, skipping a beat, then she observed him openly for a long minute. Gabrielle made her decision. She stood up, took off her clothes, and knelt naked beside the sofa. *Just this one last time,* she told herself. *He needs me. After that he will belong to Vanessa.* There had been no need for her to mention the telegram. After Mass he had gone to his desk for some papers Jinks needed and had found the message. Gabrielle had watched him read it, then put it in the desk drawer.

Gabrielle bent her head slowly, bringing her lips near his, and hovered there. His breath was warm and fragrant with brandy and coffee. She pressed her lips to his, savoring the taste. Hesitantly at first, then with an urgency building in her, she traced the pattern of his lips with her tongue. Gabrielle's emotions were like selfish vagrants, demanding the succor his body offered; she breached his lips with her tongue, brushing his teeth, probing gently. Micah's lips said nothing, but she felt his heart begin to race beneath her hand, so she moved it slowly across his belly until she found him.

"Take me, Micah," she whispered, her voice husky, in cadence with the desire that coursed like wildfire through her veins.

"Gabrielle," he moaned, a racking sound mixed with pain and insatiable desire. With quick, fluid motions he lifted her from the floor and strode with her cradled in his arms to his bed. His breathing was a barrage of short harsh sobs as he stripped the caftan from his body and lay down beside her. His hands traveled the length of her, imprinting every curve, every mound of flesh, indelibly in his brain. Gabrielle gasped with pleasure, shivering as his fingers probed and sought her intimately. Desire and primitive need spawned a wild, raging hunger, saturating their bodies. She arched her back, pushing against him. A low sound of consuming ecstasy escaped her lips as his mouth covered her breasts, taunting their peaks with moist little forays and soft sucking motions until she begged to be released from the fires scorching her loins. But Micah seemed driven by a passion that urged him to crest higher and higher until his urgent throbbing shaft governed his needs and demanded to be thrust into the narrow valley of flesh that beckoned and promised incredible ecstasy.

He used his knee to spread her legs and, unable to withdraw, yielded to unimpeded desire, a desire as primitive and powerful as any that might be found in the untamed jungle surrounding the tiled-roof house.

Gabrielle gasped as she felt him plunge into her and arched her hips to help him explore the sweetness with each thrust of his hips until they were both drawn to a crescendo of sensual, pulsating pleasure that left their bodies drained, impoverished, and satiated. She reeled under the force of Micah's passion and her pulse had not returned to normal when Micah began again. She willingly gave herself, meeting his needs, and drowned in wanton, sensual ecstasy.

OUTSIDE, it was raining and Gabrielle listened to the rain brushing against the house. Inside, there was only the sound of breathing, hers and Micah's, as they lay tangled and content in one another's arms.

"Are you asleep?" she asked, her body and mind still steeped in the wonder of their lovemaking.

"No," he said, and Gabrielle thought she could detect a smile in his voice. *He's thinking of all the times I said I didn't want him,* she thought. That was in the past now. She wondered if he was going to tell her about Vanessa, what he planned to do, but there were other things she wanted to know about first.

"Are you going to continue looking for Thuen, Micah?"

"No, he's dead," he answered, his voice curiously flat.

Gabrielle sat up. "Dead? But Benton said he's alive, cared for by an old woman. He thinks—thought—that she and Thuen escaped to Cambodia, or Thailand. How do you know he's dead?" Gabrielle thought of the picture of the smiling infant that Benton had carried in his wallet. What would become of the photograph, Benton's only link to his child?

"I found Thuen," Micah said. "The Vietcong have a deep hatred of blacks. When they overran a village, they lined the villagers up and the half-caste children and their mothers were always the first to die. They were mutilated and beheaded."

Gabrielle shuddered. "Why did you let Benton believe Thuen was alive all these years? It was cruel to let him keep on hoping."

"Cruel?" Micah looked at Gabrielle, a cynical expression on his face, but in the darkness she didn't see it. "What do you know about cruelty, Gabrielle? You've always lived in a nice, safe world." His hand was on her back; he felt her stiffen. "I'm sorry," he said. "Benton needed hope to live. I told him Loan had hidden the baby with an old woman and that I took them both into the mountains. I would have lied about Loan too, but her parents found her and told Benton. I came across Thuen about a mile from the mountain hamlet where I'd left them. The Vietcong had—'' His voice choked, remembering. ''I buried him.'' Gabrielle digested this and began to cry, for Thuen, for Loan, for Benton, and for herself.

''Shh, go to sleep,'' Micah murmured, drawing her down beside him. ''Tomorrow I'm sending you and Helen over to Toboga for a week or so while I clear out Benton's office. Everything has to be transferred back to the States. I'll be busy lining up a management team to handle the logging operation. I think I'm going to need some free time to handle a few personal matters.''

''I'll help you.''

''No, you've been through enough. When I get back, we need to talk.''

No, we don't. I'm going home. I know Vanessa is expecting your baby. I love you. Aloud she said, ''All right.'' Too much was on Gabrielle's mind and she was restless. ''I can't sleep,'' she whispered.

''Good,'' Micah murmured. ''I can't seem to get enough of you.'' His lips brushed along the curve of her cheek, and Gabrielle shifted her weight, moving close, every part of her aware of the promise in his words.

''You're not eating,'' Helen observed.

''I'm not really very hungry,'' Gabrielle answered, toying with her food absentmindedly. She didn't know what was wrong with her. The serenity of Toboga should have helped, but it didn't. Old Wu had been very kind to them, giving them rooms overlooking the water, quiet and sheltered. He had set up this table for them too, on the deck, away from prying eyes, away from the other guests, so she and Helen could be alone, to talk quietly, cry, or grieve.

''You have to eat, Gab,'' Helen said. ''Not eating won't bring Benton back. It'll just make you sick.''

Gabrielle smiled. ''I know. It's just that everything I do eat seems to go in the wrong direction.''

''Oh?'' Helen said. ''It does?'' She looked at Gabrielle sharply. ''Do you want to sleep a lot too?''

''Why, yes—lately,'' Gabrielle said, surprised. ''How

did you know? Have I got some sort of tropical disease on top of everything else?''

Helen laughed. ''I'd hardly call it a disease and it's not confined to the tropics. When was your last period?'' she asked bluntly.

Gabrielle felt the blood drain from her head. A prickling sensation seared her body; she began to tremble. She had not had a period, not since she came to Panama.

''Not since I left Houston,'' she uttered aloud. ''I thought the change in climate—''

''Change in climate!'' Helen repeated, astonished. ''Haven't you ever heard of the pill? Don't you take it?''

''No,'' Gabrielle choked, ''not since the car accident. After I got out of the hospital I had to live at home and then there was the rush to get ready to come to Panama. I just never got around to—'' Oh, God, what was she going to do? ''Helen, I've got to leave. I've got to go home.''

''Home? Why don't you just tell Micah? It's obvious the way you two behave that—''

''No!''

''All right,'' Helen said. ''No one is forcing you to do anything. Besides, you really need to see a doctor—there's no sense agonizing over something that might not be so.''

But Gabrielle knew . . . just knew it was true. How could she take care of a baby? How could she ever explain it to her parents? She voiced the last question aloud.

''You wouldn't have to explain how,'' Helen said wryly, ''just who, and then only if you wanted to.''

Gabrielle opened her eyes wide in an effort to hold back the tears. ''Oh, it's all such a nightmare. I can't dance . . . I may be pregnant. . . .'' And Vanessa was pregnant too. Wouldn't Micah just love to learn that he had gotten them both that way? What a boost to his arrogance, his ego.

''There's no need for you to make a doomsday list,'' Helen said soothingly. ''Let's finish breakfast and you can lie down a while. This afternoon, if you want, we can take the launch to the mainland and let you see a doctor. You've had too many shocks, too much trauma, too quickly. You just need time to sort it all out. I still think the best thing to do is tell Micah.''

Never, Gabrielle thought. ''I'll think about that, Helen. I do want to see a doctor, though.''

''Agh, don't look now,'' Helen said, ''but we're going to get company.''

''What have we here? The nursemaid and the lame ballerina,'' Vanessa drawled sarcastically. ''You don't mind if I sit down?'' Vanessa looked around for another chair. There was none on the deck.

Gabrielle forced a smile. ''Sorry, there doesn't seem to be another chair.'' Undaunted, Vanessa snapped her fingers to a passing busboy. He brought a chair and Vanessa sat down. Gabrielle and Helen looked at one another and silently agreed it was time to go. They began making motions to leave. Vanessa put her hand on Gabrielle's arm.

''Did Micah get my telegram?''

''Oh, was that from you? Yes, he did. But I got the impression he thought the sender had left for the States. Whatever the message was, it didn't seem to make him too happy.''

''Oh? That's too bad,'' Vanessa said, looking directly at Gabrielle. ''But I'm sure in the end he'll do the honorable thing.''

Gabrielle gathered her purse, her sunglasses—small innate acts that made her seem calm to the two women looking at her. She stood up. Helen made the same quick preparations and moved a few feet from the table. Gabrielle let her eyes swing over Vanessa, distaste clearly in her face.

''I hope you do marry soon, Vanessa. You and Micah deserve one another more than you'll ever know.''

''Where's your bird dog?'' Vanessa asked, a sneer in her voice.

Gabrielle turned back. ''My what?'' She looked blank.

''Your bird dog—Benton,'' Vanessa reiterated.

Gabrielle stared at Vanessa, surely she must know by now that Benton had died. She had to, unless Micah had been too busy to see or talk to her yet. ''He died last week," she said simply, hating to discuss Benton at all with this evil woman.

"How sad," Vanessa said, smiling. Gabrielle sensed that the news made Vanessa happy in a self-satisfied way.

"What was that all about?" Helen asked as they made their way back to their rooms.

"Nothing."

THE visit to the mainland and the doctor Helen had chosen confirmed that Gabrielle was pregnant. Ten weeks, he said.

"Things will sort themselves out, Gab, they always do. Let's just relax the few days we have left here on Toboga. Even if you won't marry Micah, he has a right to know about the baby, that is, if you plan to stay pregnant. I think you should reconsider your decision not to tell him."

Gabrielle did. A thousand times each day. And every time she reached the same conclusion. She mustn't tell Micah. Neither could she kill his baby—no, she couldn't kill *her* baby. She thought about writing to her mother. *Dear Mother: You got your wish. Sometime in September you are going to become a grandmother. Happy? Love, Gabrielle.* For it would be September. It had to be. She wouldn't be *so* pregnant from their lovemaking the night after Benton died. It had to be when they were on the *Upsure*. . .Christmas week.

Now that she had accepted her pregnancy, Gabrielle found herself fascinated with babies. It occurred to her that she had never been around any. She had no cousins, no brothers and sisters, and for as long as she could remember, all her friends had been her own age from the time she had begun dancing at three. Later, at the Fine Arts Academy and in the Civic Ballet, age difference hadn't mattered, and in any case, none had been babies. Her avid interest drove Helen to distraction.

She inspected her body every day, standing in front of the mirror naked, searching for clues. Although her breasts were beginning to swell, her stomach remained flat. It worried her. One morning after a particularly assiduous inspection during which she noted no changes, she threw on her robe and padded into Helen's room.

"Helen, wake up," she said, sitting down on the bed.

"Wha-what is it?" she asked, pulling herself up reluctantly on the headboard. "You sick again?"

"No...yes, but that was hours ago. I want to know what my baby looks like."

Helen eyed her askance and slid down on her pillows again. "I'm no seer. For that you have to wait, just like every other mother."

Later, over coffee, Gabrielle had a curiosity she couldn't contain. "Helen, may I ask you a personal question?"

"How personal?"

"I was wondering why you and Jinks don't have any children."

Helen paused, reflecting for a moment. "That is a personal question, but I don't mind telling you. It's a choice we made years ago. We couldn't afford to have any while Jinks was still in medical school. Right after he graduated the army got him. When he came back from Vietnam he put in a residency. That was another long hours-short pay job, but we discussed having a baby then too. Actually we think having children does not automatically make a person a good, loving parent. Some people are just not cut out to be parents. Jinks and I are two of them, but we adore children. My sister has seven and couldn't imagine any other way of life. Of course, she eats, sleeps, and dreams Spock. Does that answer your question?"

"Yes," Gabrielle answered as she vacantly stared at the horizon.

THEY stayed on the island another week. Gabrielle swore Helen to secrecy and Helen reluctantly gave her word not to tell Jinks or Micah about the pregnancy. She knew Helen didn't understand the need for secrecy, but then she hadn't read Vanessa's telegram.

Vanessa had left Toboga the same afternoon of the day she had stopped uninvited at their table. Gabrielle had been standing at her window in their suite overlooking the pier and had seen Vanessa board the early-afternoon launch for the mainland. By now she and Micah might already have married. What was there to stop them? Suppose Vanessa was at Chepo? It was a situation Gabrielle did not want to contend with and the anxiety, coupled with morning sickness, drained her.

Wisely Helen did not try to distract Gabrielle from these thoughts. They pushed aside the traumatic effect of Benton's death and kept Gabrielle from dwelling on the loss of her career.

Max met them on the pier in Balboa. He had a message from Micah for Gabrielle. He was working with the logging crews, introducing them to the management team he had hired. He would be there another three days.

At least he wouldn't be at Chepo when Gabrielle returned and that would give her time to think what she must do. She didn't want to face Micah. She couldn't. She was afraid she would reveal her pregnancy by some conscious or unconscious gesture. Suppose he heard her in the morning when she got sick? There was no mistaking that sound.

Back at Chepo, Gabrielle was immensely relieved to find that Vanessa was not on the premises, nor had she been there or called. Maria was happy to see her and Shadow hung about her feet until she had to chastise him. She didn't want to fall and hurt the baby.

She missed Benton but dreamed of Micah. She wanted him and the want was like a living thing, a part of her, a need that grew to immense proportions during the night when in her sleep she visualized what the flesh could not.

Despite her dreams her resolve not to see Micah strengthened. She needed a place to hide—somewhere, anywhere—until her visa expired. Then she would just show up at the consulate. They would call Micah and insist he bring her passport. He couldn't refuse the government. She wouldn't have to see him, then she could go home.

Home brought thoughts of the ballet, and how remote it seemed to her now, how unimportant in light of all the other things life had to offer. Micah had been right after all, so had her mother. She had spent her life on her toes dancing in a wonderland of fantasy. Well, there would be no more fantasy for her now, only reality, and that was the new life growing inside her, a little girl perhaps, and who knows, someday a dancer, a premiere danseuse herself. Gabrielle would be satisfied with that. She thought of Val and laughed aloud, imagining the surprise on Val's face when her good friend learned that she too was expecting a baby.

The next morning Gabrielle was sitting on the sofa recovering from a bout of nausea with saltines and orange juice recommended by Helen when a motor whining shrilly interrupted her thoughts. *Dear God! Not Micah, please. Don't let him be home early,* she prayed and ran to the front veranda, Shadow at her heels, and waited until the Jeep nosed over the rise. Father Chardin!

"Amand, come in, you're just the person I want to see."

"I am?"

He smiled at her effusive welcome, but the tone in Gabrielle's voice reminded him of his sisters. They had often had that "up" sound when they wanted him to do something, urging him against his wishes and certainly against his better judgment. He thought fleetingly of the monastery, its ordered life, so quiet, and free of women's wiles.

"Yes. Where are you going now?" Amand wore his black suit with its Roman collar. She hoped he was on his way into the jungle, it would solve her problem of where to go. "But wait," she said, "let me ask Maria to get us some iced tea—unless you would like something stronger?"

"Iced tea is fine," Amand said, showing his strong white teeth. "Well, this is my last trip into the province," he announced. "I've finally received word that my request to study in China has been approved by the government in Peking. I leave next month."

"Amand, that's wonderful. Congratulations! How long are you staying in the jungle this trip, then?"

"A week at the outside, less probably. I shouldn't be going at all, but I've still one lead to follow up, an elusive one at best, but I've got to try. There's a small band of Chibchan on the move in the southern tip of the province. An old *nele* is traveling with them, I'd like to meet him." The priest turned his vivid blue eyes on Gabrielle. "The look on your face tells me you are only listening for politeness' sake. Do you have something on your mind?''

Gabrielle answered without any hesitation. "Yes, I do. I want to go with you. I don't think I could handle a trek, but perhaps you could drop me off in a village with some of your native friends. I need a place to—to hide actually, just for a few days.''

"Hide?" Amand said, astonished. "What do you mean? From whom?" His voice boomed with amazement.

"I want to go home, Amand. Micah wants me to stay. He's—he's trying to force me to extend my visa. It runs out in a few days. If I'm not here, he can't make me. I can't stay here... I just can't." A sob caught in her throat.

"Gabrielle, what is it? What's happened?" His voice was soothing, soft, and drawing her out. Gabrielle took a deep breath, trying to form her words calmly.

"I'm pregnant, Amand," she said quietly, "and I want to go home to have my baby."

Amand was tongue-tied for a split second. He shook his head sadly. "Micah?" he questioned.

"Yes. It—I—he doesn't know. I don't want him to know. I want to go home. He and Vanessa Thomas—" She held her eyes wide to keep tears from overflowing their rims. "Vanessa told me—I mean, she sent a telegram to Micah and I read it by accident. She's pregnant too and she and Micah are to be married.''

"My God!" Amand exploded. "Are you sure?" He repeated the question, his voice etched with disbelief. Gabrielle went to Micah's desk, found the telegram in the drawer, and handed it to Amand. After he read it she put it back.

"I'm only sure of one thing, Amand, that I'm having a baby and I want to go home. I don't want to discuss this with Micah. So, where can I go, Amand?"

"Somewhere in Panama City? A convent, perhaps?"

"A convent!" Gabrielle laughed despite her tears. "Be serious, for heaven's sake."

"I'm trying to be, for precisely that reason," he answered dryly.

"It can't be anywhere on the isthmus, Micah knows it

like the back of his hand. When we were looking for Benton, he dragged me all over, and everyone knows him too. I need to hide in the jungle, in one of those small villages, but away from any of the logging teams.''

''You don't know what you're saying,'' Amand said, shocked.

''Yes, I do.''

''No, you don't. If I took a strange American woman into any of the Indian villages, it would be all over the province within twenty-four hours.''

''Well, not into a village, then.'' She looked at him expectantly.

''You'll need medical care. Go to Old Panama.''

''No. I won't need anything, not for just a few days.''

''What makes you so sure Micah would look for you?''

''He'd feel obligated to. He used to be a student of my father's.''

''Suppose he calls your parents to see if you went home?''

''He won't. He wouldn't want the publicity, but besides that, he has my passport in his safe, so I can't leave the country. I'm depending on the government to ask me to leave when my visa is up. I mean, if I just show up at the consulate and stay there, Micah would have to bring my passport, wouldn't he?''

Amand looked at her as though he questioned her sanity. ''Who knows what he would do? I wouldn't want to make any predictions.'' Amand shook his head. ''I just don't know. I'd have to think about it.''

''There's no time to think! Micah will be back from Mamoni tomorrow. I won't stay. I'm leaving with or without your help.''

Amand gazed at the stubborn, resigned look on her face. ''You know *if* I helped you....'' His voice trailed off. ''Have you given any thought to how Micah might feel about this? You should at least give him the opportunity to explain.''

''You mean give him the opportunity to decide which of us he should marry, don't you? Or maybe Vanessa and I should draw straws?'' she said bitterly.

The priest mused quietly for several long moments. "Micah would be mad if he comes back to Chepo and finds you gone—very mad, I'd say. He comes close to rattling the gates of heaven when he gets stirred up."

"His anger can rattle the gates of hell for all I care. I'm packing, Amand. I'll walk, if necessary."

"Through this jungle? With the bushmasters, wild boas, alligators, stinging and flying pests, and the screaming panthers?" he said and smiled sadly.

"I'd welcome them." She uttered the words, deadly serious.

Chapter Nineteen

"Have you decided where to take me, Amand?" Gabrielle asked as they jounced over deep ruts in the road. She clung to the side of the Jeep, feeling every bump wrinkle her spine.

"There's an outcast Indian woman. She has a *choza* near a Cuna village but not so close that you'll be noticed, because no one is allowed to associate with her."

Outcast. The word jogged Gabrielle's memory. "Is this the woman whose life you saved? The one who had her children taken away from her?"

"Yes," Amand said, surprised. "How did you know?"

"It was Christmas Day, the day I boarded the *Upsure* in Houston. Helen told me about it. I remember a man was tied to a manchineel tree and died."

"That's right." Amand nodded.

Gabrielle wanted to talk more, to curb her nervousness, but the road narrowed and the jungle seemed to be hedging them in, crowding the thin, rough path, loosely called a road because some surveyor had occasionally tied a piece of red plastic to a bush or a limb. Gabrielle shuddered at the silence around them. She could never get used to the eerie stillness of a jungle asleep. Colorful wild orchids clinging to bits of dead wood and trailing vines belied the primitive existence in tangled wilderness.

Her clothes clung damply to her by the time the priest jerked the Jeep to a halt under a tangle of gnarled vines, some as thick as her waist.

"From here on, we walk. Are you sure you want to go through with this, Gabrielle?"

"I'm sure. It's just for a few days. Don't worry so."

"But, in your condition, I wish you would reconsider. I can find you a place in Panama City," he said hopefully.

"Amand, be serious. Besides, there's no place you could

take me on the isthmus that Micah won't find me. No, this will do. I can rough it.''

"Rough it," Amand muttered, not quite sure how Gabrielle had managed to convince him this was the thing to do. He slung his machete into the thong at his waist and shouldered an olive-green pack. "You know, I hope I don't run into Micah or Jinks while you're up here. I can be devious, but I'm afraid I don't lie too well.''

"Oh, Amand, you won't even have to see either of them. They won't know. All you have to do when you come back is drive me straight to the consulate. I'll manage from there.'' Gabrielle lifted out the small case she had brought with her and joined Amand on the other side of the Jeep. She looked back through the nightmarish landscape they had just traversed and couldn't believe they had actually driven over it.

"I'm ready," she said with far more bravery than she felt.

"Follow me," Amand said, leading her into the underbrush, thick with the smell of musty decay. Beyond the odor, which Gabrielle quickly became used to, she was surprised to find that the jungle floor, spongy with humus, was much more spacious than she had imagined. The overview from the helicopter and from the Jeep had given her the impression that the jungle forest was crowded, tree upon tree, but that wasn't the case. Some areas were thick with head-high sprawling plants but Amand avoided them. Birds sang and chirped, some so brilliantly feathered she found them immediately, others so well camouflaged she never saw them. Spiderwebs, silvery and translucent, formed a canopy over their heads. There was a cathedral-like silence in the jungle far different from that which she had experienced on Toboga. Here the silence was broken only by the birds, an occasional slithering sound that made her shiver, and her own panting breathlessness.

"Amand, wait a minute," she called to him, bending over to catch her breath and gagging on a mouthful of gnats. He doubled back and put a hand under her elbow.

"I did warn you," he said sympathetically.

"I know, I'll be all right. It's just these gnats. They're

driving me crazy." Amand shook a snowy handkerchief out of his pocket.

"Tie this around your face," he suggested. Gabrielle did and quivered with relief. She was exhausted and aching with strain when they finally entered a small clearing. A ring of stones contained a small fire in front of a small thatched shack, the *choza*. A roof of fronds and banana leaves was held in place by a loose network of twigs.

"Wait here," Amand cautioned. Gabrielle watched as he went forward, then skirted the hut. A few minutes later he was back. A short, round, albino native woman followed.

"Her name is Pira," Amand said. "She speaks a few words of English, and a little Spanish." Pira peered close to Gabrielle, her pink eyes obviously nearsighted. Then she grinned and took Gabrielle's hand and led her into the hut.

Amand was right behind them. "You see what's here? A string hammock to sleep in, no running water." His foot crushed a huge red ant. "Pests. You think you can handle it?"

Gabrielle was stoic. "Yes. I appreciate you bringing me here, Amand, and I will be all right. Pira and I will get along just fine. I'll get her to teach me her dialect." Gabrielle sank down on a mat woven from madder plants. "When will you be back?"

"Four days probably, maybe seven; that is, if nothing goes wrong. You know, if I get bitten by a bushmaster or eaten by a wild animal, no one knows where you are and I doubt Pira could lead you back to the main road, and even if she could, it might be weeks before anyone came by."

"Amand! Don't say such things. You're just trying to scare me."

"I am that, child. As it is, I'll probably have to do a thousand Hail Marys as penance for bringing you here, and if anything happens to you...well, I don't think my being a priest will stop— Well, never mind," he said. He stepped outside the hut and eyed the small patch of sky visible through the trees. "I'm going to have to leave you now, or I'll get caught in the deluge that's getting ready to break loose." He bent over and squeezed Gabrielle's shoulder.

"I hope you find what you're looking for, Gabrielle. Look in your heart," he said softly. "I think perhaps the answer is there."

Gabrielle touched his fingers with hers. "Now you're going to make me cry. I don't want to feel sorry for myself. I—I just want to sort things out."

"God bless you," he said and turned to speak a few words to Pira before he left. The Indian woman nodded vigorously, smiling.

It began to rain, a brief rehearsal for the rainy season soon to come, and Pira rushed outside to scoop up an iron pot of coals. She brought them inside the *choza* and prepared their supper. Gabrielle discovered she was hungry and ate all that Pira served her in small wooden bowls. She recognized plantain, yams, and breadfruit. The rain kept them inside, and as it grew dark Pira made ready for bed. She led Gabrielle over to the string hammock and made elaborate motions with her hands to show that Gabrielle should sleep there. And to Gabrielle's surprise, the hammock was comfortable and she slept soundly, not at all disturbed by the night sounds as animals and jungle creatures came out of their lairs to seek food and mates.

The next three days passed with a certain sameness to it that began to get on Gabrielle's nerves. Each morning she woke to nausea and longed for a cool iced drink. She had to settle for the water Pira drew from a nearby brown creek. Gabrielle strained the water and boiled it, but it still had a flat, muddy taste.

It rained every day and rather than cool things off, to Gabrielle's dismay, the deluge did little more than cause steam to rise from the jungle floor. To Pira's shy delight, Gabrielle stripped off her clothes and stood in the downfall to rinse some of the sweat and perspiration from her body. The impromptu bath refreshed Gabrielle, but later that evening her limbs felt sluggish, she suffered a headache, and by the time she made ready for bed, she was having chills.

When she woke the next morning, Gabrielle knew something was terribly wrong. Her headache was much worse, she felt hot and feverish, and the nausea that came on her was much more violent than she had ever experienced. Trembling, she tried to ease out of the hammock and as she struggled to her feet her thigh muscles seemed to tear inside with incredible pain.

"Pira!" she gasped. "Please get help," she begged as the native helped her back into the hammock. The minutes ground into hours as Gabrielle lay in the hammock and prayed that Pira had understood her. She couldn't make her eyes stay open, yet she was aware of every sound, her senses keyed up, listening. A fly walked across her face and she barely had the strength to swat at it with her hand. She slept.

Harsh chanting brought her awake, how many hours later, she didn't know. A *nele,* his face a river of wrinkles, bent over her. *Oh, God,* Gabrielle thought, *what is he going to do to me?* Her eyes followed the medicine man as he unfolded a musty, tattered blanket and covered her with it. From a small bag the *nele* drew out his medicine dolls and placed them on the ground beneath the hammock. Then Pira brought in a pot of coals and those too were placed under Gabrielle's hammock. The *nele* began a monotone chant and threw cocoa beans and powdered pepper plants on the coals. Pungent smoke arose and Gabrielle's eyes began to water; the smoke made it difficult for her to breathe. Gabrielle fainted while the *nele* pleaded with spirits of the medicine dolls to descend through the layers of the underworld and find the devil who had stolen the sick girl's soul. And because the girl was so sick, he resorted to his most treasured doll, the one that carried the most powerful medicine. It looked remarkably like the Chinese God of Happiness.

Gabrielle felt a cool, smooth hand on her face. Her eyes fluttered open, too weak with fever to do more than record the blond beard of Amand leaning close to her face.

"I lost the baby." She wrenched the words through the dry roughness in her throat. Warm tears overflowed the shuttered rims of her eyes.

"I know," he said softly. "You're very sick. I'm going to get help." His voice was ragged with self-condemnation.

"Not Micah." Did she say the words aloud? she wondered. A velvet mist lay heavy in the torpid heat. Her skin felt papery and dry. She must crackle, and the thought made her smile. She swam deep and welcomed the cool dark mist.

Thunder was exploding in her ears; it seemed to be calling her name.

"Gabrielle, for God's sake, open your eyes," the thunder pleaded, begging her to obey. A heavy weight pressed on Gabrielle's chest. She wanted to tell it to get off so she could breathe. The string hammock would break and dump her to the floor. Didn't the thunder know that?

"She's still breathing."

"Give her some brandy."

"No, that's the worst thing. Here, wet this cloth and hold it to her lips. She's dehydrated."

"Gabrielle, open your eyes. Try!" Amand pleaded. Her lashes fluttered open for a millisecond.

"Is that you, Amand?" She didn't think her lips moved.

"Yes, and Micah. We're taking you out of here. You're going to be all right. Just try—try—" His voice cracked. "God!"

Strong hands lifted her gently, cradling her carefully. Gabrielle smelled Micah's cologne, felt the buttons on his shirt press hard into her side.

"Amand! Dear God in heaven. She weighs nothing... nothing. You did this to her. I could kill you with my bare hands." Micah's voice was deep, guttural with anguish.

"Not me," the priest defended himself, struggling to keep his voice calm. "You got the child pregnant. It was your baby she lost. God knows where you get your gall, man. Two women at the same time." His voice was low with disgust.

"Two? What the hell are you talking about?"

"Gabrielle showed me the telegram from Vanessa Thomas." A deep, agonized moan escaped Micah's lips, a sound of anguish so primal, so full of pain, the priest winced.

"As God is my witness, that isn't true, I haven't touched another woman since Gabrielle." The Jeep jolted over the rough road. Gabrielle moaned in pain, cushioned against the worst by Micah's arms; they tightened, lifting her to his chest. She felt his lips on the taut, dry skin in the hollow of her neck.

"Amand, slow down or I'll break your damned neck!" he said, his voice dangerously low, fear and dread cracking its edges.

"You want to drive?" Amand said, displaying unmistakable sarcasm, and so out of the ordinary that Micah looked at him sharply.

"Marry us, Amand," Micah said. There was an urgency in the low command.

Gabrielle wished the mist would lift. She wanted to tell Micah he didn't have to marry her now. The baby was gone. She could hear Micah and Amand talking. Why couldn't they hear her?

"Marry you?" the priest grunted. "You're crazy, Micah. I can't. It's against the laws of the church for me to marry anyone outside the Catholic faith."

"That's not true. You can perform an act of charity, and since when have the laws of the church stopped you?"

"More often than I care to admit," he muttered. "She's not— She wouldn't know; she's delirious with fever."

"She's mine, Amand. I want her mine before she dies," Micah said.

Amand noted the passionate determination in Micah's voice, an undercurrent of savage, unbridled emotion. "And what if she lives? She could annul the marriage."

I'm not going to die. Why can't you hear me? Don't clutch me so tight, Micah, please. . . I can't breathe.

"She's out of her mind with fever. I can't do it."

"It would be legal?" Micah pushed the priest, stubborn, refusing to give up.

"Yes," Amand sighed, "in the eyes of the state."

"Say the words, Amand."

"Shall I stop the Jeep?" His sarcasm escaped Micah.

Micah looked down at Gabrielle. She was his destiny, he wanted her beyond the realm of anything he had ever dared to want. He had to have her. "Say the words, Amand. *Now!*"

Gabrielle listened to the soft cadence of Amand's voice. Micah answered for her. Why was he doing that? She could say her own marriage vows. Salty tears washed over her lips and her tongue flicked out to the moisture. She wasn't crying. Why was Micah crying so hard? She felt his lips on hers once again and the black mist lifted for a suspended minute only to drop back, pulling her deeper, enveloping her in a curtain of darkness.

MICAH sat in the carved teak chair he had brought from his room and placed next to Gabrielle's bed. He was weary with that agitated sleeplessness that comes from prodigious amounts of adrenaline leaching into his system. But he couldn't sleep, had no intention of even considering it until he knew Gabrielle was out of danger. The gauze was pulled back from the bed and he was watching Gabrielle. She was inert and he listened for the slightest movement, but there was only her breath coming and going, sometimes catching in her throat, then coming and going again.

Jinks moved away from the far side of the bed, lowered himself to the cot at the long wall, and sighed heavily. He had been awake for forty-two hours and it showed. He spoke quietly to Micah.

"She's sleeping normally now. I think we can turn her over to Helen and Maria and get ourselves some rest." When that brought no comment from Micah, he went on talking. "You know what I was thinking I'd like to do? I think I'd like to set up a little laboratory at the clinic and study dengue fever. So little is known about it except that it's caused by a mosquito." He glanced over to Gabrielle. "She was lucky, she only contracted a mild form." Jinks continued to muse aloud to the silent Micah. "Maybe I'll write a letter to the World Health Organization. They might sponsor a grant. You wouldn't mind, would you?"

At the direct question Micah came out of his reverie. "No...no, I think it's a good idea. I'll match their grant," he said generously. Then, "You're sure, absolutely sure, she's going to get well?"

"Positive," Jinks said, making himself comfortable on the cot. "I'd stake my reputation on it."

At that Micah smiled, his first in days. "You're a clown, Jinks."

The doctor smiled, his eyes closed. "Not when it comes to medicine, my boy...not when it comes to medicine." He dozed off, planning his laboratory in his dreams, seeing himself finding a cure for the fever, and, since dreams are such secret silent things, imagining himself receiving the Nobel prize in medicine.

Micah was caught up with his conscience. It was as heavy as lead and painful. He wanted an easing and it wouldn't come. He shifted in the chair, making himself more comfortable, continuing his reflections. He was astute and intelligent in business, so why couldn't he bring these things into use with his relationships with people? Benton weighed heavily on his mind. Gabrielle had been right. Benton had been a good friend and in truth, he had loved him; despite Benton's goading, there had been a camaraderie that they both enjoyed. *We were friends for more than twelve years,* he thought, *and I never once told him I loved him, never even said I liked him.*

Now he had been given a second chance with Gabrielle. He loved her. He would tell her the moment she awoke, explain everything to her. His resolve was so strong he felt like reaching over and shaking her awake. But when she began to stir, his resolve slipped, he felt awkward and suddenly shy. The flutterings in his chest began in earnest, panic took hold, and he fled the sickroom.

Chapter Twenty

The dream was so frustrating. The *nele* was chanting in his singsong voice but he kept getting younger until she saw Amand and he was chanting too and Micah kept saying I do and wouldn't let her talk. Vanessa began screaming and pulling Micah away from her and her mother was playing bridge and kept complaining about a no-trump hand and then got up to announce that Gabrielle was married and going to have a baby and she kept trying to get her mother's attention to tell her it wasn't so but her mother just wouldn't listen. The dream wouldn't go away and Gabrielle struggled to wake up. She had to get out from under it somehow.

She opened her eyes and stared at the pivot that held the cloud of mosquito netting that surrounded her bed at Chepo.

"Nice to have you back with us," Jinks said, bending over her. His bushy eyebrows worked furiously above his tired, strained face.

"I feel awful," Gabrielle told him, her voice barely audible.

"You've had dengue fever, but the worst is over. I want you to stay awake long enough to drink some broth. I'll send Helen in with it in just a few minutes." He bustled out of the room.

Gabrielle struggled to lift herself and fell back. Remembrance jolted through her. She had lost the baby. Pira had gone for help and brought back the *nele,* but she remembered Amand and Micah too. She had dreamed of Micah, vague visions that floated in and out of her mind. And there was something she knew she had to tell Amand. But what? She couldn't remember.

There was still Vanessa. Now Micah wouldn't have to concern himself with which of his women to marry, if he

ever had in the first place. He would choose Vanessa
because she still carried his child. Gabrielle could go home
now, she thought, there was nothing to keep her at
Chepo—nothing. Somehow she would have to build a new
life for herself, a new life out of the chaos in her
heart.

"Gabby!" Helen poked her head through the slit in the
net and tucked a swath behind the headboard. "Am I glad
to see you awake." Relief was etched on her face. "My
goodness, why are you crying? Everything is fine now,
you're getting well." She plumped Gabrielle's pillows and
sat her up.

"I wanted the baby, Helen."

"I know. But right now let's get this juice and soup
down, then we can talk." Gabrielle was too weak to argue.
She swallowed as much juice and broth as she could manage. Helen set the dishes aside and began to fuss around
her, straightening the bed, washing her face, brushing her
hair.

"There. You look presentable. Jinks is going to wake
Micah in a few minutes, he'll be—"

"Yes, I want to see him," Gabrielle said. She had to say
something about the baby, the new life that didn't make it.
It deserved a requiem, some acknowledgment, if only by
saying the words aloud. "I want to tell him if he hadn't
kept my passport locked up in his safe, I would be home
now. It's his fault—"

"No, it isn't his fault," Helen said suddenly. "There are
a few things you should know, Gabby. Probably now is
not the time to say them, but I'd better. In the first place,
it's not anyone's fault that you lost the baby. You had
dengue fever—it's likely you contracted it before you even
went with Amand. And I tell you that was a foolish thing
to do. Anyway dengue fever is the reason you lost the
baby, nothing else. And there's another thing. We know
you thought Vanessa was pregnant by Micah. But that
isn't true. Vanessa can't get pregnant. Years ago she had a
miscarriage, a nasty one, probably self-induced from what
I hear, and while she was in the hospital she had her tubes
tied so that she couldn't have any children. That's why her

first husband divorced her—she had it done without consulting him.

"Micah's been agonizing over that telegram. He knew Vanessa couldn't be pregnant, but he also knows how deviously Vanessa's mind works. That telegram was meant for you, to get you out of the picture, but when you didn't mention it, Micah thought Benton had intercepted it."

"In that case, I don't want to see Micah. I have nothing to say to him."

"He may have something to say to you, have you thought of that? He's been helping us take care of you, he's had less sleep than Jinks and I put together over this past week."

"I don't care. I mean, I appreciate everything you've done for me, all of you, but I don't want to see Micah." Gabrielle closed her eyes, and the tears began anew.

Helen grimaced. "Well, it'll take a bigger person than me to keep him out of here, but if it's going to upset you, we can wait a few minutes."

Gabrielle's fingers clutched the muslin sheets and she began to cry, soft, ragged sobs of emotions gone dangerously thin. She had made such a muddle of things, she thought. But had Micah said he loved her? No. So it didn't matter. Nothing was changed. Helen untangled Gabrielle's fingers from the sheets, offering comfort, but nothing seemed to help. She gave up and kept vigil by the side of the bed, wiping away the tears when they threatened to drench the pillows, until Gabrielle slept again.

Something cold and wet pushed on her hand, worrying it until Gabrielle finally opened her eyes. Shadow's head was propped on the mattress, his big brown eyes droopy. Gabrielle smiled.

"Hello, boy," she said softly. "Did you miss me?" She scratched his ears. A movement beyond the dog caught her attention.

"C'mon, Shadow, out, boy," Micah's voice was soft, coaxing. The dog turned away from her bed and trotted out the door. Micah stood by the bed; his eyes held Gabrielle's for a brief second. She looked away, but not before she noted how tired and haggard Micah looked. She probably looked worse, though, she thought, and drew her fingers through her curls.

"You look fine," Micah said and smiled. But the smile didn't reach his eyes, Gabrielle thought. It was just a polite smile, a sickroom smile. She didn't return his smile. She couldn't. She waited for him to say something about himself, about her...about the baby. Nothing. He merely stood there, his face impassive, his jaw rigid, clenching and unclenching his fists.

Gabrielle began to sit up, and his hands shot out to help her. "Don't touch me," she rasped. Micah drew his hands back as though he had touched a hot coal. Her eyes were huge, dark, and liquid in her face. "I want to go home," she whispered and shoved her hands under the sheet to hide their trembling.

"The minute you're able to travel, Gabrielle," he said, his voice reflecting weariness and resignation. "Your passport, visa, and an airline ticket are on my desk. Helen will stay with you and fly home with you, if you like."

"No, I can go alone." She gulped air to hold back the tears. No more, she told herself. She was cried out.

Micah's shoulders drooped. "I've got to go to Coco Solito and Jinks does too, now that you're better. If you need anything, Helen will let me know." He turned and walked slowly to the door.

"Micah! Wait," she called him back. She had to say something about the baby. He pivoted, his eyes glittered. With what? Hope? No, she discounted that as an impossibility.

"I was having a baby. I—I lost it. Our baby. Did you know?"

"Yes." The single word cracked in two. "Amand told me, Jinks confirmed it."

Gabrielle looked at him, astonishment turning to anger. "Confirmed it? You had to have confirmation? Did you think I was going to—"

"No! That's not what I meant at all. I'm just telling you that when Jinks examined you, he—we—he wasn't sure if you had lost it or if the fever...." His words trailed off.

He looked so sad. Why? Gabrielle felt a heavy weight

crushing her chest; it was a profound and unfathomable ache. "Good-bye, Micah," she said in a voice much stronger than she felt, and after he left, she buried her head in her pillow to muffle her sobs.

THERE was a time, Gabrielle thought, that she would have been happy to see this day arrive. She was almost packed, almost ready to leave Chepo. So why did she feel like dragging her feet, putting off her journey home until tomorrow? Or the day after?

She had not seen Micah since the day he came into her room three weeks ago. And she wanted to see him desperately, but such wants were useless now.

Helen had gone back to Coco Solito a week ago. There had been several more cases of dengue fever diagnosed on the isthmus and because of that, Gabrielle had been asked to submit to an examination by the Ministry of Health. Immigration authorities had graciously extended her visa, but what else could they do? The government refused to let her leave until it was certain she was free of the fever.

Helen had gone with her into Panama City for the examination and after that returned to the logging camp where she was needed to man the clinic while Jinks went into the interior with the logging teams.

Gabrielle reflected on the last few days Helen had spent at Chepo. She had behaved as though she wanted to tell Gabrielle some secret, some gossip. Several times she had opened her mouth to speak, then clamped it shut. Gabrielle tried to ferret it out, but only learned that after Micah and Amand had brought her to Chepo, Micah had called Benjamin Thomas, the banker in Atlanta. What was said, no one knew, but two days later Benjamin Thomas arrived in Panama and that same evening he and his daughter Vanessa boarded a flight back to the States.

"Anybody home?"

Gabrielle left off her packing and went out onto the veranda. "Amand! I thought you had gone to China," she said, smiling at the priest, and took him by the arm and led him back into the front room.

"Tomorrow morning," he said. "I leave tomorrow. I

had some business to take care of first.'' Gabrielle went to the bar and made two gin and tonics. She handed one to Amand.

He looked at her over the rim of the glass. "You don't look like you've been ill at all. I guess it's the resilience of youth. How do you feel?''

"I feel good, at least on the outside," she said slowly. "Jinks took very good care of me. I want to thank you, Amand, for—''

"Accepted," he said abruptly.

Gabrielle changed the subject. "I never heard if your last trip into the interior was success— Oh, Amand! Now I remember what I wanted to tell you. Did you see the medicine man at Pira's? He was incredibly old and—''

"No, I knew one had been there, I smelled the herbs, but he was gone when—''

"Amand," Gabrielle erupted excitedly, "he had dolls, all kinds of dolls, and one, I think—I'm sure, it was Chinese. It had a beard and a mandarin collar carved on a robe.''

For a moment Amand Chardin looked stricken, then he laughed. "My just deserts," he said. "I'll keep that in mind while I'm studying in China. Thank you for telling me. Now I have something for you." He took a cream-colored envelope from his pocket and handed it to her. "Is Micah here?''

Gabrielle accepted the envelope with an automatic gesture, slightly puzzled. "No, he's still in Coco Solito, working with the management team he's hired to take over the project.''

"You say good-bye to him for me, will you?''

Gabrielle hesitated. She wasn't going to have the opportunity to say good-bye to Micah for herself, but there was no need to burden Amand with that. "Yes, I'll tell him.''

Amand smiled and indicated the envelope in her hand. "You needn't worry about the legality of that, Gabrielle. It's been registered in Records and of course at St. Joseph's, although naturally it doesn't have the sanction of the church. Since you're a linguist, I don't think you'll mind your marriage certificate being in Spanish, will you?''

The dream. Now Gabrielle knew what the dream meant, only it hadn't been a dream, it was real. The blood rushed to her head, and her heart began to beat erratically, causing gooseflesh to move along her arms. Her hands shook as she opened the envelope and lifted out the folded parchment. Gabrielle B. Hensley united in holy matrimony to Micah Davidson. *Gabrielle Davidson. Mrs. Micah Davidson.*

"Gabrielle, are you all right? Is this a surprise? I thought—''

She smiled weakly. "He didn't tell me, but don't worry about it, Amand, I knew. I thought I dreamed it.''

The priest had a look of uncertainty about him. He took a big swallow of the gin. "If you don't want to stay married...I mean, under the circumstances you can annul the marriage. I told Micah, tried to tell him, that is—''

"Annul? No, I don't think so," Gabrielle said slowly. "Unless Micah wants it.''

Amand remembered the grim determination in Micah as they sped through the jungle. "I think," he said, a look of immense relief on his face, "that you will be married for a long, long time, then.''

After saying his good-byes to Maria, Amand left, promising to write, to keep in touch. Gabrielle hoped he would. He was part of a past she would treasure, but the past had yet to be and she had the present on her mind.

"Maria!" she called, and when Maria hurried from the kitchen, she told her, "Unpack my things, then prepare dinner, a nice dinner. Micah will be home. And hurry.''

"Sí, señorita," Maria said, smiling.

Gabrielle laid a hand on Maria's arm. "Not *señorita*, Maria, *señora. Señora* Davidson.''

The least she could do, Gabrielle thought, was give Micah the opportunity to tell her why he was letting her go, why he didn't speak of their marriage. If he didn't love her, then it would take little to repack her things and reschedule her flight home and an entire lifetime for her to forget him. She went to the radio and called the river camp. Helen answered.

"Helen, this is Gabrielle. Is Micah there?"

"He's out riding. He'll be back before long. Is something wrong?"

"No, nothing's wrong. Helen, will you give Micah a message for me?"

"Yes, I'll be—"

"Tell him—tell him I expect him home for dinner tonight."

"Is that all?" Helen's voice crackled over the radio.

"It's enough for now," Gabrielle shot back and flipped the switch.

Oh, God, he has to come, she thought. Her hands were trembling and sweaty; she wiped them across her skirt. These clothes, they were all wrong to welcome her husband home—they were too chic, clothes to travel in—they wouldn't do. Her creamy satin lounging pajamas—yes, definitely yes. And her hair—this style was much too severe. She pulled the pins and combs out and flung them across the bed. She ran her fingers through her dark curls until they were in a state of attractive dishabille. She wished she had a pair of satin slippers with feather puffs, but she didn't, so she decided on no shoes at all. She knotted the satin belt around her waist as she left her room, then stopped short. *Tsk, tsk, not a knot, stupid,* she told herself. Her fingers were trembling already, however would she manage to undo a knot later? She redid the sash in a *very* loose bow.

Everything was ready, choreographed as fine as any ballet she had ever performed. Gabrielle sat on the sofa and waited. When she heard the helicopter coming close, she forced herself to remain seated, calmly, her feet tucked under her, sipping on a cup of coffee. She knew when Micah reached the door because Shadow bounded up off his rug and raced to the door, his tail wagging.

Micah stepped into the room. His shirt was unbuttoned and fell open to his waist, revealing the gold medallion she had seen once before. Their eyes locked and held for several long seconds, and Gabrielle tried to read the questioning look on Micah's face. She suddenly felt awkward and off balance. The cup rattled in its saucer. She looked down at it uncomprehendingly.

Micah spoke. "Helen told me I'm invited to dinner."

"Yes, yes, you are," Gabrielle managed. She watched him stride across the room to the bar and build himself a drink.

"May I fix you something?" he asked, looking at her, watching her.

"No, I have coffee, thank you." God! How ordinary they sounded, how polite, as though nothing had happened. They were husband and wife, for God's sake! There was so much to be said, so much to be talked about, questions to be asked and answered. Micah sat down on the sofa opposite her and folded his feet on the ottoman. He looked weary, Gabrielle thought, his eyes far back into their sockets, his lips pursed in thought; she loved his lips. His scars were healed, no longer pink and raw. Gabrielle felt a surge of emotion, it was the most overpowering feeling she had ever experienced in her life.

"Amand came to see me today," she blurted. "He brought our marriage certificate."

Micah's head shot up, his thoughts concealed behind shuttered eyes. "And?"

"And? And? Is that all you have to say?" Gabrielle asked, feeling a sense of confusion and anger well up inside her. "You were going to let me leave without seeing me? Without telling me? I want to talk about our baby. I want—" The words tumbled out. "I thought you were going to marry Vanessa." Oh, God, why was she crying now? Micah crossed the space between them, took the china from her hands, his own unsteady. He gathered her in his arms and held her, crushing her as though he would never let her go again.

"Gabrielle," he murmured, "I love you. The hardest thing I've ever done in my life was walk out of here and know you'd be gone when I got back. I thought you didn't want me, that you didn't want to stay."

"That's not the way it is at all," she tried to tell him, but he was kissing her, touching her, so that Gabrielle returned his kisses hungrily while butterflies fluttered and soared.

When their lips had had a surfeit, Gabrielle snuggled in Micah's arms. They didn't talk for a while. Her thoughts ran to the thousand things they had yet to discover about each other, likes, dislikes, where they would live, everything and nothing. Soon, though, these thoughts were pushed out of her mind. A subtle change came over them. Gabrielle felt it, knew Micah did too. He shifted, pushed her away. Sensing his withdrawal, she asked, "Is something wrong?"

"No." He smiled. "But I thought you invited me to dinner."

"Dinner? Who can think of eating?" She laughed. "I'm not hungry, at least not for food," she whispered.

"That's what I mean," Micah said softly. "You haven't been well, Gabrielle. It's too soon."

"Too soon?" she said disbelieving. "I'm well. Jinks said so. And I've even got a certificate of health from the government of Panama." She twisted so she could look up at his face. "Did Jinks tell you something he didn't tell me?"

Micah grinned. "No, as a matter of fact, he said you were easily good enough for another half-dozen babies."

"Half dozen!" Gabrielle made a tantalizing moue with her full ripe lips and held up her hand. "Two, that's all I'm going to have."

"Two sons would be nice," he said, his grin wider, pulling her back into his arms.

"Sons," Gabrielle repeated and thought about it. "No, if you want tiny little replicas of yourself, Micah, have them cloned. I'm having girls."

"You are?" he said, and his voice was low, seductive, causing delightful shivers to race along Gabrielle's flesh. "Have you decided when we could begin to make these girl babies?"

"Now would be nice," she murmured, pressing her lips against his neck.

"God, how I need you, Gabrielle," he said as his lips found hers, and their bodies pressed together, building a mounting passion that demanded undoing. He swept her into his arms and carried her to his bed.

Gabrielle was caught up in the incredible rapture of his lovemaking. His lips on her breasts, on her thighs, his hands gentle and urgent, drawing her to sensual heights until she begged release.

"Micah, please, I need you," she said huskily. He groaned and entered her, hesitant at first, fearful of hurting her until she thrust her hips against his with insistent rhythm. She urged him with murmured imprecations of sensual love until their bodies seemed to sway and burst with unbearable ecstasy. They lay tangled in one another's arms, their passions ebbed, yet lurking under the surface, waiting only for a touch, a word, to mount again.

"Micah, are you awake?" Gabrielle asked, raising up to rest her head in the palm of her hand.

"Absolutely," he whispered throatily.

"I've been thinking, I would like to teach dancing. I'd like to have a studio built right onto our house—when we get one—that way—"

"I already have a house on my farm in Georgia," he put in lazily.

Gabrielle sat up. "Georgia? No way. I want to live in Houston and teach in Houston—"

"I want my sons—children," he amended, "raised on my farm."

She slid a hand across his stomach, drew her nails up his chest, and circled his nipple with her fingertips. "Couldn't we compromise? Just spend summers on the farm?"

"All right," he said and pushed her hand down so she would be aware of his growing need. "But just because I gave in to you this time, don't think you can wrap me around your little finger."

"No, of course not," she answered and moved to settle her hips over his. She rested her elbows on his chest. "There is one other thing."

"What? For God's sake," he said, groaning.

"When are you going to buy me a wedding ring? I mean, our marriage certificate is in Spanish and my mother can't read Spanish, but she'll believe a ring. She'll—"

"Gabrielle," Micah moaned softly as his hands grasped her hips, "can we talk about this tomorrow?"

"Why, yes," she murmured, rotating her hips ever so slightly, "but just because I gave in to you this time—" She smiled and let him absorb the tremors building in her body. Yes, tomorrow, she thought. There would be a lifetime of tomorrows and she would add each one to the past, but only after it had been savored, lived in, loved in, adding to her treasure store of memories.

Enter a uniquely exciting world of romance with the new

Harlequin American Romances.™

Harlequin American Romances are the first romances to explore today's new love relationships. These compelling romance novels reach into the hearts and minds of women across North America...probing the most intimate moments of romance, love and desire.

You'll follow romantic heroines and irresistible men as they boldly face confusing choices. Career first, love later? Love without marriage? Long-distance relationships? All the experiences that make love real are captured in the tender, loving pages of the new **Harlequin American Romances.**

What makes North American women so different when it comes to love? Find out in the new **Harlequin American Romances!**

Send for your introductory FREE book now!

AR-SUB-2

Get this book FREE!

Mail to:

Harlequin Reader Service

In the U.S.
1440 South Priest Drive
Tempe, AZ 85281

In Canada
649 Ontario Street
Stratford, Ontario N5A 6W2

YES! I want to be one of the first to discover the new **Harlequin American Romances.** Send me FREE and without obligation *Twice in a Lifetime*. If you do not hear from me after I have examined my FREE book, please send me the 4 new **Harlequin American Romances** each month as soon as they come off the presses. I understand that I will be billed only $2.25 for each book (total $9.00). There are no shipping or handling charges. There is no minimum number of books that I have to purchase. In fact, I may cancel this arrangement at any time. *Twice in a Lifetime* is mine to keep as a FREE gift, even if I do not buy any additional books.

Name _____ (please print)

Address _____ Apt. no.

City _____ State/Prov. _____ Zip/Postal Code

Signature (If under 18, parent or guardian must sign.)